KINGDOM

OF

FURY

AND

FATE

By Sarah Teasdale

DEDICATION

For all the women who do not yet realize they
are the most powerful one in the room

And to you, the reader

MYTH AND MAGIC SERIES

KINGDOM OF MYTH AND MAGIC

KINGDOM OF FURY AND FATE

UNTITLED (BOOK 3)

MAP

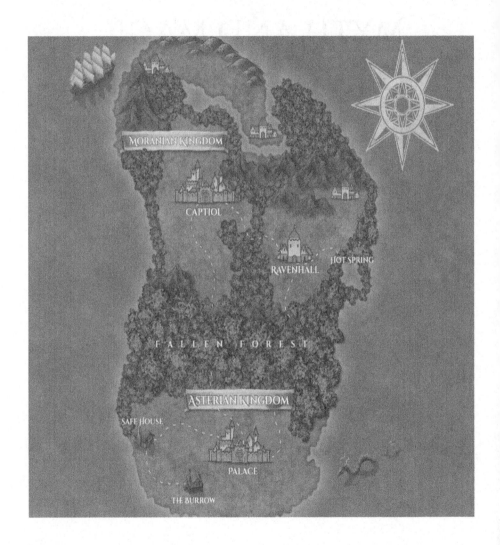

SARAH TEASDALE

PRONUNCIATIONS

Melora: Mel-or-uh

Silas: Sigh-lass

Milo: My-low

Loral: Lor-uhl

Vayna: van-uh

Arlan: are-lan

Yara: Yuh-are-uh

Kaius: kay-us

Visha: V-i-sh-uh

Nicodem: Nick-o-dem

Norik: N-or-ick

Morania: m-or-an-e-uh

Asteria: uh-stair-e-uh

Author's Note

Kingdom of Fury and Fate is a work of fiction depicting strong language and sexual content

This book is rated *R* and strictly for 18+ readers...excluding my grandmother

For a full list of possible triggers, please visit my website through the QR code below

SARAH TEASDALE

CHAPTER 1

SILAS

I will get back to you.

I promise you.

Nothing will keep me from you.

I will never forget her pleading words as I lay on the cold ground, slowly dying. I will never fail to remember tears falling from her beautiful blue eyes as she held me and confessed what I already knew was true. As she confessed that she loves me.

That she loves me.

I hear her songlike voice saying it repeatedly: *I love you. I love you. I love you.* I hear the hurt in her tone, in her words as she confesses her truth. A truth I had already known for myself.

At that moment, the moment when I knew I was dying from the fatal wound my brother had delivered, I wish I could have told her everything I felt for her. Everything she means to me. Everything I was dying to say to her. Everything I was begging time to let me tell her.

There are so many things I wanted to say as I watched Melora give her freedom for my life, as I watched her sacrifice herself. I wanted to beg her not to do it, to tell her that if she was safe, it was worth dying for. That I would die a thousand times if it meant she was alive.

I wanted to tell her she has given me life. Her love has healed me from a lifetime of hurting. She has given me so much in our time together, so much love, so much trust.

But I could say nothing as the hole in my chest seeped with blood, as it became harder and harder to stay awake. I couldn't will the words from my mouth as she agreed to the terms of saving my life. As she agreed to what Vayna had to offer.

I know I am sleeping. I am sleeping and dreaming in some far-off place in my mind because I see her in my dreams. She is all I ever see. I watch as she clutches me when the mortal queen tried to touch me. My fierce girl growled in protectiveness over my lifeless body. I see her give up what she wanted most in her life, what she craved for most of her life, to save me: her freedom.

I am not worthy of her.
Not worthy of her sacrifice.
Not worthy of her love.
Not. Worthy.

The moment plays over and over in my head as I continue to sleep. The moment on repeat in the never-ending sleep I am currently in.

I need to wake up.
I need to move.
I need to get her back.

Move. I tell myself again, urging my body to wake from the prison sleep brings me. My fingers twitch, and I know I am coming to. I clench my fist into tight balls, trying to gain more strength over my body. My eyes are as heavy as boulders as I pry them open, but they finally open.

Even when I wake, I see her saddened face, her tear-streaked cheeks, her trembling lips. Her curls wild as her, framing her strong jaw. Her bloodied hands holding my face, holding my cheeks. I see her so clearly.

I am thankful I see her. Thankful the last moments I had with her are replaying in my mind continuously. It gives me strength. It gives me motivation. It gives me something to hold on to as I try to sober from sleep.

I lay, looking at the ceiling of my room. I lay in the bed where Melora and I once slept together, held each other, and worshiped each other into the late hours of the night. I look around the room as I start to gain power over my unwilling body. It is dark and somber.

In sleep, the memories of Melora came sweetly, easily. They comforted me as I slept and thought of her, thinking only of her. Now, when I wake up and realize that she is gone, it hits me with rage and regret.

I jackknife up, stirring the bed and blankets around me. I rip off my cover and move myself to the edge of the mattress. Pure will is pushing me out of this bed, pushing me to act, pushing me to move.

I take one step and fall to the floor, catching myself on weak hands and knees. I keel over as the pain from my wounded chest radiates through my body, burning through my muscles.

But this pain I am feeling physically is nothing compared to the agony that has come from losing my Melora. It is nothing compared to the fury I feel from losing her, from having her taken from me.

I scream, my voice rough and my throat scratchy. I scream and sob, the tears as hot as my anger running down my face. The sounds coming from me were not even close to human as I wailed into the dark room, only the echo of my screams answering.

How could I have let this happen?

The one thing in this life that has given me peace is gone with an evil woman who plans to kill our people, plans to take our kingdom.

I grab onto something, a table, I think. I lift myself, still heaving from the torture her absence brings. I push the table over, tossing it aside like it is nothing. The contents spill as I continue my rampage, paper and glass flying everywhere.

Anger mixed with sorrow is a dangerous concoction; it brings out the worst in one. And right now, it is bringing out the worst in me.

I wreak havoc in the room. Glass shatters, and wood snaps under my hands. The hands that have held Melora, that have loved her from the moment they felt her skin.

The remains from my rampage lay around me as I held myself up on shaky hands and knees. The sobs have my body thrashing as I continue to let out sounds of my pain. My ears ring with the sounds of Melora's name coming from my throat, coming from a voice I don't even recognize.

The door opens, and I know who it is, not needing to look. It is not my love or my father, but Milo. It is the man who has been my brother for decades, who was with me when my mother died and is now with me when the one I love is gone.

I look at him, and his features look tired. His eyes reddening as tears start to gather.

"She's gone." I cry out to Milo, trying to hold myself up to talk to him. "They have her, Milo. She-she is gone." I don't even hear my voice as I lean harder into the floor on numb hands.

Milo says nothing as he moves towards me, kneeling on the ground beside me. "We will get her back. I promise you, we will do everything we can to get her home." his words come out strained, like he is fighting within himself, like pain is all he feels too. "What happened, Silas?" He places a comforting hand on my shoulder, and it steadies me and grounds me.

I calm myself long enough to tell him the details of Melora's sacrifice, the story of how she saved me, continuing to bring anguish. Milo listens as I explain Vayna's terms: Melora returns with her to the capitol in exchange for saving me, in exchange for my life.

Milo's face turns distraught as I tell him the treachery of what Simon has done, how he almost killed me with a sword through the back. If not for Melora, I would be dead. I may be Asterian, but even a blow right to the heart would have killed me.

"After the battle, after we found you, we looked for Simon. We discovered that he disappeared with Vayna and Melora. He's gone, Silas. He went with them." Milo explained as I tried to catch my breath, trying to stop the heaving in my lungs.

Simon's betrayal tears a new hole in my chest, like the one he gave me with his sword. My brother, my own blood, was willing to kill me for the mortal queen who plans to take our kingdom. To take everything we have built.

The pain from it all is almost unbearable. The heartbreak, the betrayal, everything is ripping me to shreds. I want to give in to the pain. To do nothing but lay on the floor and wallow in loss and grief.

But I cannot.

I will not.

Melora needs me. Her words stain my mind: *Nothing will keep me from you.* I know she would do whatever it takes to return to me and keep her promise, but it might just kill her.

Another set of footsteps enters the room's threshold. My father stands in the doorway, watching as I sit back on my heels, trying to regain some composure.

He looks old. Old and tired. His eyes are mournful, sad even.

I want to turn to my father for comfort in this time of absolute anguish like I did when I was a child.

But then I remembered what he had done.

My father lied about knowing the truth about Melora's mother. He lied straight to our faces when we asked if there was anything he knew that would help Melora understand herself—anything he knew at all.

"Get out." was all I could manage to say; even those words hurt. Milo looked between us, unsureness written over his face. "Get out before I make you." I continued to growl at my father, not giving him any room to speak.

The king took a step forward like he wanted to come to where I sat on the ground, crying for my Melora. "Silas, please. Please just-"

"You lied!" I shout at him, my voice still recovering from my earlier screams. "Melora asked you if you knew anything about her mother. She confided in you! *I* confided in you! We asked for your help, and you lied to us." I need to control my breathing before I lose it. My chest is already rattling from anger.

My father rubs a hand over his scraggly beard. "I wanted to tell you the truth—both of you. I wanted to tell her that her mother is the Goddess of Life. But I knew what it would mean—for you and me and Simon." He finishes, his eyes pleading.

It took me only a moment to understand what he was saying. I understood what it could mean for Melora to be the Goddess of Life's daughter and why it would affect him and our family—to be of *her* blood, to be of the Goddess of Life's blood. "Melora would be Queen of Asteria," I said more to myself to believe what I was thinking, at the realization of who and what she would be.

Milo jolted a bit, shock apparent in his body.

My father nodded his head. "Yes. It means Melora is the rightful heir to the Asterian throne."

"Meaning what? You knew and did not tell us because you did not want her to take your place?" I accused him. How selfish of a man must he be to keep this from Melora, who has only ever wanted to find herself.

He huffed. "I don't know what I was thinking! I was only thinking of you and your brother, of- of myself. How are we supposed to know what would happen to us if Melora took the throne?"

"She would make a better queen than you ever were king, I can tell you that much. You never even wanted to be king!" I spat the words, pissed at my father's selfishness. "Get. The. Fuck. Out." I let my head fall. I can't stand to look at him any longer, not without raging more.

My father left, leaving Milo and I in silence. Only until Milo said timidly, "Do not bite my head off for asking this." he paused, checking to see if I would genuinely bite his head off. At the moment, I would not put it past myself. "Would it have made a difference when it came to Vayna if we would have known the truth of Melora's mother? Of who Melora truly was?"

In truth, I have no idea if things would have been different. If the outcome would be changed in our favor.

But that is not the point. The point is that my father lied to me and the woman I love. He lied for self-preservation, to keep his place on the throne—the throne he never wanted.

"I am not sure," I answered, closing my eyes and trying to calm myself.

"Well," Milo began. "We now know that we are not only fighting to get back the woman who you love, that so many of us have grown to love, but we are fighting to get back our queen."

CHAPTER 2

MELORA

Everything hurts.

Everything. Hurts.

It is all I can think of as I regain my consciousness; it is all I can feel as I try to wake from the deep sleep I am in. Or unconsciousness, I am unsure. I stir and try to get my limbs moving, trying and failing. My eyes blink open as I look down into my lap, my clothing still bloodied and mangled from the battle.

The battle.

Silas.

Oh gods, it comes back to me like waves hitting the shore. I remember it all at once, all the horrible things that have happened. The reality of what has happened runs through my mind and takes over my thoughts. Silas dying in my arms, making the bargain with Vayna. It all comes to the forefront of my memories, jarring me awake.

I jerk, trying to get up, trying to get moving from where I am. Trying to move from the seated position I am currently in. My hands are tied behind my back, and a chair is beneath me, the wood digging into my skin. They could have at least laid me down. Bastards.

I gain my bearings and notice where I am being held, notice the emptiness of the room I am in. I notice the dampness and the darkness, and I realize where I am.

I am currently in an old, musty cell that smells of earth. I must be in the dungeons at the capitol of Morania, in the deepest part of the castle.

What have I gotten myself into?

I know what I have brought onto myself, though, I fully understand what I did, and I would do it a million times over just to see Silas live. To see him alive and whole.

I wish the first time I admitted to loving him was different. I wish a lot of things were different. I wish that he was not bleeding out in my arms after his brother punctured his heart, his heart that I know is mine. That I know has been mine since the night in the hot spring.

I wish we had been somewhere together, like our hot spring when we first met. A place that means something to us and our relationship. But none of that matters. What matters is that he will live.

He is safe.

He is alive.

That is *all* that matters.

It still hurts, though, knowing he is without me and I am without him. He is my soul, he is my love, and being taken away from him when he needed me most hurts. It hurts more than any physical blow ever could.

I wish I would have told him the moment I knew I loved him. I wish I would have told him the moment everything changed for me, when I stopped fighting what I knew was so true, so pure. When I stopped fighting between who I should be and who I wanted to be. Because finally, I realized I wanted to be his, consciences be damned.

I will get back to him. I will return to him. My captors must know that I would be willing to do anything to escape them, or at least suspect that I would wake up rearing for a fight, so they tied me up. The scratchy rope digs into my wrist, making this a very uncomfortable position to be in.

Something wet trickles onto my legs, causing a shiver to crawl down my spine. I look down to find a fresh slice on my collar bone, still dripping red. The blood of the fresh wound dripped into my lap and down my leg. I hiss in pain as I try to examine the cut better.

What the fuck?

My anger simmers beneath my skin, hot and ready to fight. Anger for all that happened, for all I have lost. For *everything* I have lost.

Loral.

LORAL.

She murdered Loral, murdered her in cold blood right before my very eyes. I can still hear the snapping of her neck as she pleads to me not to do what Vayna says, as she begs me not to listen to Vayna. I squeezed my eyes shut as the image of Loral's body crumbling to the ground played over and over.

I feel sick as rage boils, and I let out a violent scream, waiting for my magic to wake in my blood. Waiting for the power to free myself from my bonds.

But nothing happens. My magic that usually reacts to my temper doesn't even stir the slightest.

I concentrate on it, on the feel of my magic in my body, like Silas showed me. I can't feel it at all. There is no hum, no power to use. Like it was never there at all.

What have they done to me?

They must have found a way to either take my magic away or render it useless.

Haven't they taken enough from me?

The sound of footsteps echoing through the dungeon halls draws my thoughts from my new wound. I hold my breath, waiting to see who is about to appear before me.

They are heavy footfalls, too heavy for Vayna. I know then who is about to show up in front of my cell, and I cannot wait to get my hands on him...eventually.

I know I am bound to this fucking chair, but one way or another, I will free myself. When I do, he will feel my wrath. He will be the first to know what it feels like to be a part of my revenge. To be a part of all the things that I will end to take down the true evil of the kingdom.

The tall body stops outside the bars; even from here, I know it is him. I know it is Simon by the way he carries himself, like the spoiled princeling he is. He is nothing like his older brother; he is not as built and not as beautiful. But the similarities are there; their father's green eyes, their mother's black hair.

"You have awakened." Simon slithers, his hands clasped in front of him. "I figured you would be out for far longer. I guess we underestimated you." That crooked smile flashed brightly, but something about him looked different, distraught.

"Not the first time." I remind him. "Have you come to free me, or are you just here to annoy me?" I ask, annoyed with this conversation already.

Simon's laugh was anything but amused, his voice tired. "If I wanted to be dead, I would free you of your bonds. Seeing as I would like to keep my head, you will be staying right where you are until I decide otherwise."

I scoffed at his remark, narrowing my sensitive eyes. "Until *you* decide otherwise? I was under the impression you work for Vayna. Like a little lap dog." He grew angered by this, and it fueled me to push him more, to dig at him more. "When I get out of here, and I will get out of here, you will be missing more than your head," I promised.

Simon stared at me through the thick bars of the cell. He was probably wondering how I thought I was in any position to mouth off and make threats. I did not care that I was the captive currently being held prisoner in a cell; he deserved the wickedness coming from my words.

"Have you found out that your magic is useless here?" he genuinely questioned, looking the bars up and down. "I am sure you noticed my handiwork." He nodded toward my still bleeding cut on my chest.

"Of course, you sliced me up while I was unconscious."

Coward.

He gripped the bars like he was holding back frustration. "I bet you are curious why you can't even feel your magic. You want to know how we did it, don't you?"

He was not wrong, but I would admit nothing to this man. I would show no fear.

"Fine, I will tell you." He must be proud. "Wards drawn with your blood are placed on the outside of this cell. Whoever's blood the wards are written in cannot use their magic in the room. Well, in this instance, the cell. Something Vayna came up with, but I executed."

So they did find a way to take my magic.

"Why?" was the only question I wanted answered.

"Why what?" he quipped.

I was growing frustrated. "Why everything! Why betray your kingdom? Why try to kill your brother?" I was yelling now, my fury getting the better of me.

"You mean the kingdom that has always treated me like I was nothing? I was always overshadowed by *him!* Everything I did, he did it better. Everything I failed at, he succeeded in. He was always meant to rule, and I just follow. I mean nothing to our father. Nothing."

So he *was* jealous, but he sounded...apologetic. Like he knew that was not true, but made the excuse anyway. "Your father and brother love you! You betrayed your own blood, your own family. Silas would be dead right now if I had not come with Vayna, if I had not made that deal." I told him. He needed to hear the truth of his actions, the consequences of his actions. "Vayna wants to kill the people you are supposed to protect, people who you are supposed to love. The people of your kingdom! How could you do this? How did you even do this?"

    He chuckled low and leaned against the bars, crossing his arms. His face was stone, showing little emotion when speaking of Vayna. "I sought Vayna out about a decade ago, telling her I could help her get what she wanted; Asteria. She only asked what was in it for me. I told her all I wanted was revenge."

    He was truly delusional, toxic, and delusional. He is a little dick, but his family loves him. I would say 'loved' after all he has done, but even for all his sins, I know Silas and his father will still love him. He is their family, Afterall. Sometimes, we forget all the horrible things family has done because of our love for them...he is not my family, though.

    "So you serve the woman who will kill your home? Who killed your mother?" It's a low blow, bringing up his mother, but I am not pulling any punches.

"Do not speak of my mother!" he screamed at me, his temper getting the best of him. He took a breath and composed himself. "Do not speak of things you do not know. You know nothing of my mother, of what I have had to do for-." He cut himself off.

Okay...odd.

"You know she will kill you when this is all through, right? You are Asterian; she will want you dead." I tried to reason with him, try to make him see the truth.

"My dear, you truly know nothing." He was mocking me now. "She plans to use me, just like she plans to use you."

I shook my head. "I will never help her, I will never let her use me again, and I will never turn on my kingdom!"

"Do you really think you have a choice?" he asked, chuckling. "I will let you in on a secret; you and I will marry. We will take the throne of Asteria, and Vayna will have free reign over all the magic folk. She plans to take the throne through you because it is yours after all. Only you will not be ruling. I will, and you will be kept somewhere while the people of Asteria die." He said so surely, so simply.

What does he mean it is mine? This plan sounds awfully similar to her original plan to take over the Asterian Kingdom. However, she never imagined that I would find the truth and fall in love with the land. That I would fall in love with their prince.

I never imagined it.

"That will never work. The crown is not mine. I am not even a real mortal princess." I remind him that I am no queen, not even a princess, really.

Simon laughs again. "Gods, you are so oblivious." He groaned, frustrated. "Your mother is *the* Goddess of Life, Melora. Ismera created all the magic folk and the land they lived on. Do you see how having her blood in you would benefit Vayna?"

My mother is the Goddess of Life.

My mother created Asteria and all of the people.

She created magic itself.

There is no way that what I am about to say is true, but it is the only reason Simon would marry me and for Vayna to rule Asteria through him once I acquire the throne.

"I am the true ruler of Asteria," I whispered more to myself than to him.

"There it is. The realization that you are the Queen of Asteria, the blood of the Goddess of Life. Marrying you will make me king, allowing me to rule over the people and for Vayna to do the same. Do you see how this all works out?" Simon asked.

I did. I now understand why Vayna wanted me to return to the capitol with her after the battle and why she wanted so badly for me to take the throne of Asteria the first time I went to the kingdom.

It is because I am its rightful heir.

I am the true Queen of Asteria.

CHAPTER 3

MELORA

*S*ilas lies on the open field where the battle had erupted, the ground scattered with blood and bodies. Silas lies there, his consciousness fading in and out. He is balancing between life and death, walking the fine line between the two. I cling to him as I examine the large, gaping hole in his chest, the one his brother just gave him. The wound won't stop bleeding. There is so much blood, so much of his blood. There is nothing I can do, no way for me to save him. His bright emerald eyes lock onto mine, watching me beg for him to stay with me. To fight, to survive. In this dream, Silas dies. He dies in my weak arms as I cry for him not to leave me, as I beg him to stay with me. There is no bargain with the mortal queen and no healing hands to patch up his chest. He dies, and I cannot save him.

  I know I am dreaming. I know it is more of a nightmare, really, that this is something that did not really happen the way it played out in my dream. I can't shake myself awake, forced to watch as the love of my life dies in my arms. I know it did not happen like this, but the mind is torturous when deprived of food or water. And I have not had both in days.

It is not just my heart that is broken from being away from Silas; it is my mind as well. It is breaking every minute that I am in this prison, dreaming over and over of his death. I sit here in my anger for so long that I finally recognize it as grief.

Regaining power over my own mind, I jolt awake, quickly taking in my surroundings. I am still in the hard chair and itchy bonds that keep my hands tied behind my back. Am still in the cold, damp cell. I catch my breath, trying to stop my heaving chest. The images brought to me in sleep rattle me to the bone, scaring me through and through. Terrify me to no end. I scream to try and relieve some of the building pressure in my body. To try and let loose some of this pent-up rage.

It was just a nightmare.

He is safe.

He is home.

Just. A. Nightmare.

I have to keep reminding myself that Silas is alive and healthy, that he is home with our people, that he is safe, and that he is with those who will be there for him—those who will be there when I return.

The nightly routine I have been repeating consists of the same horrible nightmare, every night the same. Every time I wake in a cold sweat, gasping for air, trying to come down from the terror I felt in the dream. I see him again and again, dying in my arms.

I have lost track of how long I have been in this cell. Days have passed. Possibly even a week. The nights seem to run into the days and vice versa. Naturally, there are no windows in the dungeons, so I can't even track the light. It has all seemed to slip away from me as I sit and rot in my cell.

After a while in here, time has become meaningless to me. Only a thing that separates me from Silas. That is the only thing I will allow to keep us apart. That time will eventually run out, and I will be in his arms once more.

Starvation and dehydration are not helping matters of survival. Both are dangerous concoctions that have been driving me to the point of breaking for the last how many ever days. I can't remember the last time I was brought something to eat or even to drink. What I would give for a piece of fucking cheese.

I practically groan at the thought.

I refuse to cross the line of giving up, of giving in. I will not do it. I will not bend, and I will not break. I will keep pushing to survive because *he* keeps me going. *He* gives me the will to keep going day in and day out in this godsforsaken cell. And for him, I will keep going.

Another factor contributing to my delirious dreams is that I have lost a significant amount of blood. Since my magic is unavailable to me in the cell, my wounds from the battle still have not fully healed. If I were anywhere else, my body would have healed completely by now.

Being an Asterian does come with some cool tricks.

Being the Goddess of Life's daughter? No wonder my broken wrist healed so quickly after punching Milo in his wolf form.

Having magic in your blood also helps when you have just fought a battle.

I missed many of the hits intended for me during the fighting, but knives still found their way to my skin. Slashing and slicing my flesh, creating wounds that still have not healed.

I know my sanity is waning. I know it is slowly leaving me with every passing hour, slipping away with every passing day, with every nightmare that finds me in the night. The quiet in this cell is making my mind wander to places I am not sure it can come back from. I feel my grip on reality loosening every day, unsure of what is real or what is not.

Worth it.

I shut my eyes and squeeze, reminding myself it is all worth it for his life to be spared. For his life to be safe.

The sound of booted footsteps echoes in the dungeon, catching my full attention. I try to steady myself as the footfalls near. I need to focus, keep it together, and get out of this cell. I am not sure how much longer I can last, but I will push until I can no longer go.

Simon comes to the front of the bars, stopping to look at me like he always does. This is our routine, and every day has been the same. He comes down to the dungeons and stares at me through the bars of my cell like I am a caged animal. That's how I am starting to feel—ravenous and wild. It is torturous because I never know if he will come into my cell with me. I never know what his next play is.

His curly hair is shiny, most likely recently washed. Envy slips from my mind, I would love a hot bath right about now.

"Nightmares again?" Simon asks, his voice not as smug as usual...almost concerned. I didn't answer, so he continued. "I can hear you scream from up the stairs. You don't need to try and hide them." I keep quiet, unsure where he is going with this.

Today, Simon moves to unlock the cell door. His tall but thin frame moves to the lock and fiddles with keys. I try to console my surprise. I stiffen as he walks into the small space with me. I am not scared of him, but his presence makes me wary and uneasy. I pray he has enough self-preservation to not touch me...but he is an idiot.

He comes closer, close enough that I can smell his scent—liquor and cedar. I draw back as he continues to strut towards me. With nowhere to go, he stops inches from my face. The chair digs into my skin as I make space between us, not enough for comfort, though.

"I can make this all end, you know?" his voice soft, fueled with desire. My stomach clenches as his hot breath skates over my neck. I promise myself to make his death painful. "All you have to do is be good; just be a good little princess. I will take you away from this horrid place. I will even let you have your old room." He finishes, still so close.

I gather my strength, all of my might, to say, "I would rather sit here and rot than do anything you ask of me." I spit the words in his face like a curse.

His look of disapproval delights me. I smile at his reaction to my wicked words.

He pulls back from my face, and relief runs through me at the distance he puts between us. "I will break you. It is better I do than *her*. It is only a matter of time." He says this simply, like it is a matter of fact. "I am honestly surprised that you have lasted this long. I knew you were strong, but damn. I guess it is out of spite."

I laugh, but it sounds wrong. My sanity is barely there as I say, "You are right. I will spite you and Vayna until the end of my days. Until I no longer walk this earth. Good luck trying to break me. I have been broke long before I got here. I have rebuilt since then." I feel the smile curl on my teeth, wicked and vengeful.

Simon moves so quickly, my tired eyes unable to keep up. He grasps my chin and pulls my lips inches from his. "You will obey me! You will be my bride and you will be safe!" he screams in my face. "If you do as I say, like a good little monster, I will let you live. I will even let you out of this hole."

I hold my head high, even in his harsh hold. "I would rather die in this cell than be married to you."

The hit that Simon delivers comes swiftly, but I hardly feel it. There is only a slight twinge in my jaw as he retreats back like he shocked himself at his violence. I move my jaw around, dousing the pain from his hand.

"I- I...I apologize."

He what?

"My temper is short these days. I should not have struck you. I am sorry." I could not believe my ears. This is the man who cut me with a dagger the first time we met, and now he was apologizing for just hitting me? Was I hallucinating? "Listen to me, Melora. Think about what I am offering. All you have to do is behave. I- I do not wish to keep you down here forever, not like Vayna does. Just listen to what I am saying."

Simon turned and left quickly. He stalked out of the cell like he regretted his actions. He apologized. Apologized for striking me. He confuses me because I am used to the asshole kid he usually is. This was…he was acting differently.

I sat there in my cell, moving my now achy jaw, thinking about what Simon had just said. I was not lying when I told him I would rather die than marry him, than submit to him.

But I need to escape.

I need to get out of this cell.

I can't do that if I am locked in this dungeon, barely holding on to my life. I need strength to either find a way to sneak out of the capitol or to fight my way out. I need strength to get back to Silas. I need sustenance, like food and water.

I promised Silas I would do whatever it took to get back to him. I guess that now includes listening to Simon and behaving, being a good little princess. My skin crawls just at the thought of putting on a show for him. But if it means I will get out of this cell, regain my strength, and get the hell out of here, then so be it.

I will do it.

I will play the pretty princess he wants so badly—the one they all want so badly. I will play his game, and I will play it well. I will put on this act until I get my chance, then I will strike. I will get out of here and as far away from Morania as possible, and I will win.

I will get back to Silas.

CHAPTER 4

SILAS

I am about to storm the *fucking* capitol of Moronia. I am about to burn down every city and every town in this realm if it means I can get Mel back. *My* princess. *My* wife. I will burn every castle and palace from here to the other end of the realm if it means I could see her again, hold her again.

Right now, reeling in my rage, I am willing to demolish a whole civilization just to bring her home. And I would, I know I would.

My thoughts should scare me, should make me sit down and think before I act.

But they don't.

They do not even worry me because I know I would do it. I would do it and not think twice about it. If becoming a villain means I get my Melora back and have my love returned to me, I will become the villain and be an absolute menace. And I will do it with a smile on my fucking face.

I sit in a small meeting room, hand around a tall glass of whiskey. While waiting for the group to arrive, I have had a few drinks—quite a few drinks—

more than I should have had this early in the day. I am already starting to feel the slight buzz from the alcohol.

I do not usually make a habit of consuming liquor, but I need something to soothe the unnerving thoughts of what Melora is enduring. Something to numb the pain of missing her. And whiskey seems to taste better than the vile rage I feel inside.

I know what she is going through has to be ten times worse than anything I am feeling right now. I cannot even begin to think of the things they are doing to her.

Torture. Starvation. Disorientation.

I hate myself even more, knowing she is hurting, knowing she is in pain. I know she is strong. She is one of the toughest people I know. But that does not mean she has to go through something as horrible as being held captive, as being tortured.

"Started early this morning, huh?" Milo asks as he walks quickly into the meeting room, his eyes already burning into me. He understands what I am going through, but I still feel the judgment. I partly am judging myself too, I never usually drink this much. I just need a little something to take the edge off.

I don't take my eyes away from my crystal glass. "I was thirsty," I replied quietly, seemingly unbothered. "Where are the others?" I ask him as he takes the chair to my right. They were all supposed to be here by now. My patience is starting to dwindle.

"On their way." He answered while watching me closely. "Have you eaten anything today?" His voice is careful as if he is trying not to set me off.

I couldn't blame Milo for being cautious around me; I have been very temperamental this past week. The regret, the blame, all of it is driving me mad. It is driving me to react without thinking, lashing out at the friends who love me and are just trying to be here for me.

"I have not." There is no use lying to him; he can always see right through it. Even when we were kids, he could always tell when I was fibbing. "My appetite these days is rarely there," I say quietly.

Milo looked distraught as he watched me take another swig of the dark liquid. He knows what I have been going through and has been there in the dead of night when I wake from night terrors. He knows I would rather die than let Melora stay in that wretched place for another minute and endure all they are putting her through. He knows what this is doing to me.

I wish it was I who was taken in place of her.

The others started to flow in as I swallowed back the lump forming in my throat. Yara first, the twins next. I did not ask any other advisors or my father to meet me here. I knew they would never have my back like my friends in this room do. If I asked them to go to war for Melora right now, they would. They would do it without second thought, because they have come to love the wonderous woman just as I have.

"Sorry, we are late. Kane was gathering supplies," Yara said cheerfully as Kane spread out the supplies on the oak table. When he was finished, a small platter of sandwiches, a few pastries, and a pitcher of what looked to be juice or tea were set in front of me.

I have to give it to them. They really are trying their damndest to keep me strong and sane.

"You needed lunch?" I questioned starkly as the group dug into the spread.

Kane stuffed a thin sandwich in his mouth as he answered, "We were hungry; I figured you might need to eat, too."

Yara scooted the sandwiches closer to me, slyly, like I had not seen her do it. I plucked one from the tray to appease the group, plopping it into my mouth. Yara seemed pleased. The others tried not to meet my eye.

I cleared my throat, gaining their attention. "I am sure you all know why I have asked you to meet," I began, trying to keep my voice even. Now is not the time to lose it. "We need to get Melora back, away from my brother and Vayna."

The group nodded their heads like they already knew what I was going to say.

"Agreed. What's the plan?" Kaius asked, his red hair brushed haphazardly out of his face. I guess I had not noticed, but everyone here looks slightly disheveled. Like they have not slept, just like me.

"I was hoping for help on that front. I- my mind is not in the right place to do this alone. I need help. All of your help." I admitted to my friends.

They usually looked to me to lead and make decisions. This is different. I do not trust myself to make rash choices when Melora's life is at stake— not when something so precious is at stake. "So, does anyone have anything in mind that is not burning the Mornaian capitol to the ground? Because that is all I have managed to come up with." My rage was starting to leak from my pores.

My friends looked stunted, but only for a moment. They quickly caught their reactions to my input on the matter, regaining their looks of objectiveness. Milo chuckled lightly, knowing that this was my anger talking. "I do not think that would get us far, brother. It would only put Melora in more danger." Milo stated, thinking as he said, "We should take a...more tactical approach."

"What if we sent a small group to infiltrate the capitol, locate Mel, and bring her home?" Kane laid out his idea, which was not all that bad. But...

"Sending our people into the palace will only give the mortals an easier chance to capture our people. We don't need any more Asterians behind those walls." I told him a little more harshly than I would have normally.

"Send me! I would love to get my hands on that mortal bi-" Yara started way too excitedly, but was cut off.

"Not happening," Milo grunted out, ending that thought before it could take root.

"I love the enthusiasm, but we both know Melora would not want you anywhere in the capitol, let alone the palace." I tried to reason with her. I know they want to get her home as much as I do, but I will not put them in unnecessary danger.

A light knock on the door got all of our attention. I looked up to see Penn standing in the doorway. He also looked tired and a mess, like he hadn't slept. I guess Melora's absence was affecting everyone.

"Perhaps I could help?" Penn inquired from where he stood. I looked at Melora's old friend. He protected her as best he could when she was a mortal princess and stood at her side when we battled the Moranian army. I trusted him when it came to her because I knew he cared for her like a daughter.

"What do you have in mind?" I asked the dark-haired man. I can see how Melora became so tough in her combat skills. This man was built of solid muscle, forged from time and training.

Penn took a step into the room, all eyes on him. "You know I would give anything to get Melora back. To see her safe and sound." He started, staring directly at me. I nodded, understanding his grief. "Start with Ravenhall. Take it. I know it inside and out. Take it and move in position to take the capitol. Make them sweat." I like how he thinks.

"So we take Ravenhall and align ourselves to take the capitol. Then what?" Milo asked, ever the military man.

"We bargain with them. We tell Queen Vay-" He stopped himself. "We tell Vayna to release Melora, and we will stand down. If she refuses, the people will question their safety and why their queen is holding their princess captive. Her lies start to crumple if she does not hand over Melora." He has a point.

We all look at each other, contemplating Penn's idea. It is a good idea. Ravenhall will easily be taken, and once we do that, Vayna will know we are coming for her. This is a wiser plan than to just rampage my way through the mortal realm until I have back what is mine. Penn is wise, and I trust him with this.

"We take Ravenhall," I said steadily, regally, trying to resemble some type of leader. "Start moving the army into place. We will move soon." With that, Kane and Kaius rose to start getting the army ready. Penn agreed to help with the strategies of overthrowing Ravenhall. Milo gladly jumped on that task. Everyone had left the meeting room to begin their plans.

Everyone except Yara.

She sat in her chair, staring at me with a sweet expression on her face. I knew her normally cheerful demeanor had changed since Melora had been gone, but she was trying to remain herself.

"You should eat some more." That was all she said.

I dropped my head into my hands, exhausted from the quick meeting that just adjourned. "I am not hungry, Yara."

She let out a frustrated grunt. "You have barely been eating, only drinking whiskey. You need your strength, Silas. Melora needs it."

Hearing her name stung my skin.

Like a thousand knives had been thrown at me, piercing my heart.

"Don't." I felt the burn of tears start behind my eyes. I can't talk about her, can't think about her without pain swelling inside. "Please don't, Yara."

Yara, a friend for decades and a sister to me, moves to console me. Her thin arms wrap around me in a hug before I can stop her. She hugs me hard—harder than someone her size should be able to. She pulls me in so my head rests in the crook of her neck.

"I know this is torture for you. I hear you in the night, crying for her. Silas, we are here for you." That was all she had to say before the floodgates broke open.

I cried, sobbed into her shoulder. My body shuttered as screams of anguish muffled into her. Yara holds me through it, through the suffering I am going through. She lets me cry for a while, and we stay like this. Her holding on to me and gently rubbing my back.

I am lucky to have friends like the ones I have. Ones who know I am regretting what happened to my Melora and hate myself because I could not save her. They know, and yet they are still here for me, even at my lowest.

And they are ready to go to war for the one we all love.

CHAPTER 5

MELORA

I know what I need to do.

I know, yet I hesitate.

I hesitate because I know it means submitting to the younger Asterian prince, giving him what he wants. Submitting means accepting I am his, that I will marry him and stay prisoner.

You only need to put on an act until you get your chance, I remind myself. I will not wait long once I am free of this prison.

I will put on a show for Simon and Vayna if necessary. I will be the well-behaved princess Simon wants me to be. If I do this, it means I get out of this hellish cell. I get a chance to escape, and I will. The first chance I get.

I clench my teeth hard at the thought of obeying Simon, even for a short time.

But I know I must do it. I will do it so I can return to the one I truly am meant to be with.

Silas.

I say his name in my head like a mantra, remembering that this is all worth it because he is alive. Doing what I have to do to get out of the dungeons is worth it because I get a shot at getting away. As soon as I see a chance to run, I will take it. I will kill anyone who gets in my way.

I will get back to Silas, and I will tell him every day that I love him. That I am *in* love with him. I should have let him know sooner, as soon as I knew. It is the only regret I have as I sit in the cold, damp prison.

I will make up for it. If I get out of here, *when* I get out of here, I promise I will devote myself to loving him. Silas deserves so much love. He deserves to be cherished.

Footsteps interrupt my thoughts once again. I am ready this time, ready to play the part of the obedient princess. I prepare myself for the imminent arrival of Simon. I cool my constant rage to a simmer and clear my mind of everything besides my goal: escape.

"Good morning, princess." Simon greets me in a sing-songy tone.

I had no idea the night had passed.

Focus. I remind myself. Focus on what matters.

"Good morning, Simon," I say sweetly. My words must have surprised him because he stopped suddenly outside the cell. My words even surprised me the slightest bit.

His dark-haired head tilted to the side like he was questioning if I had indeed gone mad. I had, in fact, gone a bit mad in my time here, because I continued by saying, "I have thought about what you said the last time you visited me."

His eyebrows rose, "You have? Please, tell me your thoughts. I would love to know what is happening in that head of yours." He narrowed his eyes as he spoke.

"I want to obey you," I started shyly, acting timid. "I want to live, and you said you will let me live if I do as you say. I will listen. I promise." I let my eyes fall to the floor like I was embarrassed to admit such a thing. *It's all a show*, I reminded myself, and I think I am selling it.

"I knew you would come around. Knew you would understand." he said, interested. "Tell me, though, what made you change your tune so quickly? The other day, you wanted nothing but to rot in this cell rather than be my bride." He inched closer to the bars, looking for my reaction.

I would not give him one. "I reacted without thinking, and I am...I am sorry. Being your bride does not sound so bad if it means I will live." I let my voice waver, pleading with him now. "I am hopeless. I have given up. I am hanging on by a thread. Please, Simon, help me. I will be good." I lied so easily.

I could tell he was contemplating my words like he wanted to believe me but was afraid. So, I added, "Please, Simon. You are the only person who can help me. I have been here for how long? No one is coming for me. I need you."

It physically hurts to say those words. To blame my lover and my friends for not coming to save me the second I was placed in this cell. In truth, I do not want them to come for me. I actually hoped they would not try to at all because they would be endangering themselves. I would rather stay here and find a way to escape myself than have them anywhere near this horrid place.

Simon seemed pleased by my words, by my lies. He looked proud of himself, like I was something he had finally conquered. Gods, I cannot wait to kill this man.

"Alright, princess." He said, holding up his hands. "There is no need to beg. I will bring you topside with me, but you must keep your word on your promise, or I will kill you. Vayna *will* kill you." His words were menacing. His eyes told me he was telling the truth.

Simon opened the cell door with the key he had brought and stepped inside. I told my body to relax, but I could not release the tension building as he neared me. "Thank you." I looked at him under my eyelashes, hoping he would think I was admiring him for letting me free.

But he did not move to undo my bonds or remove me from the chair. Simon stood in front of me, looking over my body from head to toe. I grew wary under his scrutiny. "What-what are you doing?" I asked nervously.

He raised a hand to his chin, thinking intensely. "I believe that you will obey me. However, that does not mean Vayna nor I will let you have your magic. I am thinking of a place that would be best for it."

"What is *it*?" I asked quickly.

His gaze turned deadly, angry even, and I knew I was in trouble. "I told you there are wards around this cell that keep your magic from you while you are in here. What if I told you I could carve a ward into your skin to keep your magic from you even after you exited this cell?" He crouched in front of me now, his eyes never leaving mine.

Fear coursed through me as I watched him take out a small blade from his belt. I knew what he was about to do. I knew he was about to carve this ward into my skin, continuing to make my magic unavailable to me.

I can survive without it. I can escape without it.

"I will make it quick. You will barely feel a thing."

I doubt it.

Simon looked as though he was enjoying himself, the sick bastard. He ripped the hem of the top of my pants, revealing my stark hip bone. The skin shines milky white in the dark room. I watched as Simon lifted the blade to my skin, and I did not flinch when he began to carve.

I will not show fear.

I will not show weakness.

I sat as still as possible as he continued his work, only looking down once to find blood seeping into my lap. I felt myself slip into the nothingness I often did when I would go into Lord Chapler's study when he would 'teach me a lesson.' It helped in traumatic situations, when I wanted to be strong. When I did not want to give the abuser the satisfaction of a reaction.

So, I sat there as he finished his masterpiece. Simon's own brand on my skin. A mark that will never leave me.

Will I ever be able to use magic again?

The thought hurt. It hurt to think the only thing I have in connection with my mother may have just been taken from me. That this one symbol could take so much.

"There," Simon said proudly.

I looked at his ward, the slices bloody and swollen. The symbol was a triangle with a line going horizontally through it. One simple symbol. It did not hurt that much, but the sting was there.

Simon lifted his hand, and I fell forward, catching myself on my hands and knees before I face-planted. He let me free of my bonds with his magic. I try to remind myself not to lash out at the princeling. Not to kill him with a swift twist of his neck. He was my ticket out of here, out of this cell.

"Stand," he demanded.

I tried to lift myself up, but my legs were weak, and my arms were sore from having been behind me for so long. I tried but kept failing. I fell to the cold floor before him, and a small sob broke my lips. I regretted showing emotion, showing that I was so weak from being down here for the period of time I was.

Simon huffed out an annoyed groan as he bent, sliding his hand under my legs. He pulled me to his chest, carrying me out of the cell.

I was out.

I wanted so badly to rebel against his hold, against his arms around me. I knew I should not, that it would be unwise to anger him. He could put me right back in the prison.

The sun hit me as we cleared the steps to the main floor of the palace. My eyes burned from the bright light, but it felt good on my skin. Anything felt better than the damp air of the cell. I shielded my eyes and turned into Simon's chest more. A pleased growl vibrated in his chest, and I was about to be sick.

Knowing that he was pleased with my actions, pleased with me, made me want to vomit.

I knew the hall he took me down, and I knew where we were in the palace. My room was just ahead—my real room, not the guest room I stayed in when I first returned to the capitol. Simon opened the door and walked in.

I remembered this space so much differently than it is before me now. It is not as big and beautiful as I thought it was when I was younger, more oblivious to things.

He sat me on my bed, and I lay down. I looked up to the ceiling, where there was a painting I remembered clearly. It was of the Goddess of Life. Now, knowing what I know, the painting is very foretelling. I looked at it every night when I was a child living here. I had looked up to my mother as I fell asleep in an enemy's territory.

"You will rest. I will have food sent in, as well as bathing water." Simon told me, then left. He closed the door behind him, and I was alone again.

I sat on the bed for a while, stretching and trying to regain feeling in my shoulders. The food finally came, and I about melted onto the floor when the smell hit me. The woman who brought the covered tray removed the lid, and I was happily met with roasted meat, soup, and a hunk of bread.

I devoured the meal in minutes.

Although I knew it was a fairly bland meal, it tasted like true bliss in my mouth.

The bathing water came next. The steaming water called to me as I stood at the tiny copper tub and looked into it. I was not about to undress fully and leave myself completely exposed. I grabbed a washcloth and dipped it into the water. I quickly washed myself, maneuvering under my dirty clothing.

When I got to my hip, I had to wring the cloth out a few times because the water and blood were just being pushed around on my skin. I needed to clean the cuts out because I definitely did not want those to get infected if I was planning on making my getaway.

I finished washing, the water now red and mirky from the blood and gore left on me from battle. Some of it mine, some of it others. Either way, I felt better. I was still exhausted, but my belly was full, and my wounds were clean.

That was all I needed to make my move. This will be enough to hold me over until I make it home. It had to be. The short moments where I had obeyed Simon and submitted to him were tortuous. I realize now that I am not strong enough to endure more of the facade I had planned to play.

I need to get out now.

CHAPTER 6

MELORA

I am alone.

I am fed.

I am clean.

Somewhat clean.

Now is the time to strike, to make my move to escape, to get the hell out of here. I need to make my move, and I need to make it quick. Simon thinks I am enjoying the bed and the food, which I did, but now is the time to slip away and be gone before he realizes it.

I think back to my days as a child, exploring the grounds and all the rooms in the palace. Every hallway and door there was in this massive castle. I remember a small servant's door in the kitchens that was used to bring in the daily produce, tucked away in the corner of the room. If I can get there and make it through the door, I can be in the wind before anyone knows I am gone.

Simon believes that I will not act, especially now that I have no magic. I brushed my fingers over the still-tender spot on my hip that had started to swell where he had sliced me. I cleaned it as best as

I could without fully getting into the water. I hope it will be enough. It has to be enough.

Even if I do not have my magic, I have my skill. I know I can handle myself when it comes to hand-to-hand, I can handle myself better than most. I just hope I do not run into Simon because I know he will use his magic over me if necessary. I kicked his ass once without my magic. I can do it again.

The memory of the day in the training field when I first met Simon comes back to me. He wanted to spar with me, then insisted that we up the ante—that we use daggers. He threw one at my face, and luckily, I caught it, giving him hell afterward.

I remember Silas that day, too. He was so mad at his brother, so angry with him for touching me, for harming me. I thought he would actually kill him right then and there. I should have known then that Silas loved me, because he was willing to hurt his own blood for harming me.

Just wait until Silas gets his hands on his brother this time.

I looked around the room for something I could use as a weapon, something small and sharp and easy to carry. I don't suppose they have daggers just lying around here for me to use. There is a mirror; I could break it and use the shard if needed.

But it would slice up my hands, hurting me more than helping me.

I continued to look, frantically searching around the room. My gaze finally landed on a writing quill that sat on a small desk in the corner. I picked up the skinny pen, and the point glistened with black ink. It was sharp, sharp enough to hurt.

Good enough for me.

I held the quill tight as I went over the route in my head: Out the door. To the left. Down the stairs. Hall to the kitchen. Door by the fireplace. Once I was out of the palace, I would hightail it for the forest line and make my way to Ravenhall. Once in Ravenhall, I would go from there.

As long as I was away from the capitol, I could not be used, and I could not be manipulated. I could not be played as a pawn in this game of crowns. I would not be able to be used by Vayna any longer, and that is motivation enough to get the fuck out of here.

I stared at the door and readied myself, readied myself for what was waiting for me on the other side. I let the hatred and resentment come to the surface, filling my body with emotion that got my heart pumping. My skin did not tingle with my magic answering to my temper, but the anger still felt like an old friend coming to comfort me when I needed it most. I needed to remember what these people did to me, what they planned to do to my people. I will kill them all if I need to. And I will not think twice about it.

I opened the door swiftly before I changed my mind. The door opened easily, not locked, to my surprise. I opened the door fully, the hinges creaking as it swung. The door opened, but there was a slight problem.

A six-foot-something-sized problem.

A massive man stood before me, looking at me like he was waiting for me to run. Of course, I would be met with a tower of a person first thing when I opened the door to escape. Good thing for Penn.

Before the man could reach to grab me, I struck my quill into his throat. I reached high to hit my target, but I met the mark. Blood spurted from his jugular, the red liquid getting all over me once again. His eyes shined with shock as I ripped the quill away from his skin. He fell to his knees, trying to hold his neck together. Blood seeped through his fingers as he started to fall. As he went down, I jumped over him and ran.

I was not waiting around to watch this man die.

Out the door, to the left. I was already making good time on my escape plan. I just need to get to the kitchen before anyone else sees me or the mess I just made in the hall. Anyone could be lurking around this castle, and I was not about to let them stop me.

I ran, ran so hard and fast, because I knew if I did not make it now, I was not sure I would. I could already feel fatigue hitting me, making my movements sluggish. I guess the one meal I had was not enough for me to fully regain my strength. It will have to do, though.

Around a corner and down another hall.

Fuck.

I stop in my tracks as two guards stand outside the kitchens. My lucky day that I have run into not one, but two guards standing between me and freedom. They looked at me, then looked at each other. I am sure they recognized me and knew I should not be out of my room.

The blood all over my clothing from the other guard did not help the innocent act either. They started for me at the same time, both as big as the other guard.

Here we go.

The first man went to tackle me, crouching low enough that I jumped over him, feet first. My feet landed in a brutal hit to the second guard's chest. He drew back, the wind knocked clean out of him. I landed in a crunch and quickly turned as the first guard regained his footing. He swung at me, a giant fist coming straight for my cheek. I caught his hand and used my leverage to twist his arm, snapping the bone in two. The man cried in pain, but it fueled me to inflict more.

The other guard finally caught his breath. He came at me in hurried strikes that I barely dogged, tiredness eating at me. I was growing slow and tired. He got close enough to grab me, and that is where he made his mistake. I may be half the size of these men, of most of my opponents, really, but I know how to use my body to my advantage.

In this case, I had a weapon. I jammed the quill into the guard's side over and over, hopefully hitting something vital. He hissed in pain, keeling over as he clutched his side. I brought a knee to his face as he bent at the waist, hitting him directly in the nose. The crunch was satisfying, as was the howling from the other guard, whose arm was twisted at a weird angle.

Both were incapacitated, but I didn't stop. Something took hold of me. I am not sure if it was the pent-up anger from being in the cell or simply everything that has been taken from me. But I was going for the kill.

I thought of Loral's limp body on the ground as I came behind the broken-nosed guard; I slit his throat without a second thought. I walked to the other guard, his pleading cries breaking the ringing in my ears.

I knew what I was doing was heinous; I did not need to kill these men. I could have run after they were both unable to fight, but I didn't run. I know I could stop. I could stop myself from killing this man.

I could stop myself from becoming the monster I knew was just waiting to be released. The monster I did not want to become. I knew I could stop myself from letting all of my rage and fury be given to these men trying to stop me from going home. I thought about it, thought about stopping and caging that monster.

But I looked at the quivering man, he looked at me like I was death himself. I decided then that I would not regret the monster I was made into because no one ever regretted what they did to me to make me this way.

I stuck my quill into the man's neck, just like the first guard I encountered. He quickly bled out, his eyes never leaving mine.

I should have thought more of it, of what I had just done, but I turned and ran to the kitchen where I knew freedom awaited. The door was right in front of me. I could feel the victory on my fingertips as I reached for the knob. When I opened the door, covered in the blood of the guards who tried to stop me, I was met with another problem.

Simon stood, leaning nonchalantly against a counter. He bit into an apple as he surveyed me, looking me up and down. I knew I was screwed. I had just killed three *mortals*, but Simon could use his magic on me. And there would be nothing I could do to fight it.

"I should have known it was too good to be true," he murmured, disappointment filling his words. "Just when I thought I had you in my grasp, you try to escape to go back to my brother." He stalked toward me, and I readied myself for combat. I would not give up, not without a fight.

Simon stopped in front of me, his dark eyes radiating anger. I let loose a combination of punches before he even saw it coming. He really needed to work on his hand-to-hand. I landed a right hook, then a left, disorienting him and knocking him off balance.

I felt the exhaustion starting to weigh on me more. *NO.* I screamed to myself. I will not give up when I am this close.

I swiped the quill, slashing his arm and drawing blood. His grunt of pain was short-lived as everything started to go black. I think I was starting to black out, possibly from the pain.

No. No. No. Not yet, not like this.

I could barely hold my hands up in the positions Penn had taught me. My actions had caught up with me and I was about to be spent.

Simon caught me by the throat as I lazily swung for him again. I choked as his grip tightened. He turned me, my back now against his hard chest. His hand gripped harder, and I thought he might kill me, might choke me out.

His free hand went to the carved symbol on my hip, still slightly open from the fresh cuts he gave me. I screamed in pain as Simon squeezed the symbol that he had carved into my skin. He was not letting up, and the pain was taking over. My consciousness started to slip, but I still struggled against his hold.

I felt his lips brush against my ear as he said, "You just proved to me that you cannot be trusted, little monster."

CHAPTER 7
SILAS

I am drunk.

I am *really* drunk.

Plastered may be a better word.

I started early today, somewhere between breakfast and lunch. I honestly have no idea what time, but what I do know is that the pain of Melora being gone is still there.

It is still prevalent in my veins as I swig down another sip of the brown liquor. I feel it, her absence, with every drink I take. Not even the burn of whiskey can take away the memory of her screaming for me to stay with her.

I thought that maybe I could numb my mind and keep the thoughts of her out of my head. Perhaps I could feel anything other than the fucking agony of losing her, losing her because she saved me.

But it is still there, eating at my soul with every breath I take and every drink I drink.

I sit in the living area of my rooms in the palace. I thought about going to my cottage in the city, the 'safe house' Melora has started to call it. I like that she gave my home a nickname; I really think of it as ours now.

I couldn't bring myself to go to the safe house, though, to think of all the memories Melora and I shared in that home. I can't go there and not think about how this all could have been different.

If we were different people, living in a small cottage by the sea, no obligations, no war—just us.

But we are not different people.

We are who fate deemed us to be.

We are who we are, and that is why it pains me to go there without her, to go there and think about what could have been.

So, I sit in the living area, staring at the flickering fire in the hearth, the flames a constant heat against my skin. It is not cold out by any means, but *I am* cold. I am always so fucking cold.

Like my insides know I am missing the one thing that has brought me warmth, that has brought me love. Her absence has made a part of me cold, cold and distant.

I sit and seethe, thinking about how the battle in the Fallen Forest played out, replaying over and over the moment Melora sacrificed herself for me. I have been thinking about it for hours, maybe even the whole day, wondering if things could have been different. If maybe, just maybe, one thing could have been different, and it would not have ended the way it did.

Maybe I would still have my Melora.

I know I can't change the past, that I should not dwell on it, and that I need to focus on getting her back. I need to focus on our plans and strategies to wage war against Morania to get her back. But I can't think of anything else when I know Melora is suffering. She is suffering because of me.

I lift the glass bottle to my lips to bear another swallow. Somewhere around dinner time, I switched from a glass to drinking straight from the bottle. I don't know, really. The sun was setting, and now it was dark. I guess it is night.

The day has passed by while I sit here and soak in my alcohol. I should have been productive, should have done a lot of things. I should have trained, eaten, bathed.

I should have saved Melora.

But I didn't, and now we are here.

I feel myself gripping the arms of the chair with my free hand, so tight the leather is starting to crack. Just the thought, the image of her in a cell or being starved, is making me crazy. It is making me feel pain and rage like I have never before experienced.

A knock comes on my door. I ignore it immediately, not wanting to talk or be bothered. The thought of having a conversation right now is enough to make me open another bottle.

The knock comes again, and this time, it is harder and more urgent. I ignore it still because I know who it is. I know who it is, and I am not answering because I know what will happen. I know that Milo is on the other side of that door, pounding to get in.

He is here to make sure I am still alive.

"I will break down this door, Silas! Open the fuck up!" Milo yells from the hall. I guess I locked the door. I laughed at myself, thinking about how smart I was.

The door flies open as I take another drink from the lip of the bottle. The hinges sounded like they broke off, most likely from Milo kicking down the door.

Dick.

"What the actual fuck are you doing?" Milo asks, walking angrily into the room behind me. I still sit in my chair, staring at the flames, but I hear his steps. They sound mad.

He walks around to the front of my chair, standing right in my view of the fire. Milo looks at me, at my face, at the bottle, and at the empty one on the floor. I know what he is thinking. I am thinking it, too, but I'm just ignoring it. He is thinking that I have fallen off the deep end, given up and given in.

And maybe I have.

"Are you drunk?" he asks with a surprised stare—an angry, surprised stare. I am not sure why he is surprised; these days, my glass has been a constant fixture in my hand.

A laugh slips from my lips. "Very," I tell him, trying to focus on one of him, but it is hard when I see three. "Stop moving," I tell him, squinting to focus on him and his hard face.

"I am standing still. You are moving. Swaying, actually." He says dryly, annoyance in his tone. "Is this what you have been doing all day? Sitting here drowning in liquor?" he asks.

I lift the bottle and cheers him. "I have."

Milo scoffs, actually scoffs at me, like I have greatly annoyed him. He grabs the bottle from me, yanking it hard out of my hands. "Hey!" I yelled at him because he took my bottle.

"You need to sober up and think. Think Silas. You are sitting here doing what?" he paused to ask me. "Getting drunk enough that I can smell the alcohol coming from you? Trying to forget all that has happened. Trying to forget what has happened to Melora?" He finished, his voice angry and loud in my muffled ears.

Heat immediately radiated to my face, heat from the anger I felt from Milo's words. Deep down, deep down where I am sober, I know they are true. But hearing the truth hurts, even more so when it is from your best friend.

"Don't talk about her," I tell him, trying to keep the simmering anger at bay. "Do not talk about-'

"About what? About how we lost Mel? How she is suffering and going through gods know what and here you are drowning away your sorrow?" His words were laced with cruelness but also with truthfulness. "She needs you, Silas. She needs you now more than ever, and she needs a strong you. The you /know." Milo's face was sad like it pained him to speak to me like this. But he knew this was what I needed.

Still.

It hurts hearing the truth, understanding that this is what I should not be doing to help save my Melora. I should be fighting, tearing down cities, burning anyone in my path to her.

But here I am, drunk and afraid that she is gone forever.

I let my head fall to my hands, my palms pushing into my eyes. "Okay, help me. Help me, Milo." I plead to him, needing a friend to pull me from this stupor.

"Let's sober you up."

A cup of coffee, a loaf of bread, and an hour later, I was feeling more like myself. I had sobered quickly from Milo's harsh but true words, but the bread definitely helped.

"How are you feeling?" Milo asks across from me in the chair that matches mine.

I chuckle lightly. "Better," I tell him. "Stupid." Milo laughs at that statement.

I do feel stupid, stupid that I let self-doubt and sorrow lead my actions. I know what I need to do to get Melora back, and being a drunk is not one of them. If Milo had not come in when he did, I most likely would have drank myself to death or close.

    I was lucky to have a friend like Milo, a friend that has turned to family.

    A knock on the busted door frame grabbed both of our attention. We turned to see who could possibly be coming to my door this late in the night.

    I was not expecting it to be my father.

    "I thought I might find you two here," my father said, coming from where my door used to be. "Mind if I come in?" he asked sheepishly.

    I exchanged a look with Milo, who gave me a sympathetic shrug. "Talk to him." he urged me.

    I let out a sigh. "You are always my voice of reason, sometimes even when I don't want you to be."

    Milo chuckled as he rose, standing from the chair. He walked past my father on his way out, patting him on the shoulder as he passed.

    "Come on in," I told him reluctantly. I haven't talked to him since after I lost Melora, since he came to me when I woke after the battle. I could not bring myself to do it, to talk to him and see his lying face.

    He took the seat next to me where Milo had been sitting. "I-I want to apologize, son." he began, staring at the fire.

    I looked at him, really looked at him, and he looked old. He looked tired and ragged as I watched him speak. "I know you do not trust me," he began,

    "You are right, I don't."

    He sighed, "but I still wanted to apologize. To say I am sorry for not telling you and Melora the truth when it was so easy to do so. I- I am unsure why I lied. If I was scared or unsure of the future. But I know I should not have lied, not when all she has ever wanted is to understand herself. And for that, I am sorry. I am sorry, son." he looked at me tenderly, like a father would look at a son.

I need to think about my next words very carefully because, between him and my hangover headache, I am about two seconds from losing it. "You knew the truth of her mother, of who her mother really was. Not the first Asterian but the Goddess of Life. You knew, and you lied. Melora will not be able to forgive you and so neither will I."

He looks down, defeated. "But I do understand that you were only trying to protect what you thought needed protecting." I continued.

He nodded slowly. "I was scared for the future, of not knowing what would happen once she knew the truth, once everyone knew the truth."

I understand why he did it—I really do. I know he just wanted to protect me and Simon, but he did not need to lie straight to our faces—straight to her face.

"I accept your apology, and once Melora returns, you can apologize to her, too. *She* is far more forgiving than I; that much is true." I tell him, making sure he knows I will never fully forgive him for lying to me, for lying to *my wife*.

"I understand, son." He looked at me like he really did, like he understood why I could never trust him again, at least not when it came to Melora.

He took one last look at me, then stood to leave. My father walked until he was almost out the door, but something came over me to stop him.

"Father?" I called to him, and he quickly turned to face me.

"Yes?"

"Thank you for- for coming to talk," I tell him, somehow feeling like the little boy I used to be.
He smiled a closed-lip smile. "Of course, son."

CHAPTER 8

MELORA

❡It has been three days since Simon placed me in his living chambers. Three days since I have been placed in a different form of prison.

If I had to guess, this room is a guest suite that he has taken over. Or it could be where he has taken up residence in the palace for the last decade. This area of the palace was completely out of the way; I didn't even know it existed. It was perfect for him to keep hidden.

I am sure Vayna intended for him to be sequestered away somewhere so no one would see him and ask questions. So *I* wouldn't see him and ask questions when I was a child.

The thought of Simon lurking around the palace when I was only a child makes my skin crawl.

After my unsuccessful attempt at an escape, Simon decided I would no longer be staying in *my* rooms and that I needed to be in his. I was under constant watch by either the two guards in the hall or Simon himself. It was mostly the guards because the only time I saw Simon was at night. I was not sad about that in the slightest.

The living space was large, larger than my childhood room here. There was the bedroom of course, a separate bathroom, and a conversation area between the two. I tried to sleep on the settee in the conversation area, it sat in front of a blazing hearth that I stared at until my eyes burned. However, Simon has other ideas that allow him to keep a watchful eye on me, a *very* watchful eye on me.

Simon comes in at night, only ever after the sun has set and the darkness of the night is filling the sky. He readies for bed as I sit quietly, pretending to be sleeping on the settee. I lay as still as I can be, trying to make my breathing even. He slips into the bed, and although I hope the scenario will be different every night, it is not. Simon comes for me and demands I sleep in his bed. With him. He can always tell that I am not sleeping and threatens to carry me into his bed if I cannot walk. That usually gets me moving.

The first night when he demanded this of me, I refused and lashed out violently. Yelling and cursing his name, throwing a small table at his head, and even trying to make a break for the window, willing to jump to my death rather than sleep in the same bed as him.

But he ended that temper tantrum quickly by telling me that if I did not listen, I would never leave the room again. Therefore, I will never get a shot at escaping again.

So, I listened and slunk into the soft bed. I never sleep, though, not until he leaves in the early hours of the morning. I lay awake all through the night and pray to my mother that he does not turn to me, does not reach out for me.

He hasn't, but it does not mean that, eventually, he will start demanding more from me.

Being in his living quarters is just another prison, a warm and more comfortable prison, but still a prison. Being locked away again has made my determination dwindle down to nothing. Depression has settled deep within my bones, making me exhausted and unmotivated. I know I need to get away from this place, but it just doesn't seem doable. It just does not seem possible.

My appetite has also seemed to leave me. Just like my motivation, I no longer have the energy to act on it. Every time I am brought food, I try to eat it, but it tastes wrong—like it is stale. I should be eating, forcing the food into my mouth because I need to be healthy. I need to get stronger so I can try escaping again.

As the days pass, I just feel so lost, so useless. Every day, I try to remind myself that I promised to get back to him, promised to get back to Silas. But it seems harder and harder to continue. It feels like giving in would be the easiest thing to do right now.

But I know Silas would tell me to fight. He would tell me he needed me to come home. I feel like I can hear his words pushing me to live, to survive, to keep going. Thinking of his words, of the way he would encourage me, is the only thing keeping me sane.

The door suddenly opens, and I almost fall from the settee I had been lying on. Simon comes in, hurried and annoyed. I was not prepared for his presents until nightfall, so he caught me off guard. I had a feeling something was wrong.

Even though I did not have my magic to tell me when something bad was about to happen, I knew this was all wrong.

Simon pushed his hands through his wavy hair, frustrated. He turned to me, finally remembering I was living in his space. We stared at one another for what seemed like hours until he turned from me, not meeting my eye. His eyes seemed tired, as if he were worried.

"You have been summoned," he said, uninterested and quite annoyed. "The queen has requested that you have dinner with her." He spoke with his back to me, facing the window.

I will have dinner with *her*?

How dare she command my presence when she has not even seen me since being brought here, imprisoned here. I can feel the blood start to boil within me just at the thought of her. She thinks she can just order me around like I belong to her, like I am her little pet.

Those days are over.

"You can tell her that I will not be having dinner with her, and she can eat shit," I said harshly, then returned to staring at the flames in the hearth.

Simon walked toward me intensely, smirking slightly at my comment. "You *will*. And you will give me no problems, little monster." He reaches like he will take me by the throat but stops when I pull away from him.

I think about acting on him, about grabbing *his* throat and snapping it swiftly.

But I remember Silas as I stare at his younger look alike. I remember I needed to survive to be able to get back to him. To get back to our home. If I kill Simon, I doubt I will live to see my way home.

Having dinner with Vayna will allow me to speak with her, as horrible as it sounds. I could see how much information she is willing to give me, how much she is willing to share. Maybe even information on my mother, who I know is here somewhere in the palace. Vayna admitted it at the Fallen Forest battle, and I plan on finding her.

If having dinner with Vayna meant I could learn my mother's exact whereabouts, I guess it would not hurt me that much. However, I need to keep my temper in check. I know myself, and as soon as I see her, everything she has done will be at the forefront of my emotions.

I cannot let her get the best of me.

"When would she like to see me?"

An hour later, I am seated at a long dining table in a room I do not recognize. Vayna has yet to grace me with her presence, so I sit here and wait. Wait for the woman who murdered my first friend, who made up my entire life, who holds my mother hostage, who wants to take my kingdom and kill my people.

Heeled footsteps draw me from my angered thoughts. I know she is coming, and I know I need to reel in my anger because If I let it lose, I will kill her.

But could I actually kill her?

I have yet to fully understand what magic she possesses and the extent of her power, if it would even be possible to kill her. She snapped Loral's neck with a twist of her wrist, who is saying she will not do the same to me.

Control it. I remind myself as Vayna's lithe body comes into view. She looks as evil as ever, her blood-red gown flowing behind her smoothly. Her black hair is always pin-straight, never a strand out of place. The smile she has on her lips is not a smile of compassion, but a smile of victory.

She thinks her plan is falling into place, and the pieces are finally fitting. I hate to break it to her, but her first plan to use and manipulate me failed to work. I can guarantee her second will not be successful either.

"Melora," she walks up to the table, and a guard pulls out her seat for her. I hold back a roll of my eyes. "You look awful," she states after getting a closer look at my features. I guess I do look pretty rough right now; my skin is pale due to lack of sunlight, and my body is frail from not eating.

But she didn't need to say it.

"Maybe if I was not kept in a dungeon for gods know how long, I would look better," I answer her annoying evaluation.

Vayna rolled her dark eyes like she was annoyed. "Oh, do not be so dramatic." She laughed at me. "You, my dear, will be the Queen of Asteria," she said it like it was some prize to be won. "Simon will be your king. He is rather handsome; it could be worse." she sits and stares at me, her regalness filling her every bone.

I feel the fury starting to take over, starting to fill my blood. My hands are shaking, shaking from the anger burning inside of me. "It will mean nothing with what you plan to do to my people. You plan to control them, to use me to rule over them. They will never bow to you. Never." My voice is rough. I know it is from the violence I am holding back.

Her amused look turned stark, lethal. "Well, you do not really have a choice do you?"

The silence between us is deafening. The tension is so palpable that I am sure she could feel it on her perfect skin. I stare at her, not backing down. I do not trust myself to use words to stand my ground, but I will not let her think she can walk all over me any longer. She does not rule me anymore.

She breaks the silence as she looks away from my hardened stare. "We will be traveling to Ravenhall. We are leaving tomorrow."

She must have seen my shock because she continued. "We need to be closer to the enemy. Be closer so that when you and Simon marry, we can invade and claim what is rightfully ours."

Rightfully *mine* I want to tell her.

I still have not come to terms with being the true ruler of Asteria, the rightful queen. I had just come to terms with having magic, with my mother being Asterian, before I was taken from my people. Now, I learn that I am the Queen of Asteria, and my mother is the Goddess of Life. I have always been meant to rule.

"I have already sent Arlan, the king, and a convoy of guards to Ravenhall to prepare for our arrival," she tells me nonchalantly.

Arlan. I grimace to myself just thinking of his name. I really wish I would have killed him when I had the chance.

I stayed silent, so she continued. "I know that look; you have turned quite murderous since going to Asteria. Do not worry, I punished that shit of a son for what he had done. For trying to take power that was to be mine."

Not for almost killing and trying to rape me.

"He is his father's son, so immature. He even set Ravenhall on fire during the goddess's celebration to try and make you return to the capitol sooner. How naive."

I tensed. The fire at Ravenhall had been terrible; people were hurt, killed even. Of course Arlan was the one behind that kind of terrorizing. It is a shame that the people of Ravenhall believed it to be Asterians who had committed the arson; it was just another way to keep the mortals fearing them. Fearing us.

I was tired of this. I came to this meeting for one reason and I was going to get it. "I want to see my mother."

Vayna let out an unamused scoff. "Your *mother.*" she looked offended. "It was I who raised you when you were a child. I am more your mother than she is."

I breathed deeply because I would not let her get under my skin. She is manipulating and vindictive. I will not give her power over me any longer.

"I want to see her before we leave for Ravenhall. I need to know she is okay. I promise, if you let me see her, I will give you no issue when traveling. I will follow orders and obey." I pleaded strongly but still pleaded.

Vayna thought about it for a moment, I am sure, thinking about what she could gain, but finally said, "So be it."

CHAPTER 9

MELORA

The damp air of the dungeons hitting me in the face is almost enough for me to panic and retract my statement about seeing my mother. Being down here reminds me of my time in the cells, making me feel like I am returning to that horrid place. A shiver rolls through me at the thought of it. Although, this is a different part of the dungeons, a part where I was not kept. We are deeper into the earth and much farther away from any source of light or fresh air.

Vayna leads me to a cell in the long hallway of rusted bars, guards, of course, following behind us closely. I eye them slightly, wondering if I could take them out and make an escape. But I know Vayna will use her magic on me, even kill me if I act out right now. So, I will continue to bide my time.

She stops in front of old and rusted bars, pieces of once black paint chipping. I notice something on the outside of the cell walls, lining the outer wall of the cell we stand in front of. The markings are dark brown from here, but as I look closer, I see it is blood. Symbols written in blood cover the walls around the cell's opening—shapes and symbols I don't understand. *Wards.*

This must have been what Simon had done to me. This is why my mother could not use her magic to the full extent, why I had no power while I was in my cell, and why she could only stay in my dream for a short amount of time. Her magic has been rendered useless all this time. But somehow, some way, she mustered just enough to come to me in a dream.

Vayna turns to me before I look into the cell, scared of what I may find, terrified that she may not recognize me or know me. "Here is your *mother*," she says sarcastically, a sinister grin on her lips.

I am frozen where I stand, frozen with anxiety and anticipation because I am nervous to meet the Goddess of Life. I am about to meet Ismera in the flesh. She is a god, one of *the* gods. She is loved and feared throughout the realm. She is also my mother, but still, she is a god.

I step forward slowly, carefully making my way to the bars. I look into the shadowed cell, squinting to see through the shadows. I could hardly see anything through the darkness, only bright blonde hair shining in the corner. Like a beacon in the night.

I saw her then; my mother curled into a ball in the corner of the dirty cell. My mother, the Goddess of Life, held herself together in a dark cell. Her head was down, resting on her knees, curled to her chest. Her hair fell around her in wavy pieces, framing her thin arms.

I finally gained the courage to speak, "Mother?" I ask into the dark void, trying to not let my voice tremble.

Her head popped up at my question, at my voice. I saw her eyes now, eyes that I remembered from my dream she was in and would never forget. The same purple eyes stare back at me now. Disbelief filled them.

"Mother, it is me."

She squints, trying to see through the darkness. Recognition fills her face, and she- she knows it is me. She recognizes me.

"I am hallucinating," she mumbled to herself and quickly looked away. "Just don't look. Don't look. It will go away," she whispered.

My heart hurts for my mother, for the Goddess of Life. She thought she was hallucinating seeing me, thought her mind was playing tricks on her. "Mother, it is me. It's Melora. I am here. I am here." I crouch to the ground, hoping she will come closer to see that it is really me, that I am really here. So she can see it is truly me.

She looks harder now, looking for something I was unsure of. She moves slowly but finally moves. She crawls on her hands and knees the short distance from where she was sitting in the corner. She moves next to the bars that line the cell right in front of me. Tears well as I realize this was the first time I had met my mother in person, and not in a dream.

She reaches out, hesitating at first and pulling back, but then skims my hand, feeling that I am truly here. Her fingers are soft even after spending years in this prison. Her skin connected with mine, and her face turned relieved. Astonished.

"It really is you." She cries and reaches for me through the bars, moving so quickly that I almost miss her arms lacing through the cell bars to grab me. I do not hold back my sob of relief as I grab her back, pulling her in for a hug. "My daughter." She holds onto me as we both cry happy tears because we have finally been reunited.

I can't even begin to understand what it was like to have her newborn baby taken from her. Have life that she created, that she cared for, being ripped from her arms. For her to have known that Vayna took me and planned to use me? It must have been gut-wrenching for her all this time.

"Ugh," Vayna groaned from behind me. "I cannot take any more of this sob fest." She said annoyedly and walked away from the cell, her two watchdogs following her closely. To where I am unsure, but I do not care. I do not care about anything other than my mother right now. I care about nothing other than this feeling of rightness from being in her arms.

"Mother," I pull away from her so I can take her in, so I can see her. She is skinnier than when I saw her in my dream, and dirt from the cell smears her legs. But she still looks like my mother, still looks like the woman I have been waiting to meet.

She grabs my face with both hands, her palms cool against my flaming face. "What are you doing here?" she asks, panicky, her purple eyes going wide. "Why are you in this vile place?"

I cry more as I tell her what had happened after I saw her last, what happened after I saw her in my dream. I tell her everything. I tell her of the battle, how I lost Loral, and the betrayal of the youngest prince. I tell her how it was Silas's life or my freedom. "I would do it again if it means he lives, mother. I would." I tell her the truth, a tear streaming down my face from the anguish I feel for not being with Silas, for imagining his pained face as he lay on the battlefield.

"I know you would, my darling. You are strong, and you protect those you love," she swiped the tear that had fallen down my cheek away. "You love him—like I knew you would." Her smile warmed me.

"I- I don't know what to do." I stammered. "Vayna, she is making me marry the youngest Asterian prince and plans to control Asteria through me. She wants to end them; I know it. I can't let her do it. I won't. I will never let her." I pleaded to her, my voice hushed but angered. "Tell me what to do, please. I can't- I am so lost." I cry again, holding onto her tighter.

"Oh, my dear," she says, pushing back a piece of my hair that had fallen loose. "You are not lost. You are right where you need to be." She gave me a knowing smile. "You are meant to be here, talking with me. I knew you would come, just not when." She grabbed my shoulders and continued. "You will escape, Melora. You will go to your love and marry him. You will take the Asterian throne as queen. You have to save our people."

"No, no." I stopped her. "I am no queen. I can't rule. I wouldn't even begin to know how. I- I am not a queen. I was not even a real princess!" I stammered, growing scared. "How can I rule if you are here? You can rule, I will get you free, and then we will go home. You will take your place as queen."

She smiled softly at me. "Gods are not meant to rule. I was never meant to rule. My place is not here, not in this realm. I only came when the people

I created, the magic I created, were in need. But then I got captured." She looked to the cell behind her. "You will be queen, Melora. You were born to rule and protect our people. It has always been you. It was always going to be you."

I was shocked by her words, but I knew they were true. I knew she did not belong in this realm and that, eventually, she would need to return to wherever the gods resided.

It has to be me.

The reality of my situation hit me hard in the chest, knocking the air from my lungs. I cannot be the Queen of Asteria; I simply cannot. I cannot even be a princess, let alone an actual queen. It can't be true.

But why does it feel so right?

My breathing picks up and I am losing control of my emotions before I have a chance to calm down.

"Melora, you are so powerful. You have only just begun coming into the gifts I have given you. Your visions? The sense that something terrible will happen before it does? That is just the cusp of what kind of power you possess." she spoke softly, reassuringly. "With that power, you will help our people. You will protect them from this mortal queen, and you will end her. You must."

I took in her words, letting them seep into my skin so I could fully process them. I knew I needed to do this. I knew the people of Asteria needed to be protected and safe. I understood that.

I just never thought it would be me who would do it.

I hear the footfalls of Vanya and her guards and know our time is about up. My stomach drops at the thought of leaving my mother down here. "She's coming back," I said to my mother quickly. "Tell me how to free you, and I will. Tell me how, hurry." I begged her, pleaded with her to tell me how to free her, and I would do it.

She shakes her head, and blonde locks that look awfully like mine flow around her face. "Escape and return to the one you love. In time, I will be free. You have been so strong, Melora, my *Evaira*. Protect our people, and all will be right. I know you can do it. Do it for Asteria, for the people you love. Do it for me, my dear girl."

"That's enough. Let's go." Vayna commanded as she walked near the cell, her pace hurried.

Panic flowed through my veins at the thought of being separated from my mother, at having to be taken from her once again. "No, No." I started as a guard reached for me, grabbing my arm. "No! No! Mother!" I screamed as he pulled me away, yanking me from the cell.

My mother sat in the cell, holding the bars. She watched as they pulled me away from her, just as they had when I was just a baby. She watched and gave me her soft smile. "I love you." was the last thing I heard her say before I was ripped through the hall.

CHAPTER 10

MELORA

I am out of it as I sit horseback on the way to Ravenhall, hardly even paying attention to where we are. My conversation with my mother has been playing repeatedly in my mind since we left the capitol. She told me what I must do, what needs to be done to save our people. But I still cannot believe it is true that I am the daughter of the Goddess of Life, the rightful Queen of Asteria. So much has changed for me, and I am still accepting all these changes.

I wish I had more time with my mother, even another minute. I wish I had more time to tell her about my journey in finding who I am, finding love in the most unexpected place, and the woman I have grown to be. I wish I could have released her, that I could have found a way to help her escape her prison. But I knew there was no way I would free her right now, and she did, too. Leaving her was hard, and I will never forget the way her purple eyes gleamed with tears as they took me from her again.

I will conquer the mortal kingdom and free her myself. I thought as my fury started to spark to life again. I have become rather violent in my days as a prisoner, and I welcome it. Maybe the rage and anger have always been there, lying in wait beneath my skin for the moment when I needed it most. I welcome the viciousness; it keeps me going. It keeps me strong.

If that is what I must do to make it back to Silas, then I will.

I am trying to destroy a monster without becoming one, without becoming the thing I fear the most, but I am starting to think that destroying Vayna will make me the monster. I welcome the thought; I know I shouldn't. I know I should not want to become such a thing, but what has been done to me, to people I love, has fueled the fire I have known was always there.

"Are you awake, princess?" Simon asks from behind me quietly. They placed me on a horse with him before we left the capitol. I guess I could not be trusted to ride on my own. I couldn't blame them; I just wish my hands were not bound again. It makes me feel even more powerless than I already am, and the rope is very uncomfortable. "Are you comfortable?" he asks.

"I would be more comfortable on my own horse," I answered annoyedly. "And maybe if you were dead."

I shut my eyes as I realized what I had just said. I hadn't meant to let that part slip, but it was true. I knew I should be listening to the words I spoke to Vayna about obeying, about not causing problems while we traveled to Ravenhall. I knew I needed to if I wanted to survive. But I could not deny the truth; I would be way more comfortable if he were dead.

Simon laughed at my statement, chuckling in my ear. "There she is. I thought maybe your wickedness had left you." His hands on the horse's reins tightened. "I am glad to see that the woman my brother fell in love with is still in there."

I am going to punch him.

Once I got free of these bonds, of course.

"I have never left." I quipped, keeping my back straight so I did not touch him.

It was tiring work, trying not to be near him as we rode to Ravenhall on the same horse. I did not want to be anywhere near the vile man any more than I had to. Yet here I am, seated between his legs as he sits in the saddle behind me.

"Is that all you have to say? I thought there might be some cursing or maybe some threatening." Simon teased from behind me.

I was growing more annoyed than I already had been, but I did not say a word. I do not trust myself because the tongue is a very powerful muscle and sometimes has free will. I knew I would say something else that could get me in trouble.

"I wonder what my brother is doing right now," he asked, drawing my attention back to him. "We know what he is not doing; coming to save you. I mean, I think he would have already done it." He was trying to rile me up, trying to get my temper hot.

It was working.

"I am glad he has not," I told him. "Maybe I will get the honor of killing you myself." I felt him stiffen behind me at my threat, and I smiled. I know I shouldn't have threatened him, but my anger quickly turned to rage at the mention of his brother.

Simon let go of the reins, and his hands went to my hips. His left hand squeezed tightly on where my skin was still healing from his carving, rendering me magicless. "With what power?" he asked, reminding me once again that I am useless, that I have no magic and no power to use.

I do not need either to kill him.

Finally, after two long days of riding, we reached Ravenhall. When we began to get closer, I recognized the surrounding area, and as we rode through the small city, I knew we were at my former home. I looked at the town as we passed by, comparing it to Asteria. Ravenhall was so dirty and gloomy, nothing like the beautiful place Asteria is. I almost laughed to myself because at one time, I thought Asteria to be a place of nightmares, of pure myth.

But I was so completely wrong.

Our party rode up to the manor. Seeing it again brought back memories of my time here—good and bad ones, of course. Memories of Loral and her friendship, of the Lord Chapler's "lessons," of meeting Silas for the first time at the hot spring. What I would give to go to the hot spring right now—to slip down into the warm water and just drift to sleep.

I will go back there. One day, I will.

I examined the outside of Ravenhall Manor. It had been rebuilt since the fire that Arlan had set, which had killed so many and injured more. The windows were replaced, and the doors were put back on. Even the sides of the building that had crumbled to the ground had been rebuilt. I wonder if my room has been rebuilt.

Looking over the manor and thinking about the rebuilding process, I completely disregarded who was at the front of the manor waiting for us.

Arlan.

His light hair and petite frame stood in front of the manor's entrance, taunting me with his very existence. He was waiting for us, waiting for our arrival. My stare locked on him, and the memory of what he had done to me came back. I could practically feel his hands groping me and beating me in the main hall, blooding my face and causing nightmares.

My reaction must have been obvious because Simon whispered to me, "He will not touch you, princess. I promise that to you."

Let him try. I will not stop myself from killing him this time.

"Mother!" Arlan said with open arms as Vayna approached him and the king. They talked for a moment as Simon helped me down from the horse. I had not taken my eyes off that slithery bastard, and I would not for the foreseeable future.

Vayna and the king went inside the manor, followed by guards. Simon led me to follow them, but we were, of course, stopped. "Hello, *sister.*" Arlan hissed, his face full of arrogance. "It has been a while."

I lunged for him; even with my hands tied, I would be able to kill him. If not kill him, at least hurt him. Arlan retracted like he was scared. Coward. I didn't get to him, though; I was stopped. I was stopped by Simon, who now had a hold of my arm and was pulling me back from Arlan.

"Do not waste your time on him, princess." Simon snapped at me as he dragged me into the manor.

"I will kill him, too," I said through clenched teeth.

"You just want to kill everyone, don't you?"

He had a point.

Simon handed me off to some guards, and I was sequestered away to a part of the manor I knew well, a part I would never mistake for the place I had lived for so long. They were taking me to my old room. I was placed inside quickly, and it all looked the same as it had before the fire. They had been busy since I was last here. The fire had destroyed my room, but it was now intact and rebuilt to what it once was.

I sat down on the bed, which was still sort of soft. I definitely did not miss this. I miss the bed in Asteria, our bed, the bed that had Silas in it.

The door opened without a knock, and Vayna strolled in casually. "I am glad that they took those bindings off of you. I wish they wouldn't have had to do it, but it was necessary during our trip," she said apologetically as she looked around the room. "I came to tell you that you need to prepare yourself and start getting ready."

I felt my face scrunch in question. "For what, exactly?" I questioned. We had just arrived; what could she possibly want from me now?

She tilted her head in an almost serpentine way, examining me like I had spoken in tongues. "For your wedding. You will be married tonight."

I had not even seen her leave after she had just let that bomb off. I was so shocked by her words that I hadn't even realized she had left my room. I sat there on my bed, trying to get my mind to work out a plan—a plan to escape my fate.

Because there was only one person I wanted to marry, only one person for me.

And Simon was not it.

The door opened quickly, and a small frame carrying towels came in. When I saw who it was, my mind started working again.

"Lady Chapler?" I asked astonishedly, even though I saw the woman before me.

She smiled. "Hello, dear."

"What- what are you doing here?" I questioned her because she was in the capitol the last time I saw her. She was brought to the capitol the same time I went back, we traveled together and...oh gods...I killed her husband.

She walked over to the copper bathing tub and started pouring in soap. "I am here to help you prepare for your wedding," she said.

"No, I mean, why are you in Ravenhall?" I asked her again.

She turned to me and glanced at the door like she wanted to make sure it was shut because whatever she was about to tell me was only for us. "The queen sent me back here after you left the capitol. I was asking too many questions, knew too many rumors. Rumors that I have now learned are true." she whispered, but a sense of urgency slipped through her tone. "I know the truth, Melora. I know what Queen Vayna has done. It took me a while to accept it...to accept what was happening right in front of me, but I finally see."

Alright, I was not expecting that. "What? What do you mean you know the truth?" I need clarification because if I am to trust her, I need to know she knows everything.

She rolled her eyes at me, annoyed that I would ask again. "I know that you are the Goddess of Life's daughter, Melora. Many of us in Ravenhall know what happened to the magic folk so long ago. We know the truth of what Vayna has done."

I rose from the bed, shocked at her statement. How could people here know the truth? I thought about what Silas had said, that there were mortals still trying to escape to Asteria even after all this time. People talk, and I guess many know the truth now, a truth that has been lost over the years.

Good.

"Then you need to help me. You must know what she is planning. I need to escape; I need to get out of here." I pleaded with her, hoping she would help free me.

Lady Chapler grabbed my hands, holding them tightly. "Why do you think I volunteered to help you get ready for your wedding?" she asked with a mischievous smirk.

I knew I liked her.

But the reality of what I had done to her husband came back to me; I let him be taken in the forest. I killed him with my magic in the prison in Asteria. I don't regret it because he was a horrid man who abused me for years and years. But I don't want to hurt her after she has gone through so much to simply know the truth.

"Wait. I need to tell you something." I stop her from walking to the small bathing tub.

She turned, her hands up defensively. "If it is about my husband, I don't care. I am glad the bastard is gone. How it happened, I do not need to know." she said plainly.

Well, I guess that settles that.

She began again. "Tell me what you need."

I thought, thought of a way to get out of here. I need a foolproof plan to help me escape. What I need is to have my magic back. And I will do anything to get it back if it means escaping Simon and Vayna. I needed this damn symbol off of me that is keeping my magic from me.

An idea came to life.

A horrible, painful idea.

"I need something sharp."

CHAPTER 11

MELORA

I stand at the head of an aisle as I slip the cool coat of nothingness on. The feeling is already taking over my body, readying myself for what is about to come. I fall into the feeling with ease, remembering what I must do. I prepare myself for what is about to happen, and I am willing to do it if it means getting out of this godsforsaken manor and getting the hell out of Morania. I am willing to do anything if it means I can return to Silas.

I calm my nerves, my anticipation already eating at me as I walk towards Simon, who is standing at the end of the aisle. He is waiting for me. Vayna stands above him, a wicked smile on her face as she watches me walk slowly towards them. I feel both of their eyes travel over my body and what I am wearing. What I am hardly where is more like it.

They put me in a dress that should not even be called a dress, that should not even be in the same category as a dress. Half of my body hangs out of the white, gossamer fabric that plunges down my chest, exposing half of my breast. If I had not been so determined to execute my plan, so blank that I could actually feel what I was wearing, I know I would be freaking out.

But I am not thinking about the dress as I near the end of the aisle, as I near the man that I am to marry. I am only thinking about running. Running from this fate that is not for me. The fate that I will not let happen, even if my life depends on it.

"You look beautiful, princess," Simon says to me as he reaches his hand out for me to take. I take it and barely feel his cold fingers on my skin, trying not to feel his touch at all. The digits wrap around mine, bringing me up to stand with him at the head of the aisle.

I stand face-to-face with him, looking into eyes that remind me of Silas. I feel Vayna next to us, hovering, watching as the marriage ceremony begins. I see her out of the corner of my eye, watching me with a sinister stare that I once was afraid of. I am no longer afraid; I am just uncontrollably angry.

Words are spoken, but I do not hear them. I only heard muffled talking as I thought and replayed my plan in my mind. I only think about my plan, about running, about getting out of here. I only focus when Simon lifts his hand, and I see a blade meet his palm. He slices the flesh, and blood trickles down to the floor from the open wound. This must be an Asterian marriage custom because I did not think they did this in the mortal realm.

He grabs for my hand and I know the time is now. He is about to slice me, continuing the ceremony, continuing our marriage. I need to strike now, and I need to strike true because this is the last time I will have a chance to be free. If I don't get out now, I will never get away.

Simon stares at me as I withhold giving him my hand for him to cut. He has scarred my skin enough, and he will not do it again. He searches for something in my eyes, something that will not be there, something that will never be there, because I know he craves me, wishes I cared for him like I do his brother. I now feel nothing as I ready myself to leave this hellish place I once called home and leave the man standing before me. I feel nothing, nothing, and everything all at once.

I feel an evil smile grace my lips just before I unleash myself on him. I welcome the anger that flows through my blood, that flows hot with determination. I headbutt Simon right in the nose, blood immediately flowing down his face after a brutal crunch. I grab the knife he held and turn to Vayna, who has yet to react. I am sure she thought this would all go according to her plan.

Not if I can help it.

I plunge the knife into her chest as hard as I can, staring at her shocked face as I twist the blade deeper into her skin. She almost looks betrayed as I plunge the knife harder.

I'm not sure how her healing works or if her magic will help her heal and survive, but this should kill her or at least slow her down until I am gone. I hope it kills her.

She looked down at the knife sticking out from her chest, her shock apparent. Words do not come from her mouth that is leaking blood as she falls to the ground and tries to steady herself. I shouldn't feel this satisfaction; I shouldn't be happy that I have possibly killed her.

But I am.

I am happy that this wretched woman whom I once called mother may actually be dead. She is responsible for so much pain and so much death. I would be glad if she was gone.

I feel it in my blood as my magic surges beneath my skin, I feel the rage and fury that she has caused me, and I let it fill me. My magic is slowly coming back to me after Lady Chapler helped me carve off the scarred skin that had the symbol on it keeping my magic from me. The symbol that withheld my power was carefully sliced off, giving me back access.

It had been so painful but so worth it.

Guards came for me now, running in all directions to stop me. They would soon die. I willed my magic to come to life, willed it to move them away from me and out of my way. I was surprised when the blast of power did not instantly kill them. I guess my magic was still returning to me. It will have to do.

The guards lay scattered around the room, and I knew it was my time to run. I ran, ran, and ran through the halls to the servant's door Lady Chapler told me she would open for me. I turned the corner, and there she was, waiting for me, urging me to run faster.

"Come with me." I plead to her, beg her to follow me home because this place is not safe for her, and I know it.

She shakes her head, and I know the answer. "Go!" She yells, and I am off.

I might regret leaving her behind later, but right now, I need to go. I need to get out of here before I get caught and captured again. I will not be captured again, and leaving Lady Chapler behind will have to do because I am not waiting.

I am out of the manor and running toward the forest I know eventually leads to the Fallen Forest. I run harder than I have ever run before, I run faster than I could even imagine. I am almost free; I can taste it. I can feel it as I enter the thick forest, the branches covering me from sight.

I run and keep running, only stopping when my legs begin to give out as tiredness seeps into my muscles. I think hours have passed since I left the manor because I left Ravenhall as the sun set, and now the moon is high above me. The air has grown chilled in the darkness, my bare skin cold in the night.

I fall into the earthy ground as my legs give out, my feet raw and bloody from when I kicked out of my shoes to run faster. The dress I wore now was torn and dirtied. Parts of it ripped clean off from the branches, hitting me as I sprinted through the forest. I did not mind. I will burn this dress the second I get it off.

I do not care that my feet are a bloody mess, I do not care about my clothing, I do not care about any of it. Because I need to keep going, I need to keep pushing. I need to make it to Asteria. I need to make it home.

I got up and kept running, exhaustion slowing me only the slightest. My will to return home to the one I love is far more persuasive than exhaustion.

I feel it when I enter the Fallen Forest, I can feel the magic all around me in the nature. I can see it in the way the trees blow in the wind so effortlessly, like magic is willing them to do so. It is so beautiful, even at night.

I stop after running for hours and hours just so I can breathe for a moment. I brace myself up on a tree, resting for just a second to calm my breathing. I looked around, not realizing how deep into the forest I was. Trees and greenery are all around me, shrouding me from the moonlight, trying to come through the branches.

The slight reprieve I had was short-lived when the sound of hooves came from the direction I was running from. They followed me. The guards followed me. The guards were on horseback, so they caught up to me quickly. I guess I wasn't as fast as I thought.

I start running again as the hoof beats get closer, gaining on me. I begin running for my life. I can feel the ground shaking from the animals running towards me, their hooves pounding into the forest floor. They are getting closer, but I will not give up. I will not give in.

I will not.

I turn and quickly look at the men on horseback chasing me down, gaining on me fast. They have their arrows nocked in their bows, ready to fire at me, ready to free them from their hold.

Fuck.

They are going to shoot me, going to take me down and drag me back to Ravenhall to marry Simon. My plan is about to fail, and I did it all- I did everything for nothing.

Not if I can help it.

They will have to drag my dead body all the way back to Ravenhall before I give in to letting them take me. I will not go down without fighting, and I will die before I let them take me willingly.

I go to stop myself, to turn around and muster up enough magic to hit them with my power, hopefully stunning them or killing them if my magic has fully returned, but I run into a body. A body that is standing in the forest at what I believe to be the middle of the night. Okay...weird.

I fall to the ground, looking up at the hooded figure standing before me. They look feminine, like a woman could be beneath the dark cloak covering the body.

I watch in shock as the guards release their arrows from their horses toward us, aiming right for our heads. I am ready for the impact the sharp arrowheads will have on my skin, but they never come. I look up and see the woman before me with her arm outstretched in the direction of the guards, their arrows now frozen in midair.

With a swift flick of her hand, the arrows turn and are now pointed at the guards who fired them.

She lets them lose, and they strike the guards, sending them flying back and knocking them from their horses. I hope they are dead.

    This woman is magic.

    Thank the gods.

    The woman looks down at me, her cloak moving with her head. "Come," was all the figure had to say for me to scurry to my bloodied feet and follow her into the darkness of the Fallen Forest. Follow them to gods know where, but I am positive anywhere will be better than the capitol.

CHAPTER 12

MELORA

❡ follow the hooded woman to a small cottage tucked away in the forest. This home reminds me of the cottages in the city of Asteria. My heart grows sorrowful as I think about the first time I walked through the streets and saw the homey cottages.

I will get back. I remind myself, repeating it over and over as I am ushered into the woman's home. I look around, examining the cozy interior. The main room in the cottage is the kitchen. It is filled with greenery, herbs, pots and pans. A wooden table stands in the middle of the warm kitchen, chairs around the circle top.

"Sit." the figure says as she makes her way to the iron stove. I see her light it with her fingers, the orange flames flickering under the black burner. I sit and watch as the woman grabs a teapot and fills it with water and herbs. She draws her hood back, revealing thick gray hair. It is long, reaching her waist.

She stands at the stove, making tea and humming lightly.

"Th- thank you for what you did. I- I thought they would kill me." I say to the woman after I finally grow the nerve to speak.

The woman stays quiet as she continues the tea. She walks away briefly to another room I cannot see, but the spoon in the teapot continues to turn even after she walks away.

Magic.

This woman must be an Asteria who resides in the forest, feeling more comfortable in nature than in the city. I cannot blame her; this cottage is so homey, and the forest is so calming.

She returns with a blanket, a heavy wool fabric that she drapes over my shoulders. I finally got a good look at her face. She is old, older than anyone I have seen in Asteria. I wonder what kind of magic she possesses.

"My- my name is Melora," I speak meekly to the woman who is now pouring the dark-colored liquid into a mug. "What- what should I call you?" I ask.

She turns to me fully, placing the hot mug in my hands. I welcome the warmth on my chilled fingers. "I know, dear. I have been waiting for you."

Well that was unsettling.

The questioning look on my face prompted her to continue: "My name is very long and hard to pronounce. Just call me Visha. I knew you would be coming, *Queen Melora.*" The small smile on her face tells me she is a friend.

She knows me as queen.

How is that possible when I have not been in Asteria for weeks? "You- you know me?" I stumble out my words.

Visha nods and sits in a rickety wooden chair next to me. "Of course I do. We all know of our true queen, the Goddess of Life's daughter." She leans in closer. "People have been talking; those at the battle in the Fallen Forest have been talking. We know it is true; I have seen it. Just as I saw you coming to my home in the middle of the night." Her pale lips smirked.

"How did you know I was coming?" I questioned her as I sipped my tea.

Visha hesitated a moment, thinking about what to say. "I am very old, my queen. I was around long before the mortals turned on us, and the mortal queen tried to exterminate all those with magic. I know things that many others do not know. For example, Ismera was the one who created these lands for us to escape to, and it was not the first Asterian. It was her, the one who created us." She took a long breath. "My mother was a witch;

therefore, I am a witch. A very old and a very powerful one. I saw a foretelling of you in my cauldron one night, saw you running for your life, and knew you would end up on my doorstep."

"That is why you were waiting for me in the forest." she nodded. "I- can you help me get back to Asteria? I need to return home."

Her soft, old skin grabbed my hand and held it tenderly. "You are already home, my queen."

Tears pricked in my eyes. Her words brought emotion forth that was so overwhelming that I could not hold it back. "You will stay here until morning. I will help you return to the palace." she told me. "And we will find you some new clothing."

I dropped my head to my hands. I am going home. I am going back to Silas. Relief swelled and a sob broke free, "Thank you. Thank you so much." I cried to the woman.

"Now, let me see those feet. You tracked blood through my kitchen." We laughed together as she examined my mangled feet. Running through the forest for hours and hours is not for the faint of heart.

A knock on the door made me jump to attention, ready to fight my way back home if needed. Fear must have been evident on my face because Visha said, "It is alright. It is a friend." She reassured me. I trusted this woman; she saved me and sheltered me. If she says it is a friend, I believe her.

She continued checking out my feet as she twisted her hand, opening the door from where she sat. A man came in, a tall man with...branches and leaves wound around his skin. I tried not to react because I knew this was a normal thing in Asteria. I was just wondering what kind of Asterian I was now meeting.

"Is everything okay? I thought I heard horses and mortal guards. I came right ov-" The young tree-looking man stopped mid-sentence when he saw me sitting at the wooden table. His eyes grew large, his irises the same color as his leaves. "My queen!" he stammered out and bent at the knee, kneeling on the ground.

Um, what?

I looked at Visha who only smiled and shook her head. The man was still kneeling, his head bowed. "Please, there is no need for that," I said to him, hoping he would stand.

Thankfully, he stood. He placed a hand over his heart and said, "I am Nicodem, my queen."

"It is nice to meet you, Nicodem. I- I am surprised you know me." I said to him, trying not to stare at his leafy arms. "I am honored." I smiled at him.

"The honor is mine, my queen. We have all been waiting for your return. Praying you would return home from the mortal kingdom." he declared.

I was shocked that people knew me, knew I was the true Queen of Asteria, even though I had not agreed to be such. But I know these people want me as their queen; they know that the Goddess of Life's blood runs through my veins.

Visha stood after placing herbs on my feet. "Nicodem, would you like to help the queen return to the palace?" she asked him.

His eyes grew, and his cheeks pinked. "Of course! I will do anything to help you return home, my queen," he stated proudly.

Visha clasped her hands in delight. "Perfect. It is settled. Nicodem will escort you to the palace when the sun rises. For now, you must rest those feet."

After a night of asking Visha questions about the magic Simon and Vayna had used on me, the sun rose, and the anticipation was killing me. I was ready to return home, ready to be in the arms of the one I love. I plan to tell Silas every day that I love him, that I care for him so deeply that it hurts to be away from him. The need to do so is prevalent as I pull on the boots Visha gave me, along with the sweater and cloak.

Nicodem opens the door, ready to escort me the rest of the way to the palace. "Are you ready, my queen?" he asks, and I have never been more ready for anything in my life.

I nod but turn to Visha, who is standing with her hands clasped in front of her, watching as I prepare to leave. She comes to me and takes my hands in hers, saying, "I have been doing some thinking, about the mortal queen that is. You say the mortal queen was given magic. I believe the magic that runs through her is witch's magic. Strong, but not like mine. The symbols you explained are runes that witches use, wards. I believe the magic she possesses is something akin to what witches possess."

That would make sense. I mean, even though my mother granted her magic in exchange for her freedom, which she did not get, it would not make Vayna an Asterian. She would have to be something else, have some other type of magic similar to it. Witch's magic makes sense. "How do I stop her?" I plead.

Visha thinks momentarily, then says, "If she was born a witch like me, there would be no way to stop her. But...since she was given the magic, I do believe it can be taken back from her. The one that does it would need to be powerful to pull magic from another being, to take the magic from her blood."

I understand what she is saying; we would have to drain Vayna of her magic.

"I fear for the one that drains the mortal queen's magic; it has become something dark and twisted. Much like her." She gave me a grave look. "Please, be careful."

"I will," I told her, then moved to hug her. "Thank you," I whispered to her.

She hugged me back tenderly. "You are very welcome, dear. You are always welcome in my home." She told me, then I pulled away.

Nicodem and I walked away from the cottage and headed for the palace. He said it was only a short distance away, but as we walked, tiredness ate at me.

Finally, we were near the edge of the forest, and I saw a large area of grass, swords ringing in the distance. "This is the farthest I go, my queen. We dryads do not like to venture far from the forest," he explained.

I turned to him, and hugged the man who resembled a tree. "Thank you, Nicodem. Thank you so much." I was so grateful for him and Visha, they made me feel protected, loved.

He hugged me back, his leafy arms surrounding me. "It has been my honor," he murmured, bowing when I pulled away.

I walked on shaky legs out of the forest, out of the thick greenery, and into the warm Asterian sun. It reminded me of the first time I stepped foot in the Asterian Kingdom. I stood there and let the sun hit my face, just as I had done on my first day here.

I walked toward the sound of swords, and as I crested a small hill, I saw that there were men training. A lot of men training. Like the whole Asterian army was out preparing for battle.

I walked toward them, hoping they would recognize me and take me to Silas. But a tall, dark man at the head of the group caught my attention.

Milo.

Even though I was exhausted, I ran. I took off toward the man I had come to be friends with, the man who I knew would protect me and stand by me as he had done before.

I was sprinting, and he finally turned and saw me coming. Recognition hit his features just as I closed in and jumped. I jumped onto him and wrapped my arms and legs around his thick body.

"Milo," I cried into his shoulder. I sobbed as I tried to catch my breath.

He held me, held me so tight I thought I would break. "Melora. What- how did you-" he stammered, trying to make sense of me appearing out of nowhere. "I need to get you inside," he said and he turned to walk to the palace.

I did not let go as he walked quickly through the halls. I did not let go until he sat me down outside a door I knew.

Silas's study.

Milo opened the door without knocking, hurriedly rushing into the room. "What is it, Milo?" Silas questioned his friend without even looking up from what he was doing on his desk.

I stepped around Milo's broad body, which was heaving from getting us here so quickly. "Silas," I spoke to him, watching as he heard my voice. Watching as his head rose and his eyes met with mine. "Silas." I cried.

He stood so fast and so smoothly that I almost didn't realize he was before me until his arms were around me—the arms I'd been longing to be in, to be comforted by.

He held me flush against his body and we collapsed onto the floor. "Melora." he cried into my hair. I felt him shake, a tremor running through him.

I felt his skin on mine and knew I was not dreaming. I was not hallucinating.

    I was truly here.

    I made it.

    I held on, held on to the man that I would do anything for. To the man I would kill for.

    I held on to the man I love.

CHAPTER 13

MELORA

I hear the water drip, drip, dripping in the cell I am being held captive in. I can feel the damp air on my skin from the dungeons being so deep in the earth. I feel the scratchy rope binding me to the chair I sit in.

I hear him before I see him; he comes to me when I sleep. I know what he is here to do, know what he has already done. He approaches me and pulls out his blade. I feel the sharp steel cut into me.

The sound of screams woke me from my dream. They were my screams. I am still screaming, wailing into the darkness as I feel arms wrap around me. The arms are small but ground me as I continue to lash out from what I saw in my sleep.

"I'll get Silas." the sweet voice says, but I barely hear it. I only hear my cries, my sounds of internal pain.

The bed dips, and Silas is before me, sitting on his knees in a bed I have yet to recognize. He holds my face, bringing me close so I can see it is him. I stop screaming as I realize I am here with him—in his bed.

I look around the room and realize where I am. I am not in the cell in the Moranian capitol; I am home, home with *him*.

I look at Silas again, taking in his appearance for the first time since I have been here. He looks tired and distraught. He looks thinner; his muscles are still there, but his face looks hollow. It seems like he has hardly been eating or sleeping. "Mel, you are safe," he assures me as I fall into his arms.

Silas holds me to his chest, bringing me so close that it is like he never wants to let go. I would be fine with that. He rocks me gently as I cry and come down from my terrifying dream. He rocks me and tells me I am safe; I am home.

Hours pass by as I lay in Silas's bed, held in arms that comfort me. I slept on and off through the night, never staying asleep long enough for dreams to plague me. I only know it is morning because the sun is shining in through the window of the room.

"Hi," I say to Silas, who has not taken his eyes from me all night. Every time I woke up, he was already awake, watching, making sure I was not scared.

He moved his fingers through my hair, tenderly brushing it from my face. "Hello, princess." My heart warmed at his words. I truly had thought that I may never hear those words again. Emotion came to life, and tears started to fall. "It is alright, my love." He soothed me as I cried softly.

My love.

"Silas," I said breathlessly, needing for him to hear this, needing to speak the words I have longed to say. "I love you, Silas. I have regretted it every day since I was taken that I did not tell you sooner, that I did not tell you when I knew it was true. I love you, and I will never not love you. My world begins and ends with you. My heart, it beats, loves, and aches only for you."

He stared at me, compassion filled his face. "I love you, Melora. I love you. I love you. I love you." He whispers. "I knew it from the moment you graced me with a smile. I knew it from the moment you held a dagger to my throat. You are mine, and I am yours." He grabbed my face and kissed me. Kisses my lips, kisses away my tears, kisses every inch of my face until he is sure he covers every part with his love. "Nothing will ever separate me from you again. Nothing," he growled, most likely thinking about the way our separation played out.

We stayed like this for hours, and I would have been content with never leaving this bed again. We lay there, staring into each other's eyes, telling one another how in love we are, making sure to never take another minute together for granted.

"As much as I would love to lay here for eternity with you," Silas began, and I already hated the words. "I need to know what happened, Mel. We need to know what happened."

I knew I needed to tell Silas and our friends what occurred while I was in the mortal kingdom. Silas wanted to know what they did to me, but I needed to tell them what I saw. All I found out.

"You are so strong, so fierce, but if you tell me you cannot speak of it, then I won't push it. I just- it is eating at me, making my blood boil not knowing all that has happened to you. I just want to make it better; I want to make them pay." he said softly.

I knew that if I said I did not want to talk about it, he would let it go. They all would. But I knew I needed to tell my story, tell them everything I saw. I know it will hurt; it will hurt Silas to hear what his brother has done, and it will hurt me to relive what has happened. But getting it off my chest, sharing the weight of my trauma with those who love me, it may help me heal, help us all to heal.

I thought for a moment about leaving this room, and panic started to take hold. "Bring our friends. I will not be leaving this room."

Silas gathered our group of friends, only leaving me for a quick minute. Even though he was gone for no more than five minutes, the darkness of being alone overtook me. Thoughts and feelings I have suppressed came to life, rattling me. The feeling of being in the cell, of carving off my own skin to remove the symbol, stabbing Vayna. It all came into my mind.

But then the door flew open, and Yara ran in. My friend hugged me, taking me into her thin arms just as she had when I was sleeping and woke terrified. "I missed you," she said, her voice strained.

"I have missed you so much, Yara." We held each other as the others gathered around the conversation area in Silas's room. The hearth was lit, warming the room and casting a yellow glow around the walls.

"Hi, princess," Milo said as he took me in his muscular arms for a bear hug. "Thanks for almost tackling me the other day." We both laughed, happy tears streaming down my face.

The twins came next, both hugging me tightly. "I hope you gave them hell, Mel," Kane said as he broke away from our hug. His words amused me, but I did not answer. If I had felt myself, I would have said that I did, that I gave them what they deserved, but what I have done, how many I have killed, it weighs heavy on me.

Kaius stepped up next, holding something in his hands—two somethings. "We found these after the battle in the Fallen Forest. We kept them safe until you returned like we knew you would," Kaius said, handing me my twin daggers. The purple gems in the handles shine brightly like they had been cleaned.

I take the daggers, the lightweight weapons grounding me, reminding me of my strength. I needed this more than they will ever know. "Thank you so much," I tell him, emotion clogging my throat.

I looked at who came into the room next, and I almost crumbled to my knees. "Mel," Penn said, eyes watery and red. I hugged him, pulled him in by his neck, and did not let go. Just like the day when he came to Asteria to warn me about the queen, I cried into his shoulder, comforted by his fatherly presence. "I knew you would make it back. I knew you would return to us," he said as I continued sobbing into his shoulder.

"I have missed you every day," I said to him, realizing that we had not truly had a moment together since my days at Ravenhall.

I released him from my hold and turned to the group, there was not a dry eye in the room. Everyone, even Milo, had tear-stained cheeks and reddened eyes.

I was home. I was home and around people who loved me.

Everyone gathered around the fire and looked at me as if I were not real, as if I was not truly back. I wrapped my arms around myself under the stares of my friends. I know it is out of worry for me, but I am still uncomfortable.

Silas grabbed me by the waist, pulling me to his lap as he sat in one of his oversized chairs. I will never get used to his touch; how it makes me feel so cherished and desired. Right now, it grounded me in sight of having to relive the past month.

Silas brushes my hair away from my face and caresses my back as I tell our friends everything that happened, from the moment I woke up in the cell to when I ran home to Milo. I tell them of what Simon had carved into my skin, of him making me sleep with him at night, of the symbols that kept me from using my magic.

I explained Vayna's plan to them, how she wanted me to marry Simon and rule Asteria through us. I- I told them of the people I murdered, the guards I killed with my writing quill, and the ones I hurt when I left the capitol.

I hadn't realized I was crying until I felt my wet, heated cheeks. When I finished my story I looked around at the faces surrounding me, supporting me. Yara was crying, wiping away her tears quickly. Milo looked as though he could tear someone in half. Penn did not even meet my eye.

I felt Silas behind me, seething from all that I had just shared. He grabbed the arm of the chair so tightly his knuckles were white. I knew he was furious at his brother and himself. I knew he blamed himself for all that had happened, but I blamed no one other than Vayna.

"And I would do it all again if it meant I would save you," I said to Silas, whose eyes were reeling with rage. I held his face, running my thumb over his stern lips. "I would do it again without a second thought if it meant you were safe."

I need a fucking drink after that, something to calm the utter chaos that is warping my mind. The burn of whiskey sounds better than the burn of tears in my eyes.

I stand to get myself a drink from the cabinet, and Silas reluctantly lets go. I walk over to the liquor cabinet and pour myself a drink. I turn back to the group, drink in hand. Their faces have gone grave. Yara is crying again, her hand covering a sob trying to escape. Milo curses under his breath. I look to Silas to try to understand why they are reacting like this right now.

I just stood to get a drink.

I look at Silas, who is looking at my body like he will tear apart the realm. I look down at myself and realize what they all see.

I am wearing a nightgown, a silky long one that I love. But the firelight behind me has made the shadow of my body visible through the material. My body that has been starved, beaten, abused. I know they can see the stark outline of my waist, the bones of my hips jutting out.

I know they see what my body has been through.

I panic, anxiety coursing through me. I drop the crystal glass and move to cover myself with my arms. I hate them seeing me like this, hate them knowing the extent of what I have been through.

The glass breaks on the floor as Silas stands up. He comes to me quickly and scoops me into his arms. I curl into his chest, crying hard.

"Leave." he barked at the friends still sitting in the conversation area, and he took me into his room.

He sat in bed with me still in his arms, holding me and rocking me, comforting me as the crying finally stopped. A memory flashed to the forefront of my mind—a memory that has been sitting with me since it occurred.

My mother called me something just before I was taken from her. She called me... "Evaira," I say aloud to Silas, who is still holding me. He stops rocking and looks at me, surprise written in his expression. "What does it mean?" I ask.

He tilts his head, black strands brushing his strong jaw. "I am surprised you know such a word. It means 'Gift from Gods' in old Asterian, a language that has not been around for centuries."

Old Asterian.

"My mother called me that when I saw her in the capitol."

Silas smirked down at me. "I think I like that nickname better than 'princess.'"

CHAPTER 14

SILAS

It has been a week since Melora returned home.

It has been a week since she fought her way back to me, since she fought her way home, just like she promised to do. Like I knew she would if she had the chance. All that she has done, everything she did was to get back home, to get back to me.

I hate that she did what she needed to do to return home; the killing, the hurting, the pain, all of it. I wish she did not have to go through any of it and anything that came after.

I know it haunts her, I know she feels the terror of it all still. I am with her in the night when she wakes, her screams ringing through the room as she thrashes around, forgetting where she is. I see the extent of what she went through in her eyes. They are as beautiful as ever, but something is missing. I think she lost a piece of herself when she was held captive, a part of her that slipped away. I cannot blame her; no one ever would.

I just wish I could help her. I wish I could take away all her pain and agony so she would never have to feel such things ever again. I would take it all and bear it myself if it meant she did not have to. I would do it because I know what she did for me, saving me, that is, it cost her more than I could ever give.

My Melora is strong, so damn strong, and so damn fierce. I know she will get through this. And I will be there every step of the way to make sure she does. I just hate seeing her like this, dealing with all of this.

Our army was ready to take Ravenhall, to demand that the mortal queen return Melora to us. But she had other plans, plans where she saved herself and escaped. Plans where she killed her way out of that wretched place to free herself.

And I could not be prouder of her, of the warrior she is and all that she has become, of what she did to get back home to me, to get back to our family. I am proud of her working with the trauma she has gone through but continuing to push on. I do not deserve this woman. I do not deserve her love, her fight, her *everything.*

But she has given it to me, and I will never let it go. I will never let our love go unsaid again, never not tell her how deeply I care for her, how passionately I love her. Her love...it is the love that poets write about. The kind of love that prevails even in the darkest of nights. Like I am the night, and her love is the moon.

"You know what I think?" Milo interrupts my thoughts as he bursts into the conversation area in my rooms.

"I am sure you are going to tell me," I answer sardonically from the chair I sit in. I have not been in the best mood this past week. I only ever find happiness when Melora rests or when we lay together in bed, finding peace in each other. I quit drinking because I realized I had started to depend on it while Melora was being held captive. I need a clear head right now; I need it for her.

Milo flopped into an oversized chair, which was not oversized on his large body. "I think she really needs to get out of this room. I mean, it has been what? A week? I think some fresh air will do her good."

I thought about what he said, and I do think that getting her out of my rooms will do Melora some good. But I do not want to push her. The thought of her leaving my room to go anywhere makes her start to lose her grip on her emotions, panic taking her over. So, I will not push her on this. But...

"I know, but she is—I think she is scared or anxious about being anywhere other than here." I gesture to the rooms around me. She is currently in my bedroom reading. I gave her some space to just be, but I would never be too far from her again. "The last thing I want is for her to be forced into something she does not want to do."

"I cannot argue with that. She is rather stubborn, after all," Milo said while looking at the closed doors that separated the conversation room from the bedroom she was currently in. "Have you talked to her about what must be done?" he questioned, tensing at his own words.

I let loose a breathy sigh. "I have not. I don't want to push her, Milo. I don't want to put too much on her plate too soon. I mean, what she has gone through...I just never want to see her the way she was when she first arrived." I finished, drawing a hand over my face.

The first night Melora had returned home will haunt me for the rest of my never-ending life. My beautiful, brave girl was too afraid to sleep because she feared my brother would visit her in her dreams and torment her. I will kill him for what he has done to her, what he has done to *my wife*.

I think about the things I will do to him every night when I am watching Melora sleep, watching and waiting for the nightmares I know she will have to find her. I gave him too much grace the first time he put his hands on her; I should have ended him right then. But he is my brother, *was* my brother. He is now nothing other than the thing that plagues my love, and I will end him for it and all he has done.

    I feel the heat rising in my blood, slow and steady but hot enough to make me rage. "She knows she is the true Queen of Asteria, but I do not think she fully understands what that means. I don't think she realizes that she will replace my father and take over as protector of our kingdom. It's a lot of weight to put on someone who is still healing from such trauma." I explain, trying to cool my heated blood.

    "I agree," Milo says. "But we need to give her the choice. People already call her queen; they already cheer for her in the streets. They love her as they love you. She will be one hell of a queen," he says proudly, smiling at the thought.

    "The question is not if she would be able to do it; she would be an amazing ruler, passionate, protectful, fierce. It is just if she is ready to take on such a change right now, after everything." I rose to stand, the conversation making me anxious and fidgety.

    "She will be all of those things." he glanced at the doors again, his face turning sincere. "But I still think we should talk to her about it."

I stare into the blazing hearth. The weather is always warm in Asteria, but ever since Mel has returned home, she has been cold, like I was when she was away. So, I keep it blazing.

"Talk to me about what?" I hear her sweet voice coming from where she stands at the double doors to the bedroom, both doors open. "Are you two talking about me?" she asks playfully, eyeing both of us.

I know she is trying to tease us, joke around, and seem like herself, but I still see the suffering in her eyes. I see the pain.

I go to her, naturally, and wrap my arms around her body. I hate the way I can feel her ribs when I hug her, and I hate how the bones in her collarbone jut out now. She has been eating better over the time she has been back, but she is still not anywhere near where she needs to be. I hug her tightly, never wanting to forget the feeling of her body in my arms again. "Yes, my love. Milo and I are always talking about you." I say into the top of her head, inhaling her scent deeply.

She giggles, and I swear the sound stops my heart. "You two are always up to no good." she wiggles in my arms, trying to get closer in our hug.

I finally release her, and she walks to the fire, warming her hands near the flame. The way her hair shines in the light has me so transfixed that I don't even hear what she and Milo are talking about. All I can focus on is her. It is always her.

"Silas," Milo snapped me out of my stupor. "Mel wants to know what she just walked in on." he looked at me with a questioning stare, like he was unsure the time was right to talk to her about all of this.

Milo was right, though; she needed to know and have the choice to do what she wanted. I would never take such a thing from her, not after all her life has been nothing but giving up her own will for others.

I returned to my chair, saying, "Are you up for a semi-heavy conversation, my love?" I ask her as she turns to me.

She picks at her nails, a nervous habit I recognize now. "I can handle it," she says more harshly than I am sure she meant. I understand how hard this has to be for her to be vulnerable and healing.

"Sit with me," I say and pull her into my lap, taking her hips and pulling her close. I need her close, not just for my own selfish reasons, but because her presence reminds me she is here.

She is home.

"We want to talk to you about something you already know, Mel." Milo looks at her intently but is not pushy. "You know you are the true Queen of

Asteria, right?" he asks her calmly, and I feel her body go rigid in my hold.

Melora did not meet either of our gazes, staring at the floor in front of her. "I do. My...my mother confirmed it for me. I know what I must do." she answered like she was reading a script.

"But do you want to?" I question her. "You have a choice in all of this, Mel. You get to choose. You have a choice. You will always have a choice here, Melora." I say to her carefully, letting the words sink into her beautiful skin. I want to ensure she knows she chooses her fate in all this. "If you chose to take your rightful place as queen, then so be it. But you tell me you do not want anything to do with it, to let my father continue to rule, then that is what we do." I stroked her hair, the wild strands soft under my touch.

"We are with you, Mel," Milo said to her. "In whatever you choose. We are with you."

Melora looked at both of us with watery eyes. She knew we meant what we said. Milo and I would stand by her, as would Yara, Penn, and the twins.

"I do not want to push you. I do not want to make you worry. We just want you to think about it; we do not need to make decisions right now. But Mel, you are the rightful ruler of Asteria. You are the Goddess of Life's daughter. You are a *fucking queen."* I said to her, proud of all she has done, all she had to do.

She raised her head slightly higher and sat up straighter on my lap. "Is it true? That the people already call me such?" she asked shyly.

"It is," Milo answered her. "They know the truth. How? We are unsure, but we believe that word spread after the battle. They cheer for you, Mel. Prayed you would come home."

"They love you," I whispered in her ear. "I can't blame them one bit." She giggled softly at that remark, and her demeanor lightened, changing into the woman I knew was still in there.

"I...can I think about it?" she asked us, still messing with her nails.

"Of course, my love."

CHAPTER 15

MELORA

I have been thinking...and I think I would make one hell of a queen.

But could I actually do it?

Doubt and anxiety have been eating at me every time I think I have made my choice. Every day is a different one. Today, I feel as though I could rule, that I could protect this kingdom and destroy the mortal queen.

But that is just today.

Every day, I have been getting stronger, mentally and physically. I still have not left Silas's room, but I think today may be the day for that venture. I am eating better, finally having an appetite after the images of all the bloody mortal guards have left my mind. I am starting to return to my normal body type, a healthy one.

Every day, I start to feel more and more like myself. The darkness is still there but less prominent. I sleep more, not having the recurring nightmare of Simon coming to carve me up any longer.

I just see his face now. I see his and Vayna's faces staring at me in my dreams.

It is better than the nightmares, but it is still unsettling.

A light tap on the door draws my attention away from the window I am looking out. Silas walks in, his black hair shiny and touchable. His lips curled into a smirk that I could kiss for lifetimes.

"Hello, my love," Silas says as he walks over to me and crouches. "How about you and I go out for a bit today?" he asks, and I feel my heart jump. I want to get out of this room, have the sunlight touch my face again, and smell the flowers and greenery around the palace, but I have just been too afraid. I am not afraid of what I will find once I leave Silas's room, but I am afraid of how I will react.

I do not want to lose control of my emotions.

After two long weeks, I think today will be the day I step out into the light again. "I think that is a wonderful idea," I answer, then get dressed for the day. I pull on brown pants and a leather vest over a blouse. This has become my favorite outfit, other than my long nightgown.

"Ready?" Silas asks, and I know he is asking more than if I am ready to go. He is asking if I am okay, if I am okay enough to step foot out of this room.

And I think I am.
"Ready."

We walk a less-traveled path wherever we go as we walk. I know this because it is not our usual route to get to places around the palace or city. I know Silas is doing this on purpose, trying not to overwhelm me. I appreciate it, but it is time for me to start living again.

I already let Vayna take so much of my life away; I will not let her take one more second.

Silas and I walk around the city, into the shops, and around the gardens. We talk to the people, shop owners, and some children who run up to us.

"Queen Melora! Queen Melora! Prince Silas! Please play with us! Please! Please!" one small child pleaded with me; I was just about to agree when Silas spoke up.

"I'm sorry, but Queen Melora has some things she needs to take care of. How about this? I promise we will come back and play another day. We'll play hide-and-seek. How does that sound?" Silas bargained with the small boy.

I swear the children's eyes grew as large as saucers. "Yes! Yes!" They all answered. I laughed as Silas and I continued on our walk. I guess it was true; even the children acknowledged me as queen. Why couldn't I do the same?

"Mel! Silas! Fancy meeting you here!" a sing-songy voice rang out, and I immediately knew who it was.

"Hello, Yara," I said as I scooped her in for a hug. She has been such a crutch for me these past few weeks, coming to keep me company, bringing me books, and even offering to spar in Silas's room. I know she and Loral would have been great friends.

Loral.

Just thinking her name hurts, hurts like something gouges my heart out of my chest. Even though we have so many good memories together, the only thing I can think of when I think of her is the sound her bones made when her neck broke.

"So, how about it, Mel?" Yara asked, I have no idea what she just asked me; her and Silas's conversation went right over my head as I thought of my friend.

"I'm sorry, what?" I asked her. Concern grew on her face, and Silas put a reassuring hand on my back. I calmed instantly; his touch grounded me. It reminded me of the here and now.

"Do you want to go check out a dress shop I think you would really love?" Yara asked again, more timidly this time, like I would say no.

I hated that my friends, even Silas, felt like they had to walk on eggshells around me. I understand why, I understand what they saw me go through. I am grateful for them, but I am done making them feel like I will lash out at any moment.

They do not deserve that.

"I would love to," I answer, and her face returns to the bubbly woman I know she is.

"Let's go!" Yara squeals, tugging my arm.

But Silas gets to me faster. "You are okay?" he asks quietly.

I give him a smile and brush my hand over his cheek. "I am good," I reassured him. "I promise."

He nods, understanding. "I love you." He says, and the words almost bring me to my knees.

"And I love you."

A few moments later, Yara and I are in a small boutique trying on dresses. We tried on gowns made of silk and other soft fabrics and skirts that twirled when we swayed. We laughed and giggled at each other as we fiddled with the skirts.

It was fun. It was simple.

"You must try this one on, my queen. The color suits you!" The boutique owner says, her fiery-red hair gleaming. I believe she is a nymph of some sort.

"Please, Melora is fine." I remind her for a hundredth time.

Yara grabs the dress and shoves it towards me. "You have to try it on! The color is so you!" She is very excited about this one, but she gets excited about everything.

So, I grab it from her and change into it. When I look in the mirror, I am speechless at what I see before me. It is me, but- I have never looked this beautiful. Never thought of myself as beautiful until this moment. Not until I saw myself in this dress.

The garment is simple. The color is a baby blue, and the fabric is cotton, soft on my fingers. The skirt is long and flowy, swaying around my ankles. The cut of the dress is an off-the-shoulder neckline that hugs my chest perfectly. Overall, the dress is sweet and simple, airy and light. But it is the most beautiful I have ever felt in a piece of clothing.

"Oh, Mel." Yara sighed as she watched me in the mirror I was staring into. "She'll take it," Yara tells the boutique owner.

"She'll what!?" I blurted out. "Yara, I have no use for this dress. It is- it is too beautiful to sit in my wardrobe for the foreseeable future."

The saleswoman moves to the register with a bright smile. "I presume I am putting it on Prince Silas's tab?" the nymph asks.

"Yes, that's right," Yara tells her. I feel my eyes go wide with surprise.

"Yara, what...what is going on?" I ask her because she is definitely up to no good.

She shrugs her shoulders and grins mischievously. "Come on, we have someplace to be." She grabs my hand.

What is happening right now?

"What, Yara, what is going on?" I question but laugh at her excited look. "We can't just put this dress on Silas's tab and then walk out of this store wearing it."

"Actually, you can. He told me to," the worker says shyly from the register. "I think you have somewhere to be, Your Majesty." She bowed her head slightly.

I look at Yara, questioning her with my stare. She gives away nothing.

"Fine." I gave in to the small, wonderfully cheerful woman. Yara squeaked her happiness and then pulled me out the door.

We walked through the city, past the stores and taverns, past the people who bowed their heads or full-on bowed at the waist when they saw me. I felt so silly walking through the streets in this magnificent gown, but everyone we passed admired the gown's beauty.

Yara and I traveled the path I knew would take us to the safe house, Silas's personal home. I had been there quite often after the first time he showed it to me, after he shared a part of himself that not many others get to see.

Yara continued walking us toward the cottage I had come to love. "Why are we going to Silas's house?" I asked her as she dragged me on.

Yara only gave me her signature smirk as she continued pulling me toward the door. After stepping through the entrance, I was immediately reminded that I had not been here in some time and had missed it. I missed the way the home was just for Silas; he apparently shared it with more than just Milo and me. I am not surprised he did; Yara is one of his closest friends.

I am just curious as to why she brought me here.

I turned to go into the living room, hoping to find Silas waiting for us, but he was not there, leaning against the fireplace...or sitting in the chair.

"There she is!" Kane said as he pushed himself from the fireplace. "We have been waiting." He was smiling broadly now, looking at the dress I was wearing.

"We were beginning to think you ran off." Kaius jokes. "Silas would have been very sad if you would have left him at the altar." he mimicked a frown.

Wait.

Left him at the altar?

"What is going on here?" I asked the group, now composed of the twins and Yara. I was starting to grow annoyed. I had been dragged around this city wearing a very beautiful dress, and now I was brought to Silas's house. I just wanted to know what was happening.

"We were supposed to keep it a secret," Yara growled as she elbowed Kaius. "Well...surprise! It is your wedding day!"

It is my what?

"Yara, what on earth are you talking about?" I questioned her, because I know she did not just say it was my wedding day.

"You are getting married!" Kane blurted excitedly. "If you want to, of course." He added.

"I—I am so confused," I said, laughing at myself and the friends before me. They seemed so excited, but I still had no idea what was happening.

"Silas set it all up. I was to take you to get a dress, then bring you here. I think I executed my part of the plan well." Yara smiled to herself. "Are you surprised?"

Am I surprised?

I am beyond surprised. I am ecstatic, nervous, and slightly confused, but ecstatic if this means what I think it means.

"Silas and I...are getting married?" I asked for clarification because I would be overjoyed if that was the case. Marrying Silas has meant a lot of different things to me over the duration of this adventure.

In the beginning, before I loved him, marrying the Asterian Prince was the last thing I wanted to do. Then, when we decided to stay engaged, even if it was only fake, I was disappointed because I had started to think maybe I did want to be with him. Now, the thought of marrying Silas, of being his wife, made my heart burst with love and excitement.

I wanted nothing more than to spend the rest of my life with Silas, loving him every day.

I wanted to be his *wife*.

"You are if you want to. Silas instructed us to make sure you knew you had a choice. If you do not wish to marry him-"

I cut him off before Kaius could even finish that sentence. "I want to marry him!" I yelled quickly.

The group smiled at my words, and Yara finally said, "Okay then, let's do this."

CHAPTER 16

MELORA

The twins led Yara and me out to the back of the cottage, where the patio sits on top of the sand. I think of the first time I was standing on this patio with Silas. It was the first time I had ever seen the sea, and I was awe-struck with its beauty. It was also when I knew I could not keep my feelings for Silas to myself any longer, that I needed him to know I cared for him.

I look to the sea, wanting to take in the gorgeous blue water. I peek around the broad shoulders of the twins standing in front of me and see that there are already people standing in the water. It is Silas. Silas and a man I do not recognize stand ankle-deep in the gently lapping sea. Milo and Penn are present, too, standing on the shore. They all look in our direction.

As soon as my eyes find Silas, I know this is right. I feel it in my gut, that tug that tells me this is how it should be. Silas stands in the water, linen pants and an airy shirt that is lightly blowing in the breeze. He stands out against the brightness of the sea, his dark hair and tanned skin contrasting with the bright water.

He is simply the most handsome man I've ever laid eyes on.

His eyes meet mine, and everything slips away; everything around me becomes a blur. The sound of the waves hitting the sand is the only sound I hear as I slip my shoes off and slowly start walking to Silas, to my husband. I hadn't even realized Yara and the twins went to stand by Milo and Penn on the shore, just out of reach of the lapping water.

I feel my feet hit the sand, warm from the sunny day that has now turned into a setting sun. I feel my legs taking me toward him, toward my future. A future that I have chosen for myself.

And I have chosen Silas.

I pass our friends, whom I hardly see because I can only focus on Silas. I feel their eyes watching as I step into the cool water, the wetness traveling up my legs as I wade deeper to where Silas waits for me. The memory from the first time I felt the sea slips into my mind. Silas and I had played and splashed in the cold water that night. It is one of my favorite memories.

My focus is solely on Silas, on the man I love so deeply, so truly, nothing ever made sense before I was with him. "Hello, my love," Silas says to me as he grabs my hands, his rough palms embracing mine. He is smiling, a type of smile that is only ever for me.

"Hello," I whisper to him, his bright emerald eyes holding my stare. "Silas, this is-"

"If you don't want to marry, I understand," he says hurriedly. "I just wanted to give this to you, a wedding you deserve. A better memory than the last wedding you attended." He gave me a solemn look, and I knew he meant when I was being forced to marry his brother. He was right; this will be far happier memories of a wedding because he is who I am to wed.

I squeeze his hands and beam up at him, "Silas, I want nothing more than to be married to you. To be tied to you in every way possible. I am yours—heart and soul." I assure him, wanting him to know I chose this.

His eyes gleam, emotion coming to the surface of his features. "You are mine, as I am yours," he promises like an oath, like an oath he will never break.

The man I did not recognize cleared his throat, grabbing Silas's and my attention. "If you two are ready, let us begin!" he exclaimed with an excited smile.

The man speaks a few words, then hands Silas a small knife. I remembered from my brief wedding with Simon that they cut their hands during the ceremony. Why? I am unsure. I will have to have Silas explain it to me later.

Silas cuts a small slice into his palm, and I wince; seeing him bleed is not one of my favorite things. It actually makes me sick to think about it; it reminds me of the battle. When he was stabbed through the chest. When he was dying in my arms.

Silas offers me the knife, but I hesitate. Since my escape from the mortal kingdom, I haven't touched a weapon other than my daggers briefly. I freeze, unwilling to touch the knife. "Would you like me to do it?" Silas asked, his voice grounding me and comforting me.

I nod my head, yes, and he holds my hand, palm facing upward. I watch, waiting for the sting the blade will bring. "Mel, look at me."

I listen because, of course, I listen to him. I look into his eyes, and I can't help but think that his shade of green, the color of his eyes, is my favorite color.

Silas smiles as he looks down at my hand, which I am only now realizing has a small slice in it. I hadn't even felt the steel on my skin; my mind was too enraptured by him.

He places the thumb of his uncut hand into his slice, pressing until blood covers the pad of his thumb. He looks at me, giving me a reassuring nod, and I follow his lead, placing my thumb into my sliced palm to cover it in my blood. Silas then reaches for my face, and I am unsure what he is about until he holds my cheek and swipes this blood-covered thumb over my lips. It is like I am in a trance because I do as he did and hold his cheek while running my bloodied thumb over his lips.

Silas shakes his head as a smirk laces his now-red lips. "You are always surprising me, my queen."

My queen.

I am feeling like a queen right now, like his love is giving me the strength to rule an entire kingdom.

Before I knew it, Silas's lips were on mine, and he kissed me like he had never kissed me before. Like he had never tasted my skin and was starving for just the littlest taste. I kissed back, moving my lips against his in a heady dance we ultimately lost control of. Our blood mixed during our kiss, and then I understood why we did such a thing.

We are now bonded by blood. Our love runs deeper than connection, deeper than lust. It runs in our blood, in our very beings. It's deep, soul-deep. Our love will forever course through us, through our veins, for the rest of our lives.

I only tuned into the cheering of our friends after Silas parted our kiss. I looked at him, our blood coloring his perfect mouth, and I wished that we were alone—that we were the only two people on this beach—because I would have him. I would have him in ways that I have yet to understand.

The group hoops and hollers as we turn towards them, hand-in-hand. I look over their faces and see the friends that have turned into family standing before us. Yara is, of course, crying, Milo is clapping and smiling brightly, the twins cheer for us, and Penn...Penn hides very well that he is crying. But I know him too well for him to hide it from me. My own tears start to well at the sight of our closest friends before us, watching us bind our love.

I thought my first memory on the beach would be my favorite, but this is a memory that will be with me forever—a memory that has outshone all others.

Not long after the ceremony, a celebration broke out. A small party on the beach where Silas and I had just got married started to form. People, some whom I have not met yet, some whom I have only seen around, came bearing food and drinks. A small bonfire was erected in the sand to light the now dim evening; the flames danced in the light breeze. Conversation and laughter were all around as people ate and drank to celebrate Silas and me.

This was not a fancy ball or a wedding feast like I had been used to seeing in the mortal kingdom. This was better. The energy was laid-back and fun. Many people danced to the music being played by some of the guests. Others talked amongst one another on the sand. It was truly perfect.

The only way it could be better is if I was only with Silas. With my husband. I am happy so many people came to celebrate with us, so excited to see so many friendly faces, but I just want to be with him. Be the only one to have his attention. I am selfish, I know, but only ever for him. I looked over the crowd, trying to find Silas's eyes. I found him, talking to two men I believe work at The Burrow, the tavern in the city.

He must have felt my eyes on him because he looked right in my direction and locked his gaze on me. His look was heated, hungry even. He knew what I wanted, what I craved. I bit my lip to try and contain the smirk that was trying to break free. I loved how he anticipated what I wanted. I loved how he knew me so well.

That he knew me better than I knew myself sometimes.

I could see him trying to end the conversation with the two men, trying to escape so he could be with me. Watching the awkward interaction made me laugh. But the men would not let him leave their conversation, continuing to chirp Silas's ear off. He was getting frustrated, but not enough to abruptly end their talking and come straight to me.

I guess I was going to have to play dirty.

"Milo!" I yelled for him. He was talking with the twins. "Care to dance?" I ask him, giving him a mischievous little grin.

A devilish grin graces his lips. "I would love to dance with the bride." he bowed dramatically and extended his hand for me to take. "However, I am not sure if your husband will approve. He is the jealous type." He teased as he pulled me to his chest, starting to sway to the soft music.

"That's the point," I murmured under my breath, trying not to laugh.

Milo twirled me around the flames of the fire, gracefully swaying us to the slow music. "I see," he rolled his brown eyes. "You *want* to get his attention." he chuckled. "If that is the goal, let's see what kind of mischief we can get into."

I knew I was about to get into some trouble.

Milo whistled at the small band that had grouped together to combine strings, drums, and sounds of pure beauty. They took the hint and changed the soft, light tune to a much more upbeat one. The music picked up, and people joined in on our dancing. The sand was filled with feet dancing around, some together and some alone, but still dancing.

    Milo and I danced around the fire as more people started to join in on the fun. Milo is quite the dancer, picking me up and swinging me in the air. I had completely forgotten what we had set out to do as a laugh of genuine happiness left me. This was living. This was feeling. And suddenly, I felt like myself again.

    Milo twirled me out, letting go of my hand to let me spin on my own. My skirt twirled and flowed as I danced around the sand barefoot. I closed my eyes and let my head fall back, enjoying the moment.

    I was suddenly stopped dead in the sand by a strong body, a body I would know anywhere.

    Silas wrapped his arms around me, embracing me as I tried to catch my breath from all the dancing. He looked down at me, his handsome face predatory.

    Mission successful.

    Silas smirked the kind of smirk that promised passion. "I am done sharing."

CHAPTER 17

MELORA

"It's about time." I teased with a returning grin. "I was beginning to think you would let me stay alone all night long."

Silas pulled me closer, tighter to his chest. I could feel his corded muscles straining against his shirt, the hard surface pressing against my breast. "Not a chance in the godsdamn world am I sharing you with anyone tonight." he cupped my heated cheek in his hand, bringing his face close to mine. "You are *mine. My* wife. And I hate sharing."

His words made me bite my lip, knowing what his tone would bring. Anticipation settled deep in my gut, filling me with the warmth of lust. "Then don't." I stood on my tiptoes and brushed my nose to his, begging him to kiss me. To take me away and have me all to himself.

A low growl left Silas, vibrating his chest. He took a step back, and I thought I may have pushed too far, teased too much. But Silas bent and flung me over his shoulder like a sack of potatoes. I squeaked as he laid a swift slap to my ass.

He took off, carrying me to the cottage. I was giggling, laughing at the way he was carrying me, and I could hear him laughing as well.

"Have fun," Milo said as we passed him, I heard a chuckle in his tone.

Finally, we were in the cottage. In the small room, the sexual tension between Silas and I grew, making us breathless as he sat me down on the wood flooring.

I looked at him, at my spouse. "Kiss me, husband," I demanded sweetly, tugging at his shirt.

That was all the pleading it took for him to have his lips on mine, moving at a languid pace. He kissed me like he had forgotten what it was like to kiss, like we had not just kissed a matter of hours ago when we wed. I did not mind, though. I would take this slow, tortuous kissing any day.

He held the back of my head, my curls entangling around his fingers. I pressed my hands to his chest, feeling him breathe deeply. I wanted more of him, more of his kisses, more of his skin. Just more. Always more.

"Silas," I said his name like a prayer. "Silas, please."

He rested his forehead against mine, his eyes closed. "Are you sure?" He asked tenderly.

I knew what he was really asking; if I was ready to have sex after everything I had been through. After the torture, the abuse, the trauma. We had hardly touched each other these past few weeks. That was partly because I wanted to be alone and because I knew if I got my hands on him, I wouldn't be able to get enough. It's not that I didn't want to have sex; it is just that I have been through a lot, am dealing with a lot, and physical intimacy seemed nerve-racking after what I went through.

I knew Silas would respect whatever I chose; if I said I was not ready, he would understand, he would care for me and be here for me.

But I am ready. I am ready to have him, to feel his skin and know he is alive and he is mine.

"Yes," I answered before planting my lips on his once more. I stepped away, grabbing his hand. I tugged, and he followed, a grin spreading across his face. I pulled him up the stairs and into his bedroom until we were next to his bed.

We stood there for a moment, only a second, and took each other in. "You look so beautiful in your wedding dress, Mel. So godsdamn beautiful," he said, drawing a hand over the curve of my waist. "But I am afraid I cannot keep it on you for one more moment."

Silas bent and pulled the bottom of my dress up and over my head, exposing me completely. I was happily not wearing any undergarments under my dress. I wanted to pat myself on the back for my boldness, but that would have to wait.

Silas's gaze on my body was absolutely sinful, drinking me in like water on a scolding day. "So fucking ravishing, my love." His eyes had turned dark, filled with hunger. I reached for him, tugging at his shirt. I wanted it off; I wanted to see his perfect skin shine in the moonlight seeping in through the windows.

He complied and tore his shirt free, buttons flying over the floor and bouncing around. I was not wasting a second. I wrapped my hands around his neck and jumped, wrapping my bare legs around his waist. Our mouths were back to battling each other for dominance, a mix of lips and tongue. Silas groaned as I sank down onto him, brushing against his hardened erection I could feel through his pants.

The feel of him at my aching center was barely enough to ease the tension. I was already so undone for him, so heated and hot that I could melt from one touch. I wanted, no need, to feel him inside me.

Silas walked us backward to the bed and dropped me down onto the bouncy mattress. I giggled as I flopped down, but my giggling died down when I saw his face. He was looking at the scar on my hip, the one from when I had to remove

Simon's handiwork. The spot had healed over, a nice patchy scar to always remind me what Simon had taken from me. It also reminded me how I persevered, how I survived.

I have seen Silas angry, I have seen him murderous even. But the way he stared at my hip, like he would burn this world and everyone in it for what has been done to me, made me realize that he felt the same fury as I.

Silas kneed in front of me, placing his hands on my knees and staring up into my eyes. "I swear to you, I will kill every single person in that kingdom that put their hands on you. I will kill my brother, kill him slowly and painfully for what he has done to you." I can only describe his look as carnal, primal in a way I knew he meant what he said.

I laced my hands through his hair and pulled him close, kissing his trembling lips. "Silas, I am here. I am safe. I am *yours*." our foreheads connected, and our eyes closed. We need this; we need each other.

I held his cheek and tipped his gaze to meet mine. His eyes were dark with lust and anger, but I did not want Simon or Vayna to take this moment away from us. I would not give them another thing to ruin. This was our wedding night, and I *will* have my husband.

"Silas," I kissed his lips, then his cheek, then his jaw. "I love you," I tell him between kisses to his face.

"Say it again," he whispered, his shaking hands caressing my thighs. "Let me hear it."

I smiled as I continued to kiss over his skin. "I love you. I love you more than anything."

Silas let out a deep sigh, a sound of relief, like he was finally realizing I was here. That I was his and his only.

His hands moved up my sides, taking in every curve of my body, mapping every dip and valley. Silas held my face so softly, so gently, as he kissed me. His lips touched mine, and all thoughts of violence or his brother or Vayna completely disappeared from thought. I only thought of him, only felt him.

The pace had changed from earlier. This was now slow and sensual, letting us revel in every moment. We were no longer ripping at each other's clothing or trying to rush into the intimacy. Silas's lips moved against mine in tedious, torturous moments. His hands traveled down my body just as slow as his lips, feeling every inch of me.

I braced my hands on his shoulders, feeling his muscles move under my palms. Silas started kissing down my neck, my shoulder, and across my collarbone. "I want to kiss every inch of you," he said against my skin, causing goosebumps to rise. "I want to cherish all of you, Mel. Cherish every part of you."

I let my head fall back, his words and lips making me feel a mix of lust and love. He moved lower, kissing my breast eagerly. Silas held both as he scattered kisses and licks across my nipples that were now aching for more. His mouth was hot and claiming against my sensitive skin, making me writhe for more.

Silas kisses down my bell, over the parts that are soft and sometimes make me self-conscious. He kissed and worshiped me like my body was art, like it was something to behold and never take for granted. He made me feel confident as we worked his way down, his hands following along with him. Silas placed his hands on the outsides of my thighs, kissing the apex of my hips, making me moan for more.

He took his time kissing the scar on my hip, making sure he kissed and loved every inch of it because it was a part of me, a part of my story.

I tugged his hair at the root, pleading in the movement for him to kiss my center. Praying that he would move to the pulsing area that I knew was ready for him. "Gods, Mel." he moans as he spreads my legs slightly apart. I laid back, supporting myself on my elbows. He looked at my slicked center, he looked and looked and turned ravenous. Silas struck, putting his mouth on me and working against me in a friction that was utterly delicious.

"You taste..." he moaned against me, his voice vibrating against my clit. "You taste like *mine*," he growled, sucking me into his mouth. I cried out his name, my orgasm dangerously close.

I was shaking with want, chasing that high that only Silas could bring me. Then...I was devastatingly cold. Silas pulled his mouth away from me, when I had been so close, so close to that magnificent spark between my thighs.

"I need to feel you," Silas said, rising from where he kneeled down on the floor before me. "I need to feel you come, Mel," he promised as he undid his pants, dropping them to the floor.

He was on me only a second later, and that heat, that scorching warmth, was already back, waiting to be ignited. Silas sank in between my legs, his head falling to mine to connect our foreheads. His hand travels to the nape of my neck, holding me close. I was ready for him, ready for all the love I knew he would give me.

"I love you," I whispered to him as he entered me, his hard cock making a dominant entrance.

"Again." He begged as he thrust, settling so deeply inside of me.

I moaned as he moved, his hips slowly pumping into me. "I love- I love you," I said again, this time a cry as I could feel my orgasm coming to life once more. "I love you, Silas."

He grunted out as he continued working me, continued pushing me closer to the edge of ecstasy. "Let me hear you, Mel. Again." He commanded, and I complied as the static traveled through my body.

"I love you," I cried as my climax rampaged my body, making me quiver around him. "I love you, Silas." I whimpered out as he drove me through my orgasm.

He hasn't stopped thrusting, still chasing his pleasure. "That's it, my love. Let me hear you. Let me hear those words on your lips as you come all over my cock, Mel."

My vision was spotty, still hazy with lust, as I whispered again, "I love you."

Silas growled as he flipped us, moving onto his back in one swift move that had me on top of him in a second. The quick adjustment to the new position was sinful; the part he hit inside of me already made me shake with anticipation.

He grabbed my hips and moved me up and down on him, and I watched as his cock disappeared into my entrance. It was the most erotic and captivating thing I had ever seen, and I could not get enough.

I started moving slower, steadier in my pace, wanting to soak as much of this in as I possibly could. "You are killing me, my love," Silas said, sitting up to hold my body as I rode him languidly. "You take me so beautifully."

I rocked back and forth, Silas's arms holding onto me tight as I torturously moved us closer and closer to climax. I could feel my walls beginning to flutter, knowing that I was about to let loose another wave of earth-shattering bliss. "Mel, keep going." Silas pleaded, whispered into my shoulder as he held on. "Keep going, just like that, baby. That's it."

And that *was* it.

Silas and I broke apart at the same time, holding each other through our orgasms that had me spasming around him and him twitching inside of me. It was beautiful the way our bodies melted into each other's. The way we fit perfectly into each other's arms.

The only sounds in the room were my name on Silas's lips and my sighs of pleasure. It was glorious and wonderful, and I never wanted to leave this room again.

CHAPTER 18

SILAS

Melora is my wife.

Melora is *my wife*.

I have to keep reminding myself that this is real, that she has chosen me, and we are alive and together. That she has returned to me. It feels like a dream, like the whole night was made up in my mind to play a cruel trick on me. Our wedding, the celebration, our first night together as Mr. and Mrs., it all feels too good to be true, like at any moment I will wake from the best dream I have ever had.

But I know it is real because I can see my Melora sitting in my living room, reading a book and looking adorably concentrated. I watched her from the kitchen, where I had just finished washing up our dinner plates. We haven't left the cottage all day, spending breakfast, lunch, and dinner here. We have done nothing but lay around, talk, read to each other, and cook meals together.

As well as indulging in each other throughout the day.

This is the first time we have not been on each other, this is the longest we have gone without tasting each other, feeling one another. I think both of us feel as though this is a dream, like we need to constantly remind ourselves that we are together.

That we are happy.

I watch her, watch her reading her book and twirling a piece of blonde hair in her fingers. I could stand here all day just looking, looking at the love of my life. Even though we spent all last night and all day today exploring and loving each other, it was not enough.

It never will be with her.

The need to have her near me all the time, to have her love, is overwhelming and all-consuming. But I welcome it because it is all for her—for the woman who sacrificed the most important thing to her to save me: her freedom.

I try to remind myself that all is well, all is safe now that she has returned. But she and I both know that this war has only just begun. I know Vayna, have grown up hating her and all she has done to my kingdom and family. I know she will never cease until she gets what she wants.

But we know more now that Melora has returned, and hopefully, that will be enough to end her. Hopefully, it will be enough to help us defeat the one who threatens our kingdom. It has to be.

I wish Melora and I could stay in our little happiness bubble forever, never having to leave the safe house. It would be ideal to have her and not have to share. I would truly be in heaven.

But unfortunately...duty calls.

"Hey," I say quietly to her, trying not to startle her from her reading. Her head pops up, and a small smile graces her berry lips. "Would you like to go on a walk?" I ask, kneeling in front of her chair and placing my hands on her knees.

She closes her book and sets it in her lap. "The last time you asked if I wanted to go on a walk, I ended up married," she teases me, running her finger through my hair.

"That is true." I cup her face, brushing my thumb over her lips, reminding me of the ceremony. "I think we could use some fresh air."

Truth be told, we could definitely use fresh air and some sunlight. I was happy to stay in this cottage for as long as possible, but I needed Melora to see the city, the people, as hers. Her city, her kingdom. The people already think of her as their queen, many found out the truth after the battle in the Fallen Forest and have thought of her as such since. The Asterians know she is the daughter of the Goddess of Life, and they already worship her as their queen.

It is time Melora starts seeing herself the way others see her, seeing herself the way I see her, the way our people see her.

A queen.

A warrior.

A fighter.

"I could enjoy that," she said, answering my question. "Let me put on a sweater." She rose and ran upstairs to the wardrobe I had brought in for her. I could not have her be here all the time with me and not have clothing. Well, I could...I could manage Melora not having any clothing to wear; I would actually be very okay with that.

"Ready?" I asked when she reappeared with a cozy brown sweater on.

"Ready!"

The sun was setting as we made our way through the streets of the residential part of the city, where most of the cottages and homes were. Melora and I walked hand-in-hand through the streets, and I couldn't help but feel a flutter in my stomach every time she made a light circle on my hand with her thumb. Her touch made me giddy, like a small child receiving a gift.

I love taking Melora to parts of the city she has never been to, showing her the parts of our kingdom I know she will love. Her love for Asteria, for this land and its people, moves me in a way I cannot describe. All I ever wanted was for Melora to come to love this kingdom as much as I do, and here we are, strolling through the city, Melora with a smile on her face.

I want her to stay in this happiness, but the time has come for her to decide, and that is why I said, "Have you given any thought to what we talked about the other night?"

She hesitated, looking down at our moving feet. "You mean if I have decided to be queen or not?"

I watched her, watched the slight tensing of her jaw. "Yes,"

"I have thought about it every day...and my choice changes every day," she admitted, looking off into the distance. "I want to do what is right for these people, for this kingdom, but I am unsure if the best thing for them is *me*."

She finally looked at me, and indecision was whirling in her eyes. "Mel," I began, making her stop walking and fully face me. "You have no idea how strong you are. How brave. How caring. Those are all qualities of a leader, a ruler who cares for her people. You may not see it in yourself, but we do, *I* do."

Her river blue eyes began to gleam, emotion coming to the surface. "I just...I am scared." she answered quietly, for only me to hear.

I wanted to wrap her up, to hold her until there were no fears and doubts turning in her beautiful mind. "I am too." I said truthfully. "I want what is best for you, what will make you happy. But I have seen you with our people, have seen you lead an Asterian army into battle against the mortal kingdom. You are more like a queen than you will ever know."

A tear slipped down her soft cheek. I wiped it away, hating seeing her cry. "If it was up to me, we would run away from it all. Hide away in the safe house and just be two normal people living and loving." I brought her closer, and her hands went to my chest. "But it is not up to me. It is up to you. And I know you will never forgive yourself if you do not care for these people like I know you long to, like I know you are capable of."

She blew out a shaky breath, nodding her head slowly. "You are right." she whispered. "I know I can do it. I know I can be the queen these people need. But...I was never meant to rule. It was never meant to be me."

My strong, ferocious girl's voice broke, making me want to pull her into my chest and guard her from everything this life has handed her.

"It has always been you, Mel."

Melora began to speak, but little voices caught us off guard. More children, like the ones from the other day, came running up to the two of us. It was a small group of children who looked like they had been playing, all dirty and red-faced.

"Queen Melora! Prince Silas!" they shouted as they crowded around us. I looked at Mel. Her face was beaming as she looked down at the children. She looked so happy to see all these little faces, all these children of her kingdom. A few adults gathered around us, too, watching and laughing along with us as the children continued their fun.

Melora greeted all of them, hugging them or holding their tiny hands. She looked so amazing like this, loving the people of her kingdom. A tug on my shirt drew my thoughts away from her. I looked down to see a little boy with his arms outstretched to me; he wanted up. He was holding what looked to be a bundle of flowers in his hand.

I gave in to the cuteness and swung the little boy up into my arms. His giggle of delight warmed every crevice of my heart and suddenly made me yearn for children of my own. "We made something for the queen," the boy whispered shyly. I looked at what he was holding in his small, dirty hands.

Mel is going to love this.

"My queen." I said to get Melora's attention; she rolled her eyes at me and turned to see what I was doing. "It looks like you have a gift."

The little boy in my arms handed her the flower crown, and all the other children cheered and clapped as Melora took it into her hands. She looked at it, at the beautiful arrangement of white and red flowers formed into a ring that would sit as a crown atop her head. Melora looked down at the small gift the children had given her like it was the best thing in the entire realm…and it really was.

"It is a crown!" One child yelled excitedly.

"Our parents helped us make it!" another chirped. Melora looked at the adults watching from a distance; a few bowed slightly when her gaze met theirs.

"Well, this is the most beautiful crown I have ever seen," Melora told the children, and I could hear her voice choking up. "I thank you all so much," she brushed the small boy's cheek I still had in my arms.

"We made it for you to wear at your coronation." he said softly to Mel. The little ones around us cheered and jumped up and down. "Please wear it! Please wear it!"

Melora looked at the crown, at the small children before us, and then at the parents and other adults around us. I could tell she was moved by this gesture, and it may have just sealed her decision.

I wanted her to see how much these people love and respect her.

"Of course, I will wear it. Look for me at the coronation; I will wear it proudly." She smiled as the children hugged her legs and squealed in delight.

After a while of playing around and talking with the children, Melora and I continued our walk. We ended up on the beach, one of her favorite places. The wind blew her hair as she stood facing the water, eyes closed.

I did not say anything; I just watched her stand in silence because I knew her mind was probably loud enough.

"I will not do this without you." she finally said, still facing the sea, not taking her eyes from it as she continued to speak softly. "I will not do this without you or our friends at my side. I refuse to."

I stepped closer and placed my hand on her back, wanting to remind her she never had to do anything without me again, that she never had to endure anything without me ever again. "I will be with you. I will always be with you, my love," I told her, a vow I would take forever.

A vow I would never break.

CHAPTER 19

MELORA

We returned to the safe house, the cottage a warm welcome after walking through the streets of Asteria for the better half of the evening. I was ready for a bath and maybe some wine—maybe a lot of wine—and possibly even a neck rub. Yes, definitely a neck rub.

After the decision I just made, after what I just chose to do for myself and for this kingdom, I think alcohol needs to be involved.

An idea popped into my head as Silas and I entered the living room of the cottage. A fun idea that would allow me to be near all of the people I loved. I needed that right now. I needed to be around the people who would help support me through this mess of becoming a queen.

"I have the best idea ever," I told Silas as I plopped onto his lap after he sat down onto the couch. "I think you will love it. I know Yara will love it, and I know Mi-"

Silas cut me off with a quick kiss to my lips. "What is this wonderful idea?" he questioned, I guess I had been rambling.

"Well," I began as Silas drew a hand up my back, caressing my spine and the hair that lay over my shoulders. "It involves drinking, dancing, and all of our friends having fun. What do you say?" I asked, giving him a mischievous smile I knew would get him to cave.

He took in a long, deep breath. "It is hard to say no to anything when you are on my lap like this."

That is a yes.

I jumped up, excited to feel like myself, excited to want to have fun and enjoy this life I was given. I was tired of keeping myself cooped up in either Silas's room or the safe house. I needed to get out like I normally would and see people and places. I wanted to do this; I wanted to do this for myself because I have been through a lot, but I am finally healing.

I clap my hands together, ready to get going. "Let's go then!"

Silas laughed as he stood, following me upstairs to his room. "Where are we going?" asking as if he did not already know.

"We are going to The Burrow, of course. Now, no more questions, let's go!"

A quick change and an hour later, Silas and I walked through the threshold of the first tavern I had ever been to...the only tavern I had ever been to. My memories from the last time I was here were a mix of good and bad, fun and ugly. Good because I was with Silas and all of our friends, drinking and dancing the night away. Bad because his brother had threatened me, admitted to knowing who I really was, then disappeared to the mortal kingdom to reveal the traitor he really was.

Overall, I had fun and thought of the memory fondly, but I would like to make more.

I spotted Yara immediately, waving us down in the corner booth, the same one we sat in the first time I was here. I stepped to walk down the short steps and towards our table, but something stopped me.

The tavern-goers, the drinkers, the dancers, even the bartenders stopped what they were doing. They stopped the music, stopped dancing about, and stopped handing over drinks. Everyone stopped what they were doing, because they were all looking at me.

"My queen," the first man we passed said and bowed at the waist. It was like a wave after that; everyone started bowing over and acknowledging me as their queen. It felt good, I have to admit, to see my decision confirmed by how the people see me. I do not deserve their love or their loyalty, but I will take it and use it to help me protect them.

I froze, not knowing how to react to this. But Silas placed a hand on my back and I knew I was safe, and I knew I was loved. By Silas and everyone in this tavern.

We are in a place of fun, of life, and love, and I do not want to be a queen who expects people to stop what they are doing every time I walk into a room and bow dramatically. That is not the kind of person I am, and not the kind of queen I will be.

I looked around at the still-bowing people, moved by their love for me. "Please," I began, talking loudly for all to hear. "Please stand. There is no need for that. We are here to have fun! Here, we are one and the same. Let us have fun and dance and drink!" I yelled to the crowd, who answered with a gleeful cheer.

Silas and I pushed through the once again rowdy crowd, finally making it to our friends. I let out a breath when we got to our table, letting the nervous energy be released. Hopefully, that was all the public speaking I will have to do for the night.

"Hello, my queen," Yara said teasingly, motioning for me to come sit by her. "I got you some ale," she told me, pushing the tall, foaming mug to me.

"Thank you," I whispered to her, taking a large swig. "Where is everyone else?" I asked her as Silas took his spot across the table from me.

"Well, it looks like Milo has made a move on Jessa," Silas said amusedly, looking to the dance floor at his friend, who was currently dancing with a dark-haired woman. "He has only had a crush on her for like ever."

I giggled at the thought of Milo having a crush. He seemed so serious most of the time, but I guess everyone needs somebody, and he deserves to be happy and to have someone. I looked again to find him on the dance floor with a tall woman, a woman who looked as much a warrior as him.

I watched as they danced, not really doing much dancing; they talked more. They laughed together. Milo whispered something into her ear, and she giggled. It was sweet seeing this side of him.

"Yes, Milo is off with Jessa, and the rest of the dumbasses are either at the bar or dancing; I am not sure which one," Yara told us, her nose scrunching as she tried to remember where they were exactly.

I laughed at her as I looked around and spotted one of the dumbasses she spoke of. Kane was currently walking back to our table, carrying six mugs of ale. It was actually kind of impressive as he walked slowly through the crowd, careful not to spill the alcohol.

"Hi!" He greeted Silas and I with rosy cheeks and a grin on his lips. "I got enough ale for everyone!" he said happily, distributing the mugs around the table.

I had a mug and was content on finishing this one before getting into another, but Silas did not have a mug of ale in front of him. "Not drinking tonight, my love?" I asked and took his hand on top of the table.

He smiled softly and shook his head that he was not. "None for me, but plenty for you," he said with a grin.

I respected that he was not drinking right now and had not been drinking since I returned from the mortal kingdom. He told me about what had begun to happen while I was gone and how it had turned into a crutch for him to deal with my absence. He did not want to be something he knew he wasn't, and he knew he needed to have a clear head for me.

I gave his hand a little squeeze, hoping he understood how proud I was of him.

Kaius and Penn strolled up to the table just then, laughing together over something one of them had said. I enjoyed seeing Penn like this; happy and having fun.

"Hello, my dear," Penn said, smiling ear-to-ear. "Care to have a go?" he asks, nodding towards the dance floor.

I gave him a questioning look, surprised he would ask such a thing. "You know how to dance?" I laughed a bit, trying to imagine him twirling about with a partner to soft music. The thought made me laugh more.

He chuckled. "You have no idea," he said playfully. "Come on, it will be like old times...with less punching and kicking."

A moment later, Penn and I were dancing around the tavern's dance floor. We danced in time with others twirling about to the upbeat music played by the men who played at Silas and I's beach party after we married. It made me happy to see many of the people here who were at the celebration and to recognize people other than my friends.

Penn was not bluffing when he said I had no idea, because he was truly a great dancer. I guess fighting and dancing go hand-in-hand; both have to do with footwork and rhythm. I was actually impressed with his moves.

He spun me and twirled me about, laughing and cheering along with the others dancing around us. Milo and Jessa passed us along the way, smiling at each other as they danced. Yara and her dance partner, Roslyn I do believe, twirled past us too, both women smiling giddily.

Eventually, the music turned slow, allowing us to catch our breath from the rapid movements we were just making. Penn and I slowly swayed to the music, enjoying time together. We have hardly talked since I returned from the mortal kingdom, and barely even before that.

"How are you doing, Penn?" I asked him, holding on to his shoulders as we swayed.

He returned my question with a curious look. "What do you mean?"

"I mean, how are you doing *here*, in Asteria? Are you adjusting well?" I asked him, looking up into his gray-blue eyes.

He took a moment to respond, twirling me under his arm once before he spoke again. "I am doing well. I- I actually like it here. Like...I can breathe for the first time in years." he looked at me, like he was admitting a truth he did not want to. "I knew I would stay here. I knew I would follow you wherever you ended after I first arrived in Asteria and found out the truth. But I never thought I would love it here, love the people, love the land. I truly feel like I have a place here."

I smiled, happy to hear he felt the same way. "You have no idea how happy that makes me," I told him, hugging him tightly. "I wanted you to love it; I knew you would. But I also knew that it was a lot to take in."

"It has been," he responded. "But it makes it easier when you have people who take you in like you have been friends for years." He looked over to the group of friends at our table. "And it makes it easier when you know the queen," he nudged me playfully.

I rolled my eyes and smiled, thinking of all the love and happiness these people had brought me. Yara, Milo, Kane, Kaius. They have been friends to me ever since I stepped foot onto Asterian land, even before I trusted them, even before they should have trusted me. They had always trusted me and took me in as a friend because they knew how Silas felt about me.

I am forever grateful to have the people I do in my life. To have friends who support me through my healing, through this change that is happening within me, and who would burn cities to the ground to make sure I returned home. I am grateful, but I need them now more than ever.

Because tomorrow, I will be crowned queen, and they will be right by my side through it all.

CHAPTER 20

MELORA

I know I am having a nightmare.

I know that this is not real.

I can feel that it is not real, but I cannot will myself to wake. I wish to open my eyes and know that I am safe, but my body just won't. I have not had one in a while; the nightmares have passed with time, with time and healing, but tonight, they return to me. They return to me in waves, plaguing my mind with terror. It is one of the ones that occurred on repeat when I had just returned home from the mortal kingdom.

When I was still raw and torn inside from all that I had been through.

It is Simon, Simon and Vayna. They stand at the end of the wedding aisle, dressed and waiting. They wait for me as I walk towards them, towards the marriage that fate had not chosen for me, that I had not chosen for me. I know this is a dream because it does not play out how it happened in real life. In reality, I did not marry Simon, did not kiss him, or bind us together blood and soul.

But that is not what this dream shows me, not what my mind has in store for me tonight.

My eyes finally open, waking me from my torturous sleep. I feel a soft and soothing caress on my forearm. I turn to find Silas watching me breathe deeply to calm myself, watching me come down from the horrors of the night. Seeing him here next to me calms my racing heart, reminding me that I am not in the mortal kingdom or being forced to do anything against my will, but I am here next to him in our bed.

We don't say anything, because nothing needs to be said. Silas knows of my dreams, is there for me when I wake screaming and panting for air. He knows his brother torments me even in sleep, that he invades my dreams to torture me more. So, we lay there, not speaking of what I dreamed about because he and I both knew what it was.

Silas continues to soothe me, drifting his fingers up and down my arm and over my face, keeping his touch feather-light against my skin. It is a calming thing to have your partner, your love, be there when you wake from nightmares, wake from the things that have torn a piece off of you in the process.

He reminds me that I am whole, that I am in one piece. It takes time, cleaning up the pieces from all that I survived, but we did it.

I did it.

I see the sun peek in from the window of Silas and I's bedroom at the castle. After I returned from the mortal kingdom, we pretty much combined our rooms into one, seeing as I was not leaving his. "What time is it?" I asked Silas in a sleep-coated voice.

"It is morning, my love," he answered, pulling me closer to his broad, naked body. "Would you like a bath before the meeting?" he said into the top of my head.

We planned for a meeting with the crown's advisors, with King Norik's advisors, to take place this morning. I was not looking forward to it, to say the least, but I knew it needed to be done. I still have not confronted King Norik about his lie, about how he did not tell the truth about my mother when Silas and I had asked.

I was not hurt that he lied about who my mother was because, after all, he owed me nothing.

It was the fact that he lied to his son to keep himself as king.

I can only hope he does the right thing now: step aside and let me take my place as queen.

"Only if you join me," I answer his earlier question playfully, feeling his hard want pressing into my belly.

Waking with Silas was dangerous, tempting, but very dangerous, because it always seemed as though we could never get enough of each other, even in sleep. I went to bed craving him, and woke up craving him. Craving his body, his love, all of him. It was a never-ending cycle that I would happily live in forever.

A growl of approval vibrated his chest, sending a thrill of pleasure racing to my already heated center. "If I ever say no to joining you in the bath, please just kill me." He said with his lips against mine, grazing over my smile.

I giggled as he picked me up from the bed, easily scooping me up in his arms and taking me to the bathing chamber. I loved being in his arms, pressed against his body with my hands entangled in his soft onyx hair. I never wanted to leave them; I only wanted to stay in them and get in the steamy bath I knew awaited us. I simply wanted to live in this small slice of happiness forever.

We walked through the conversation area between the bedroom and the bathing chamber, Silas's long legs quickly covering the distance. I guess he could not wait for the warm water either.

I laughed at his urgency, at his quick pace.

"Morning," a deep voice said from the living area we were walking through, causing Silas to halt to a stop in the middle of the room. Silas and I both looked to the front of the fireplace. There stood Milo, coffee cup in hand, a smirk on his handsome face. "I was wondering if you two were ever going to get out of bed."

"Milo!" I squealed, realizing that I was, in fact, very naked. "What are you doing!?" I tried to nuzzle closer to Silas to conceal some of my nudeness.

"You better turn around right now and stop staring at my wife before I gauge your eyes out," Silas growled at his friend, at his brother. I want to say that he was kidding, but I knew that he was not.

Milo's brow rose in surprise, making him grin more. "Feeling protective this morning, are we brother?" Milo said as he turned to face the fireplace, taking Silas's warning to heart. "You know, I could always just join you-"

"Do not even finish that sentence." Silas sighed annoyedly as he set me down and went to retrieve clothing for the two of us. He wrapped me in my robe and pulled pants onto himself. I already missed his skin on mine, the warmth his body brings me.

"What are you doing here?" I asked Milo, annoyed that he just interrupted what I am sure was about to be a very fun bath. I thought about what he said earlier, though, about joining us. Did he mean *join us,* as in bed together? I never really thought about having more than one lover at a time, but the thought...well, "It better be good." I smiled as I took his cup of coffee from him for myself, trying to get the image of him and Silas together with me out of my head.

"Besides coming to annoy you both," he began. "I do have some urgent matters to speak with you about." The playful tone in his voice was now gone, and I knew this was not about to be good.

Silas sat down in the chair next to mine, nowhere near as close as I would like. "Not good, I presume?"

Milo shook his head, looking down at his feet. "It could be worse," he paused, taking a deep breath. "The advisors are planning to have this meeting without you. They uh...they are meeting right now." he looked at Silas. "Without either of you."

Without me? I was the whole reason for this meeting, for this assembly. I called them together so I could tell them I was taking the crown, tell them my plans. I wanted to keep the advisors in the loop; after all, they have been in their positions for decades, and I would need their knowledge. If I was going to do this, I would need everyone's help...well, not everyone.

"Let me guess," I began, anger radiating through my voice and blood, stirring the magic beneath my skin. "Aro is trying to sway them against me?"

"Not happening," Silas said, rising from his seat abruptly.

"Couldn't agree more," Milo said, following Silas in the direction of the door.

"Where are you two going?" I said, rising from my seat as well.

The men stopped, their anger evident. "We are going to have a word with Aro," Silas said as if it were obvious.

I appreciated them both for their protectiveness and love for me, but if I was going to do this, I was doing it my way. "You will not."

They looked at each other, wondering what I was about to say. "You will wait for me, and *I* will have a word with Aro. With all of them." I had no clue where this confidence was coming from, but I loved it, and I needed to keep it.

I needed to have it when I faced the advisors, when I faced the people of Asteria. I wish I could always have this confidence, not just when I was only around Silas or my friends.

Silas smirked proudly, and Milo gave that devious little smile I knew meant trouble. "As you wish," Silas purred. "My fierce queen."

I summoned Yara to help me prepare quickly; that is what I told the men, at least. I really wanted her to help me because I was feeling rather nervous about what I was going to face, about what I was to say aloud and claim. I was about to tell the advisors, some of whom did not like me very much, that I was taking my place as queen.

"I don't know why you are so nervous; you are fidgeting like a damn child." Yara groaned, trying to contain my wild curls into a braid down my back.

I tried to sit still, tried so hard to not let the anxiety get to me and make me a nervous wreck, but I couldn't help it. I was just so damn nervous. "I just want everything to go smoothly. What if- what if they do not want me as queen? Do I kill them? What even happens? Or what if they *do* want me as queen, what happens next?" I was rambling, a telltale sign of my anxiousness. Next, I was going to start picking at my nails.

"I am going to stop you right there," Yara said, yanking my hair back by the braid so my chin pointed up. She looked at me in the mirror, just like she had when she had told me she knew the truth of what I was going to do, of when I was planning to kill Silas. Back then, she looked hurt. But now, she looked determined. "You are a *fucking queen*. You are the daughter of the Goddess of Life. The rightful Queen of Asteria. You are the Queen of Life. You are the Evaira. You need to act like it." Her voice was harsh, but I knew she meant it sincerely, that she wanted me to see myself as others saw me.

Easier said than done.

I stood up and faced her. "But-"

"No buts." She silenced me, grabbing my shoulders. "If you were a man, there would be no issue, no second-guessing yourself. You are not a man; you are a woman—a woman whose pain has shaped her into a warrior, into a queen. And you will rule this kingdom with the love and the fury that fate has granted you."

She was right.

This is my fate, my reason for all I have gone through.

For the pain, the fear, the regret.

I will rule this kingdom with it all.

And I will be the queen these people need.

The one who will take down the mortal queen who threatens them.

CHAPTER 21

MELORA

"My queen," Milo says as he greets Yara and me in the hall, bowing dramatically at the waist.

I roll my eyes and punch him in the shoulder. "Do not do that." I whisper-yell at him.

"Ow." he grinned as he rubbed his shoulder. "You may be a queen but you pack one hell of a punch."

"Don't you forget it." I teased.

The three of us walked quickly through the halls of the castle, ending in front of the door I knew was the advisors' meeting room. I remember this from when we were briefed before the battle with the mortal kingdom.

Penn and Silas were waiting for us upon arrival. Silas was dressed in all black looking like the prince I was once taught to fear.

That fear has turned into love...and maybe some lust.

"My queen," Silas said, bowing his head. Penn was next to him, his hand already on his sword. Did he think these advisors would harm me? Maybe.

Milo laughed. "I would not say that if I were you."

Silas pulled me to his chest, his arm wrapping around my waist. I looked up into his dark green eyes and all of my anxiety melted away. "You look ravishing, my love." He swiped a curly strand out of my face that had fallen from my braid.

I did feel ravishing and queenly, even though I wore my typical outfit; brown breeches, a loose white shirt, and a brown leather vest over the top. It was simple, but I felt strong in it, strong and determined.

"Are you ready?" Silas asked me quietly, only loud enough for me to hear.

"Kiss me." Was all I had to say for Silas to plant his lips on mine. His kiss was consuming, taking over my thoughts and body. I welcomed it, because it made the nervousness and anxiety slip away to somewhere it could not reach me.

A throat cleared, Penn's, I am guessing, and I smiled against his lips. I could feel his smile as well. "Let us interrupt their meeting," I said, drawing in a big breath and filling my lungs with the air that I needed.

"I am with you," Silas said as he turned to the door to open it.

I was unsure what I expected to find in the meeting room; I knew the advisors were there conversing about me without me even present. That alone was enough to piss me off. But when Silas opened the door, and all the men went silent when they saw me, the fury in my blood rose, as did my magic.

How dare they talk of my future without me here.

How dare they talk about the kingdom's fate when their rightful queen was not even present.

I was starting to scare myself, because never in a million years would I think to myself that I sounded like a queen. But I did.

"Melora," King Norik's voice boomed over the men sitting around the long table, their eyes plastered to me. Some of them looked fearful. Good. "I was expecting your arrival sooner rather than later."

"Were you?" I questioned him, a little too much malice in my tone.

He did not answer, and the point was made: I did not trust him. I respected him as Silas's father and *former* king, but I did not trust him.

I walked to the head of the table, where I had stood when I declared my love for Asteria, my love for Silas. The feeling of rightness flowed through me, making my fingers spark with magic. I could feel it coming to life, feeling it vibrating under my skin.

My magic knew this was right, as did I.

"You all know why you are here," I stated from the head of the table, Silas and Milo standing behind me, Penn beside them. "You all know what I am here to say, to do. And yet you meet without me."

A few men's heads fell forward, not meeting my eye. The tension was palpable as I stared down Aro who was sitting at the other end of the table straight across from me. He looked as though he had a lot he wanted to say to me.

He would not get the chance.

My confidence is astonishing; it is like a switch has been turned on, allowing me to embody a queen, a ruler. My hands were shaking, but I held them together in front of me to try and keep them at bay.

"It is known that I am the true ruler to the Asterian throne, the daughter of the Goddess of Life. I am here to take my place, to take my crown. I am here to rule and protect Asteria until my last breath. I will do so with a love and ferocity that will uplift the kingdom, the people." I paused, looking around at the sitting men; they watched as I spoke. Some looked proud, excited. Some looked wry. "My mother told me to protect our people, the people she created. I will do whatever it takes to keep our people safe, to keep them safe from the mortal kingdom and their queen. I-"

Aro cut me off before I was finished. "You cannot just come in here and start making proclamations about being queen and-"

I simply held up a hand, and he paused mid-sentence; a few of the men looked at him and shook their heads. "I was not finished speaking. Interrupt me again, and you will no longer have a place as an advisor; I am sure I could find someone much more capable of keeping their mouth shut when their *queen* is speaking." I sounded like a godsdamn conqueror, like a fucking ruler. I would like to think my mother would be proud.

"The mortal queen will die, her plot to overthrow the Asterian kingdom with it. I will not let her take this kingdom. Never." I paused again, trying to keep my breathing steady and my anger from Aro to a simmer; I could already feel my magic stirring violently within me. "I know there is doubt about me; believe me, most of it has come from myself. But I promise you that I will not let our people live in fear any longer; I will not live in fear any longer. The mortal queen will die, and their kingdom will know their place when I am through with them."

I finished, breathless and riled up. Everyone was silent, still staring at me with looks of surprise on their faces. I thought I may have failed, have failed before I was even crowned, but King Norik, well, I guess just Norik now, spoke up. "My queen." he bowed and placed his hand over his heart.

I was not expecting that.

Others started to join him; all around the table, the advisors stood and bowed.

Bowed to me.

To their queen.

Aro still sat, looking at me with defiance. I tilted my head slightly and gave him a look I knew would provoke fear. He stood and bowed reluctantly.

As he fucking should.

A minute passed before everyone rose, looking to me for instruction. I honestly have no clue what would come next.

"The sooner you are crowned the better, my queen," Norik said from beside me, standing with his hands behind his back. "The people already see you as such, but the sooner we make it official the better."

I straightened, knowing I had to make a choice. "We will do it today," I told him. Norik smiled and bowed his head in acknowledgment.

"You can't do it today. These things take time to plan. There should be a feast beforehand and a ball after. The coronation is a major deal and needs to be planned accordingly." Aro, of course, stated this to deter me from being crowned today, I guessed.

He will not do such a thing.

"I do not need the feasts and dances. I need the people to know I am their queen, and I will fight for them, for their kingdom." nods of approval came from around the table. "It will be done today."

"We can do it later this evening; just give us time to gather the people," Norik said casually as if Aro had not expressed his concern.

"Please do not forget those who live in the forest. I would like them to be there as well." I told them and turned to Silas, who was still behind me. His stare was sensual and proud. "Everyone out, please."

And just like that, the men rose and left the room.

I looked at my friends, standing proudly beside me. "You too. I would like a moment alone with my husband." I told them.

Yara groaned but left with a little skip. Milo only chuckled as he walked out. Penn came to me though, grabbing my hand into his. "I am proud of you, Mel," he said.

I smiled, looking into his emotion-filled eyes. "Thank you."

"Could I have a word with you, my queen?" Norik's voice catches me off guard.

I turn and he looks timid, like he does not want to piss me off.

I do not speak, so he continues, "I- I wanted to apologize for lying to you when you came to me about your mother. I should have told you and Silas the truth, it was stupid and self-righteous of me."

"You are right," I tell him, my face never giving anything away. "You should not have lied. Not to me, and definitely not your son."

Norik's face falls, and he knows what he has done, he knows and he is owning up to it. I respect that...but I do not trust him.

"I accept your apology and thank you for coming to talk to me. I respect you as former king and Silas's father, and I would like for you to help advise me during this crazy change. But I need to know that you will not lie to me again, because now I am queen...and I will not easily forgive a second time." I finish, the cool coat of satisfaction covering me.

He nods his understanding. "Never again, my queen."

A moment later everyone was gone.

Except for my husband.

Silas came up behind me, slipping his arm around me to pull me back against him. "My vicious girl," he whispered into my ear, his breath tickling my skin. "I could not be prouder of you, my queen." His voice was pure sex.

I let my head fall back into the crook of his neck, wanting to be closer. Silas kissed my cheek, my jaw, my brow. He kissed me like he was marking me as his, every kiss a brand on my skin.

"Let me worship you," Silas said, turning me around to face him. I immediately laced my fingers through his soft hair, needing to feel the strands on my skin. Silas's lips cost featherlight over mine as he said, "Let me worship every part of you."

I couldn't take it anymore, his lips this close to mine and not having them on me. I lunged forward, pressing my mouth to his in a fast motion that he returned. Our lips moved together in a wild dance, needy and crazed in our pace.

Our hands were just as frantic, grabbing and tugging at each other's clothing. Needing it off so we could be as close as possible. I slipped my hands under Silas's shirt, feeling my way up his muscled stomach. He moans into my mouth as my fingers reach his chest, as I press my nails into his hard flesh.

"Off," I spoke, pulling his shirt up and over his head.

"Demanding," Silas grinned on my lips. "I love it."

He pressed against me, his body flush against my front as he walked us backward until my ass hit the table we had all just been meeting at. I put my hands on his shoulders, hoisting myself up and back until I sat on the oak table in the advising room. Silas moved between my spread legs, placing himself as close to my aching center as possible. I could feel his hardness as he pressed against me, still moving his lips against mine.

The feel of him on me, the feel of his need pressing against mine, was enough to drive me absolutely feral, was enough to make me forget that I was about to be crowned queen. I needed this, I needed him, I needed to have this peace.

I wrapped my legs around his waist, pulling him closer than he already was. He groaned at my movement, at my lust for him.

I needed more, but I was still so dressed. I let my chest fall away from his, making space between us only for a second. I moved to undo the clasps of the vest I was currently wearing, wanting it to be off so I could feel Silas on my skin. I removed the leather top off quickly, Silas helping me remove the garment and the one beneath it.

His hands moved to my now fully exposed skin, caressing my curves and hips. I loved the way his hands left a trail of fire in the path, igniting something so deep inside me, that he was the only one who knew how to extinguish it.

His mouth moved to my chest, licking and sucking my skin as he worked his way to my breast. He was truly worshiping me, praising every inch his lips touched. He continued to kiss and feel my body, making me feel like the most precious thing in the realm.

"Silas," I moaned as he knelt in front of me, his hands planted on my hips. "I need you. I need you now." I begged, my hands still laced through his luscious locks.

Silas grinned that devilish little grin as he slid down my breeches, leaving me fully naked on the table. The oak was cold on my rear, but I was so hot, my skin burning up for him, that I hardly noticed. "You have me, my love." he purred as he kissed the inside of my thigh. "Never doubt for one moment that you have me."

Silas moved so slow, so painstakingly slow up my thighs. His lips and tongue leave me writhing with need for him. Finally, *finally,* he reached my center. I knew what he would find; I could feel the wet want of need continuing to grow as he explored my body with his mouth and hands.

The anticipation was murder, his mouth so close but still not close enough. "Silas," I pleaded, wanting him to lick me and consume me in every way imaginable.

"Look at you," he growled, watching as he traced a single finger through my wetness. I whimpered at the teasing feel of his digit, just enough to make me need more. "So *fucking* wet for me, my queen." he continued saying as his finger slipped down and into my entrance, eliciting a sound of pure lust from my throat. "Such a good wife, always so needy for her husband."

Silas watched as he moved his finger in and out of my entrance, curling as he went in and hitting a spot in me that made me feel as though I could ignite right here. He watched as my naked body shook with want, as my hips bucked against his hand. The look on his face can only be described as carnal, hungry.

"I want to see my wife come all over my fingers," he murmured against my thigh as he added another digit into me. I was so full, felt so full of him that I knew I would burst. It was too much, but never enough when it came to Silas.

I felt my skin prickle and knew my climax would shatter me any moment, but my world completely broke when Silas sucked in my throbbing clit, taking me over the edge happily. His mouth moved with his fingers, drawing out my pleasure and making me cry out his name.

I was so blinded by my lust, by pure desire, that I had not even seen Silas undo his pants and pull himself out. I had not even known until he entered me, causing me to melt against him and fully take him.

Silas's forehead fell to mine as he entered me, moving into my slick heat, still pulsing from the first orgasm he delivered. My arms held me up on the table as Silas thrust into me, fully filling me with his hard erection.

"Fuck, Mel." he gasped against my lips. "The feel of you -*fuck*- you are so beautiful," he said as he continued to move in and out of me, never leaving me for more than a second.

I let one hand go to the back of his neck, pulling his lips to mine as he continued his steady pace. We kissed hungrily, mouths missing each other's lips, breathing into each other, trying to catch our breath. Silas picked up his rhythm, slamming against me and making me shake with need.

"Come with me, my love." he coaxed as he wrapped an arm around me, pulling my sweat-slicked body closer to his. You would think the table would make this uncomfortable, but the position it was letting Silas have me in was absolutely sinful.

I held on tight to his neck as my second orgasm hit me, ravaging my body and making me pulse around Silas's cock. I felt him jerk inside me, his hips moving rapidly as his pleasure left his body.

The room was filled with only the sounds of our pleasure, of our pleasure and our love. Our movements slowed as we came down from our highs, spent from the passion that just ensued. Silas lifted me into his arms, taking me from the oak table beneath me.

I instantly wrapped around him, never wanting to leave his body. He walked us over to my chair, which sat at the head of the table. He sat down and pulled me into his lap, looking down at me with a happy little smile on his face. I nuzzled closer to him, needing to be as close as I could get.

Silas brushed a fallen piece of hair from my face, looking at me with so much love and passion that I was sure my heart would explode. "I love you," he said, bringing my lips to his in a sweet kiss. "I am in love with you," he told me again.

"You better be," I teased him and he grinned as he played with my hair. "Because we just had sex in a very public place where any of those old crone advisors could walk in on us at any moment." We laughed at the thought, laughing together in our little piece of happiness.

"I don't think this room has seen this much action in decades." he smiled as he looked at me, studying my face.

That statement rattled me as we continued sitting in my chair, just being with each other for a little longer. It shook me as I thought about it more, because this room will most likely see more action in the near future. There will be plenty that goes on here because after all...we are at war.

CHAPTER 22

SILAS

The sounds of the crowd seep into the room connected to the balcony that we are about to step out onto. The Asterian people have gathered together and await the crowning of their queen. The commotion that is coming from the people can only be described as excited, cheerful.

I look at my Melora, my strong girl. She waits to step out onto the balcony. She looks like a vision, a vision so beautiful it hurts. She is wearing the brown pants and vest she had on earlier, her hair is down and out of the braid, and her wild curls cascade down her back. She even has on the flower crown the children made her, requesting that she wear it. This is what a queen looks like, the kind of queen Melora wants to be.

She is not interested in fancy gowns and gaudy dinners. She is more focused on the people, on keeping them safe. She is astonishing, and sometimes I cannot believe she is even real. She has always been a queen, but she may finally see herself as one.

Although the confidence she exuded earlier with the advisors is still there, she seems nervous. She is doing her telltale sign of being anxious; she is fidgeting with her nails.

I close the distance between us because I can no longer stand to be this far away. Melora takes her eyes from the crowd for a moment to look at me. Her brows are furrowed, and her lips are pressed in a firm line. "Relax," I tell her, taking her soft hand in mine.

"Tell me again, what will happen?" She asks, squeezing my palm.

I have told her about five times now what will proceed after we take our place on the balcony, but if she needs to hear it once more to feel better, to calm herself, then I will gladly repeat it.

"We will step out, then you will address them. My father will address them next and then crown you." I told her as I pulled her to my chest. I wanted to calm her nerves; having her close always does it for me. "I will be beside you the whole time. Milo will be with us as well. Penn will be there, too. We are with you, my love." I assured her.

Milo must have heard our conversation because he added, "We are with you, Mel."

"Always," Penn added.

This calmed her slightly, knowing that I, Milo, and Penn would be with her as she faced this. As it becomes real.

My father stepped up beside us, and I instinctively pulled Melora harder to my chest. I know he would not dare hurt her; he knows what I would do and how fiercely protective I am over her, but I do not trust him—not after he so blatantly lied to Melora and me. I am glad he is taking this with grace, not causing an uproar and giving Mel a hard time. He knows she is the rightful queen, and he has done well to respect it so far.

I just refuse to trust him. Especially not with Melora.

"Are we ready?" my father asked Melora and me in a cheery voice. He seemed excited.

Melora nodded and stepped out from my arms. "I am ready."

She changed then. She took a deep breath, drew back her shoulders, and readied herself to address our people. Her nerves and anxiety seemed to leave her as she raised her chin, and regalness dripped from her. I know the anxiety is still there, but how she transforms into the Queen of Asteria and slips into the role with ease makes me even more amazed by her.

Melora steps out onto the marble balcony that overlooks the people who have gathered.

There are thousands, even those who reside in the forest, who have gathered to see their queen. The diversity of people in Asteria is one of the many reasons I love this kingdom, but seeing it before me is so moving. Seeing the different people and the different types of magic all around us is enough to bring a tear to my eye.

I stand beside Melora and watch as she places her hands on the rail of the balcony and looks over to see all her people standing before her. The crowd has silenced, watching their queen and waiting for her to be crowned.

"Many of you know me, and many of you do not. Many of you know who I am; I am the daughter of the Goddess of Life, Ismera." Her voice is steady and loud. "Today, I will take my place as queen, as the rightful ruler of Asteria. Today, I will honor my mother's wishes to protect our people and ensure the kingdom's fate will be safe. I am the blood of the Goddess of Life, and her magic runs within me; her power runs within me." she paused, looking over the crowd intently. "I promise you, I will be a loving and protective ruler. I will hear you, listen to you, and aid you in any way I can. I promise this to you, to the people of Asteria, on my life."

The crowd of Asterians cheered at her proclamation. They hollered and clapped for their queen.

"The threat of the mortal kingdom is real, but it will be no more. I will end their reign of terror over us. I will end their plan to take what is ours. With the help of those with me today and those who are not, we will make sure every Asterian knows peace." She finished.

Chills broke out on my arms from the crowd's reaction to her words. They cheered and cried out in joy for their queen, for her words of faith.

Melora grabbed my hand quickly, squeezing tightly. I could feel her shaking. "You did it. You did it, Mel." I whisper to her, trying to steady her.

My father stepped forward, carrying something in his hands. I realized that it was the crown of Asteria, the crown my father always wore. I have not seen it in many years, but its beauty still surprises me.

My father holds up the silver crown, the red rubies shining brightly in the evening sun. "The crown of Asteria," he states. "It is my honor to crown the rightful Queen of Asteria, my daughter-in-law, Melora. My son will now crown his wife."

I did not know that was going to happen.

Melora looked at me, panic claiming her features. I gave her a sure smile, letting her know to not worry. I stepped forward and took the crown from my father.

I slowly turn to the waiting crowd, thinking of what to say. "This crown crowns the Queen of Asteria. The daughter of the Goddess of Life. The *Evaira*. The true heir to the Asterian Throne." I pause for dramatic effect. "I crown Melora, the Queen of Life!"

The crowd cheered again as I finished and turned to place the crown on Melora's head. I laid it softly on her silky curls, and atop the flower crown I knew she would not want to remove, it sat perfectly on her—like it was made for her. "Ravishing," I told her as I fixed some loose curls around her face.

Melora smiled, eyes watering as she took a breath and stepped forward as Queen of Asteria. I watched as my love, my wife, stood before our people and looked like the fucking queen she was.

I could die right here and be happy that I was able to see this moment. Melora has been through so much, but she has prevailed, showing her resilience and strength.

I knew always knew what she was, but maybe now she will see herself as I do.

Time seemed to have passed in the blink of an eye; moving from the balcony and back into the castle was a whirlwind. Melora was ushered by an excited Yara into the Great Hall. Apparently, she and Milo planned a surprise get-together for Melora.

Which I absolutely had no part in whipping together.

Alright, maybe I did.

Melora and I sit at the head of the Great Hall, where the Asterian Thrones sit before the people who have gathered. The hall is crowded with people, people who have come to celebrate their queen. I had Yara and Milo invite many of the folk Melora had met in the city.

There is food and drink for all, and music playing joyfully from the guests who played their instruments at our beach party after our wedding. Melora recognized many of them immediately, happy to see them all.

I looked over to her, where she sat on the large throne. She looked like she belonged there as she sat and watched the partygoers, still wearing her crown. The silver throne extenuated the silver of the crown on her head, making her shine brighter than she already was.

Melora laughed as she watched Yara and Kaius twirl around on the dance floor, swinging to the upbeat music. She sat at the edge of her seat while she watched the partygoers enjoy the food and dancing. She looked content, happy.

"Would you like to join them?" I ask her.

She looks at me, her cute nose scrunching. "I would very much like to, but I am unsure if it is appropriate for the queen to dance and get along like our friends are doing." She laughed again, the sound ringing delightful in my ears.

I grabbed her hand, drawing her gaze back to mine. "You are the queen, my love. You do as you please." I paused, grinning. "Besides, this is your party." I gave her a wink, and I swear her cheeks pinkened.

She stood abruptly. "You are right. Dance with me?" She asked, playfulness in her tone.

"It would be my honor."

Melora grabbed my hand and dragged me to the center of the Great Hall. She was so excited, her face lighting up when I wrapped my arm around her to ready us to dance. She held on tightly as we began to sway with the beat of the music.

The band picked up their tune, the sound vibrating the air around us. Melora grinned as we began to dance around the center of the room, twirling and gliding with so much gracefulness that you would not think this was our first time dancing with one another.

The music crescendos as I pick Mel up by the waist and spin her around in the air. People around us clap and cheer us on as we continue our dance. By the time the song ends, we are both out of breath and smiling ear-to-ear.

"You are one hell of a dancer," she tells me, her eyes hooded with mischief.

"Only for you, my love." I practically growl into her ear. All this dancing, moving so beautifully with one another, has awoken a fire in me that only burns for her, and suddenly I needed to have her skin on mine.

I believe Mel was feeling it, too; her hands rested on my chest, pressing her nails into my shirt. She looked up at me like she would devour me, and I would happily allow her to. "I want you, Silas," she whispered. "I need my husband."

"Just say the word, my queen."

Melora's gaze heated at my words, and she said nothing as she pulled me towards a small hall behind the thrones. I knew where this hall led: the stairs to Melora and I's room.

We quickly walked the path to the stairs, stopping only once in the hall to have my lips on hers. I couldn't help it, not tasting her lips. I pushed her against the wall in the hallway and planted kisses along her jaw, down her neck, and on her lips. Just this little taste was already driving me mad with lust.

She giggles as she slips under my arms that had caged her in against the wall. Melora's hair bounces under her crown as she takes off toward the bedroom, looking over her shoulder to laugh. "Get back here," I called to her, trying my damndest not to laugh along with her. She is going to be the death of me, easily making me hot with want and then running away from me. "Get back here so I can kiss you!" I yelled at her again.

She turned to look over her shoulder as I began to follow her down the hall. "You'll have to catch me first," she giggled, a mischievous little grin on her lips.

She wants a chase?

I will give her a chance.

I run after her, running to catch the woman in front of me, her laughter ringing through the hall. She ducks into a room, and I only realize once I enter that it is our room. I chased her down the hall, up the stairs, and around a corner to our room. Now, she was done for. I had her where *I* wanted her...or maybe where *she* wanted me.

I stop in my tracks as I enter the room and find Melora standing and waiting for me, her chest rising and falling as she tries to catch her breath. She's standing there so beautifully, looking at me like I am the only thing she has ever wanted, like I am the only thing she has ever needed.

Gods, I am so crazy for her. So needy and frenzied with love when it comes to Mel, when it comes to my wife.

I take a step towards her, meeting her in the middle of our room. My hands easily embrace her, pulling her face toward mine so I can taste her again, so I can feel her lips on mine again. She rips open my shirt, the little vixen, exposing my heaving chest. Her hands are instantly on me, making me forget any thoughts I have ever had.

I want to do the same, tear off her clothing and leave her bare for only me to see, so I can see every inch of her. But I don't move to tear her clothes off in one swift motion like I crave to; I simply take a step back from her, creating space I already hate. Mel looks at me, her eyes boring into me with downright want, with pure need...for me.

"Silas," she pleads to me. "What are you doing?" she asks, her cheeks pink and her face confused.

I reach out to her top, starting to remove it slowly—so slowly that I can see every part of her, every inch of her that is all mine. "This is something I never want to rush, my love," I tell her, unbuttoning her blouse and helping her shimmy it off. "I never want to take for granted seeing you, really seeing you again," I tell her, and her look turns understanding, like she knows I was thinking of our time apart.

I knelt before my wife, before my queen, and undid her pants. I slide them down slowly, making sure to look and kiss every part of her skin, even the scar on her hip, *especially* the scar. I look up at her from where I kneel, her breast perfect, her wild curls laying over her shoulders, her silver crown gleaming in the dark room.

I am surprised she hasn't wanted to take it off yet.

That crown will be staying on, though.

"Kiss me," she begged, pulling me up from the floor to meet her lips. She melts into my hands as I wrap them around her, grabbing her waist and tugging her body forward. I will never get used to the feeling of her on me, of her skin against mine. She makes that soft purring noise I love so very much, letting me know she can feel my cock through my breeches. I am so hard for her, so fucking hard for my wife.

But tonight is not about me, not about my selfish wants or needs. I want to show Mel who she is; I want her to see herself as I see her.

She is ready for me, pulling and tugging me closer to the bed, but tonight will not be taking place in our bed. I stop us, still kissing her like my life depends on it, like she is the air and I am drowning. Melora places her hand on my erection, feeling me through my pants. She could end me with such a thing; her touch could end me, and I would thank her.

I moan as she rubs me through my breeches, making me wild with lust, making me want to be inside her so bad I practically am dying for it. I quickly undo the buttons on my breeches and slide them down with help from Melora, who is lowering herself to the ground. I stop her, not wanting her mouth on my cock, because there is no way I will last long enough to do what I want to do.

I turn her around, and she gasps when she sees herself. I turn her around to face the full-body mirror that sits in the corner of our room. I nudge her forward with my body, my hard want pressing against her perfect ass. She moves, but continues to stare at herself in the mirror, continues to stare at us as we get closer.

"Silas," she whispers out, not knowing what I am doing. She is still watching us, still staring at me in the mirror as I stand behind her, both our bodies naked out on display.

"Look at you," I tell her as I move her hair from her shoulder, pressing kisses along her skin there. "Look at yourself, Melora. Tell me you do not look like a fucking queen. Tell me you do not look strong, beautiful." I tell her, because she is all of those things, but it is time for herself to see it.

She watches herself, looks at the crown still on her head, and looks at me. Her gaze is sinful, claiming as she grabs my hands and pulls them to her center, wanting me to touch her—*gladly.*

I put my other hand on her chest as I began to feel her wetness. I slip my fingers into her center, feeling her hot want waiting for me, all for me. I watch my hand move in the mirror, watch as her body forms to mine as I continue to fuck her with my fingers.

"Beautiful," I tell her, making a circular motion on her clit that I know will have her writhing. "Strong," I whisper into her ear, still watching her in the mirror, still watching as I move my hand against her. She watches too, watching as my fingers go in and out of herself. "Fucking vicious." she purrs at my words as she bucked her hips back, grinding against my hardened cock.

I know what she wants, and I will never not bend to her will.

I remove my hand from her center, already missing the feeling of her wetness, of her want for me. I grab her hands and place them on the wall on the sides of the mirror, so she can still see us as I fuck her. She braces herself, letting her arms hold her weight as she watches me in the mirror behind her.

I move behind her, aligning myself with her entrance. She pushes back, so fucking needy for me. I enter her in one long push that has her gasp for air, moaning in delight. I seat myself fully, letting her adjust to the size of me, her walls wrap around me, welcoming me into her body.

I grab her hips and begin to move at a languid pace, never leaving her for more than a second. I watch her face in the mirror; she is looking at me, looking at us, and watching our bodies move as one. She smiles as she watches, our eyes meet, and she holds my stare. I grin at her as I roughen the pace, becoming more ruthless in my strokes.

"Silas," she moans, purrs only for me, only ever for me.

She is getting close, getting close to the edge that I am about to jump off with her. "Watch yourself come, my queen," I tell her, loving the view I have of her, the mirror giving me a beautiful sight of her as I claim her from behind.

I place my hands next to hers on the wall, allowing me to be closer, go deeper. "You are a queen," I tell her.

Thrust.

"A ruler."

Thrust.

"My fucking wife."

Thrust.

Melora shatters before me, taking me with her. I feel her spasming around my cock, her climax bringing on my own. We never break eye contact in the mirror as we crumble apart, as we both give in to the pleasure each other has brought. Her sounds are like a song, and my name on her lips as she comes is my favorite song ever.

I pull her to me, her body still shaking as she comes down from her orgasm. I hold her close, hold her and keep hold on as she clings to me. I remove her crown, placing it on the dresser before turning to go to our bed.

I know tonight will be full of love, full of passion into the early hours of the morning. But I also know, I hope, that Melora has finally seen herself the way I have. That she sees herself for who she truly is, for the strong woman she truly is.

CHAPTER 23

MELORA

¶ sit in the advisor meeting room at the head of the table and wait for everyone to arrive. I, of course, will never be left out of a meeting again, so I will be here as early as needed to ensure that never happens again.

They are lucky I did not kill them on the spot. *Stop.*

I tell myself, squeezing my eyes closed hard. I try to remind myself that I am not like Vayna, not a queen who kills because she can. I will not be evil like she is. Dark like she is. I will not.

The door creaks open, and I sit straighter, waiting for the arrival of the men who will most likely hate me by the end of this meeting. Oh well.

"My queen," Theon, one of the advisors who has supported me, walks into the room. "I wasn't expecting you to be here yet, but I am happy you are," he says with a closed-lip smile as others walk in behind him.

The other men, the ones who have supported me and given me respect, file in behind him; Orin, Jasper, and Lonan.

"I thank you all for joining me today. I believe you already know why I called this meeting?" I ask them, trying to let softness take my features. *They are not the ones who will hate me, so I want to be nice.*

"We figured you would either be canning us or keeping us," Orin said, a chipper smile on his old face.

The men laughed slightly, like they would be content either way, and I enjoyed that about them—that they were happy and content that I was queen. "Well, you are correct," I laughed slowly along with them. "But it is not you all who will be being canned." The door opened again; this time, it was the one I had been waiting for, Aro and the other two men who usually had his side walked in with him.

The three of them looked around the room, questioning what they had just walked into.

"Sit," I spoke to them without any of my earlier amusement.

They sat, for once, listening to me.

Silas walked into the room then, and I felt the air leave my lungs. All my focus was centered on him, even in a room of men who hate me; all my attention was on him. I thought of last night, how he put me in front of the mirror and fucked-

"My love," Silas said as he bent to kiss my cheek. "You look extraordinary," he stated simply, caressing the hair on the top of my back.

My skin tingles at the thought of his hands on me. At the thought of last night. How he made me feel like a queen.

"There they are," Silas said, interrupting my lustful thoughts.

Milo, Yara, the twins, and Penn walked through the door then, filing in to stand around the table. "You wanted to see us, Your Majesty?" Milo asked, a small grin tugging at his lips.

"I did," I said, giving him my usually annoyed glare. "Everyone, please have a seat," I said, trying to let regalness fill my tone as it did yesterday when

I addressed the people of Asteria. I still cannot believe how I did it, how I stood before all of them and declared myself their ruler.

I need that confidence now.

"I would like to start handling things now that I am queen. First of all," I began, looking at Aro, who was surprisingly silent. He must know what was to come. "You may leave," I said to him and looked at the other two sitting by him.

Aro drew back like I had hit him. I wish I had. "Wh- what?" he asked. "You can't just tell us to go! We are advisors to the crown!"

"Actually, I can. I said, you may go. All three of you." I looked at them as I spoke. "I do not need advisors who did not support me when I was only a princess; I need advisors who support me now that I am a queen."

The three of them stand there, stunned at my proclamation. They were not moving, so I said, "Go." a small bit of viciousness lacing my voice.

They got the message and left the room.

Finally.

"Good. Let us move on," I said cheerfully. Silas chuckled in his seat beside me, and I smiled a bit. "I need three new advisors, and I have the perfect people to fill the position."

"And who would that be, my queen?" Kane asked, genuinely curious.

I smiled. "How about you?" I asked, trying to hide my excitement. "How about the three of *you*?" I looked at Kane, Kaius, and Yara, who looked like I had just spoken in a different language.

"You cannot be serious," Yara said, unwilling to believe I just placed her on my advisory board. "I mean, we are- we are just-"

"You are all my closest friends, my closest confidants. I trust you to tell me your opinions, when you think I am wrong, and help me lead Asteria. Can you do that?" I ask them.

The three friends still looked shocked. "We-we can," Kane spoke up, astonishment in his voice. "We will."

"We will." Yara and Kaius both said, eyes wide but with expressions of gratitude and excitement.

"Perfect," I said, clasping my hands together. "Now, Milo,"

He looked at me with raised brows, his head tilted slightly. "Yes, my queen?"

"Keep it up, and I will take back what I am about to say," I tell him playfully. I would never take this back or change my mind, though. "I name you commander of the Asterian army. You will oversee the army, train them, and prepare them for battle. Will you do this for me?" I asked him because he honestly looked as though he might pass out.

Milo stood abruptly, his chest puffed out and a look of determination on his face. "Mel, I-" he stuttered, then kneeled to the ground on one knee, his hand placed over his heart. "I- I am honored. I will not let you down, I promise you," he vowed.

"You could never let me down, Milo," I said with a smile. His honor and surprise at this placement just cemented my decision. I knew it could be no one other than him. He would command with pride and honor.

Milo sat back down, and I swore his eyes glistened as he looked at me. I gave him a slight nod, acknowledging how this had moved him.

"Penn," I turned to where he had taken a seat next to Milo, I believe the two of them had become somewhat of friends. That makes me happy. "Will you honor me by being my personal guard? Apparently, it is custom for a queen to have one. As you know, I can protect myself, but I would have no one other than you to help me." I smiled at him, at what he meant to me.

He taught me to protect myself, helped me get through some of the hardest times of my life when I was in Ravenhall. I am forever grateful for him and love him dearly.

He chuckled, his old cheeks pinkening as his body shook with laughter. "I would have done it if you liked it or not," he said to me, making everyone join him in laughter. "I know you can protect yourself. Trust me, I remember how many times you *almost* kicked my ass. But I will be with you, like it or not. You are like the daughter I never got to have, Mel. I will protect you like you are my own." His demeanor changed and he got serious, sentimental.

I promised myself I would not cry, but his words, his promise to me, brought emotion forth. I never knew what it was like to have a father, but Penn has filled that role tenfold.

"Then it is done," I said, trying to hold back the tears gathering in my eyes. "Now that all of that is taken care of, let us talk about what is the most important task now that I am queen; Vayna."

"We need to kill her," Milo says, determination filling his voice.

I nodded, listening to him. "I could not agree more."

"But how?" Jasper asked, wondering on his face.

"I am glad you asked. Visha? Please come in." I called to the door that was closed.

After a moment, the large door opened slowly, and Visha, the witch who saved me in the Fallen Forest, walked into the room. She looked slightly scared or maybe nervous. I knew she most likely had never been out of the forest, never away from the comfort of nature. I could not blame her for being uneasy.

But I needed her here. I needed her help.

"Everyone, this is Visha. She saved my life and knows how to kill Vayna." I told everyone in the room. My friends knew of the witchy woman who saved my life in the forest after I had been chased down by mortal guards, but the other advisors did not know her.

"I *think* I know how to stop her," Visha stated harshly, reminding me that her idea was only a theory. "I am unsure if it is a foolproof plan."

"I know," I told her, looking at her intently. "But it is the best we have."

Visha told everyone what she had told me that day in the Fallen Forest; to kill Vayna, we must drain her power. According to Visha, since Vayna's magic was given to her, she believes it can be taken away, killing her.

"It would be dangerous. You would have to be close enough to have a connection to her. Draining magic from an object is one thing, easy even," she explained. "But draining a person will be difficult and dangerous." Visha looked at me like she wanted to tell me more; her eyes were worried.

"So you are saying that once Vayna's magic is drained, once it is taken from her, she will be no more?" Yara asked, curiously scrunching her brows.

Visha nodded, saying that it would hopefully kill her.

The thought of killing Vayna, of ending her bloodied reign, has been at the forefront of my mind since I knew she knew the truth about Asteria. Since I found out that she mass murdered innocent people, people with magic who did no harm other than have more power than her.

"Who will do it? Who will drain her?" Milo asked, giving Silas a side-eyed glare. I knew he already knew who would do it; Silas did, too.

"It will be me," I stated plainly, as a matter of fact.

"No," Silas growled. "You will not risk your life," he said to me, his eyes wide with anger and fear.

"It has to be me, Silas." I grabbed his hand, trying to assure him. "It was always going to be me."

"She is right." Visha spoke up, drawing heads to where she stood. "She is the strongest here, blood of the Goddess of Life. I believe she is the only one capable of using that much magic, that much power. She is the only one who will live." Visha said, dropping her gaze to the floor.

"I have to agree with Silas here," Penn interjected. "How do we know it will be safe, Mel?"

"We don't." I straightened my posture. "But if it means saving Asteria, saving our people? Then I must risk it."

"Mel-" Silas started, turning to me.

"It is settled. I will be the one to drain Vayna of her magic." I cannot believe what I am about to say. "As your queen, I command it."

Everyone went rigid, even Silas. I was surprised at my command and at how harsh my words sounded, but I knew I needed to pull the queen card. If not, I knew one of them, most likely Silas, would stop me when the time came.

I would not lose him to her.

It was silent; not even breathing could be heard. However, I felt as though the pounding of my heart was loud enough that those around me could hear it.

A throat cleared, Penn. "What is our next step of action, my queen?" he asked.

I thought for a moment, took a deep breath, and continued. "Well, that is where you and Milo come in," I said, looking at the two men who sat side-by-side. "Ravenhall. We take it like you originally had planned. We will bring the fight to them."

"I like where this is going," Milo said, a bloodthirsty grin on his lips.

"We take Ravenhall and tell the people there the truth, the truth about Vayna, about what the mortal kingdom has done. We will not kill anyone who does not act against us. We will be closer to the capitol, closer to Vayna." I told everyone who was listening closely. "I need the two of you to concoct a battle plan to overtake Ravenhall. Ready the army, Milo. We must move quickly before Vayna makes another move."

"Will do," Milo said before standing, Penn in toe.

Everyone left the room slowly, filing out after saying goodbye to me or asking questions like, 'What can I do?' 'What do you need from me?' and 'How can I help?'

These people have my back—I knew they would—but seeing their dedication to our cause makes me feel like I belong.

After a moment, Silas and I were the only ones left in the room. He looked solemn, his head hanging. "I cannot lose you, Mel," he said quietly. "I will not lose you again." His voice grew harsher.

I moved to kneel on the ground in front of the chair he was still seated in. I grabbed his hands. "I promise you, you will not. Never again." I promised him, vowed to him because I would never allow that to happen.

I moved to kiss him, but before I could, I felt the familiar feeling of slipping into darkness come over me. I can recognize when a vision is about to appear to me, like right now.

    I think I close my eyes, letting the vision take over my mind. I feel Silas's hands steady me. I feel the darkness pour into my mind, into my thoughts. I am in the forest. I can see Visha's cottage in the distance. I see something else, something black, like a shadow moving over the land. The shadow engulfs the grass and the trees, swallowing them whole until only darkness is all I can see in the forest.

CHAPTER 24

SILAS

The sounds of swords are all that ring through the air as Milo, and I watch the men of the Asterian army train and prepare for the battle we are heading into. Milo and Penn have been preparing new additions to the army, training them, and equipping them for war.

"I worry for her." Milo blurted out. "I- I worry about what she must do." He stands next to me overseeing the army, arms crossed and eyes ever watchful.

"As do I," I tell him, averting his gaze. "I know she has to do it, I know she has to be the one to do it, but if there was a way I could, you know I would."

I have thought about it over a million times since Melora gave her order yesterday. Maybe there is another way, maybe there is a way that doesn't involve endangering Melora.

But I came up with nothing.

Like Mel said, it was always going to be her.

"She is strong. She will live," Milo said, almost as if he were reminding himself. "She has to."

Before I could agree, I heard the voice of the woman we were talking about, like a melody in the wind. She was walking over to us, talking to the men training as she passed. Of course, they tried to bow to her, but she would not allow it.

She was dressed in her fighting leathers, the black ones that made my mind think of all kinds of delicious thoughts of her. She caught me staring as she closed the distance between us, her lips curling into that devilish smirk.

"Hello, husband," she said, standing on her tiptoes to kiss me. I instinctively grabbed her waist, the curve of her body fitting perfectly into my palms. She kissed me, graced me with her lips on mine in a heated motion that made me hungry for more.

To my avail, she pulled away and separated our kiss. Her cheeks were heated, lips pink. So fucking beautiful.

"Hello, commander," she said to my friend. "How is the training going?" she asked him.

He laughed at her, shaking his head. "They are doing good, my queen. Although, I am sure they will do better now that their queen has joined them in the training field."

She smiled brightly. "I will not let these men sacrifice their lives in battle while I sit inside and play pretty queen," she told him, her annoyance growing. "Now, who will spar with me?" she asked.

Milo barked out a laugh. "Good luck finding a partner; no one would ever think of raising a hand to you."

Melora groans, flustered. "That will not do; I will train, too." her fist was balled, and I knew she was growing madder by the second. I liked it when she got fired up, showing her more vicious side. "Penn, will you spar with me?" she asked him.

Penn paused, stopping his fist from hitting a man he was sparring with. "Um, no," he answered. He must have read her annoyance because he continued. "Melora, you are our queen, I will not spar with you and risk actually hurting you."

"That did not stop you when I was a princess." she pointed out, crossing her arms. "Why is this any different?"

"Because you are no longer a mortal princess; you are a queen," Penn told her.

Melora groaned loudly, and I had to stop myself from laughing. She was so cute when she was annoyed with us men. However, I knew that annoyance could turn to anger at any moment, that is why I said, "I will train with you, my love."

"You will?" She asked, excited.

"You will?" Milo asked like it was a bad idea.

"I will," I told both of them.

This was definitely not one of my best ideas.

Melora is beating the shit out of me. Her fist and feet have connected with my flesh one too many times, and I am starting to feel her wrath. I knew she wanted to train, but damn, she had some pent-up anger in that body.

I dodged a punch that was aimed at my jaw, a hard swing that definitely would have hurt. I have been giving it back to her, not wanting her to think I am taking it easy on her because she is queen and my wife. She would probably kill me if she knew I was pulling my punches, but there was no way I was actually going to fight her.

I would let her have a go at me, let her get all her pent-up energy and rage out. I knew she needed that, knew it would help her...but she is kicking my ass.

"She is kicking your ass," Milo said, chuckling to himself.

"He's pulling punches!" Mel shouted to him as she kicked out, aiming for my gut.

I react without thinking and pull on the arm that is outstretched to hit me. I pull her body to mine and turn her so her back is against my chest. The feel of her body on mine, her leathers hugging her curves and her ass so perfectly made me crazy for her.

"You are so sexy when you are like this," I tell her, whispering in her ear. I feel her arch into me, arch her ass into my already hard cock. "So sexy when you are being a vicious little creature," I say as I nibble on her ear.

She giggles as she wraps her hands around my arms that are holding her to me. "You have no idea how vicious I can be, *husband*."

Before I know what she is doing, she uses her body to flip me over her shoulder and slam me on the ground. I have to give it to her. Her strength is becoming fierce. It is the Goddess's blood that runs through her, making her stronger.

I land hard on my back, knocking the wind out of my lungs. I hear Milo and others cheer and holler as Melora stands above me, looking proud. I was proud of her, too.

She moves to stand over me, but she freezes up entirely before she does.

Melora goes down, falling to her knees as she holds her head. I roll to her, trying to keep her upright by the shoulder as she screams in pain. "Melora!" I yell at her. "Melora! What is it?" I yell again, but she doesn't answer, only screams as she continues to hold her head.

"S-something is h-happening." she groans out in between screams. "I-I feel it."

Her blood-curdling screams are enough to kill me right here. That sound, the sound of her pain, was the most horrible sound I have ever heard. "It's okay, Mel. I am here. It's okay." I try to calm her, try to soothe whatever madness is eating at her mind as she screams louder.

Milo crouches next to her. "What the hell is happening?" he asks, his face filled with fear, fear for Mel.

Men have started to gather around, watching in horror as their queen knees on the ground, screaming. I know Mel would hate this, but she doesn't even seem to notice through the pain she is enduring.

"We need to get her inside. Now." I tell Milo, who instinctively stands, protectiveness radiating off of him.

I pick Mel up, whose screams have turned to whimpers. I hold her in my arms, close to my chest, and hurriedly walk back to the palace. At some point, Penn joined and was now behind Milo and me. The three of us raced Melora into the palace, into my study where I sat in a chair with her curled in my lap.

I brush her hair away from her tear-streaked cheeks, my heart hurting from seeing the signs of her pain. "Mel, what happened?" I ask her gently.

She is breathing heavily, trying to slow it down, but the screaming has stopped, and her panic has set in. She still holds her head. "I- I..." she began slowly like she didn't know where to start. "There was pain; I felt like my soul was being ripped from my body. Like a part of me was being torn off."

She said it so plainly, so simply, that a chill ran down my back at the thought of what that may feel like. "You are safe, Mel. I have you." I held her cheek and looked into the eyes that I would happily drown in.

She started to speak again, looking around the room and spotting Milo and Penn, but the study's door opened before she could.

A breathless Yara came bursting through the entrance, having looked like she may have just run to come find us. "Something has happened in the forest," she said, huffing.

"What do you mean?" Melora asked our friend, her worry growing. "What do you mean something happened in the forest?" She asked again, fear making her voice wobble.

Yara looked at us all, her small frame still with what looked to be shock. "You all need to come with me. Now."

A minute later, we were all standing outside the castle again. I had my arm around Melora, not letting her get too far from me. Milo and Penn were beside her, close enough if anything were to happen.

My father is waiting for us on the grassy plain we had been training on earlier, looking grim. "My queen. Son," he greeted us. "The forest...Vayna has struck."

I feel Melora's body shake under my arm; I try my hardest not to give in to the chill spreading down my spine at my father's words.

I hear Melora suck in a sharp breath, I turn to her, and she looks pale, horrified. "My vision," she whispered to herself. "What has she done?" Melora asked my father, her voice full of fury and fear. "What has she done!?" she yells, her body almost collapsing again.

My father shakes his head, his eyes beginning to water. "She used her magic," he starts. "She has whipped out half of the Fallen Forest, Melora. The best we can figure is that she sent out a wave of her magic, a spell perhaps? As soon as the scouts came to tell us, I sent Yara to find you."

"There's more." I guessed, knowing that he was not telling the full extent of the situation.

"There is," he released a shaky breath, his fear written on his old face. "Half of the people in the forest are gone. They...she killed them with whatever magic she was able to use."

A collective gasp came from the group as my father relayed this information. Melora sobbed as she placed a hand over her chest. "I knew this was coming. My vision showed me. What I felt in the training yard...it was her killing our people, killing the land." She cried at her realization, but she couldn't have known; she couldn't have guessed that this would happen. "I am going to be sick," she said as she turned and vomited harshly.

I rubbed her back as she sobbed and puked on the grass. "There is no way you could have known, Mel," I told her.

Yara comes to crouch in front of her, moving her hair from her face. "He is right, you couldn't have known," she tells her.

Yara looks at me, and I see the worried look she passes to me. I see the fear in her eyes as she gives me a pleading look.

Melora stands, wipes her mouth, and turns. "I need to see." her voice changed into that ruthless queen I knew she was when it came to Vayna. "I need to see what she has done."

And with that she started walking toward the forest without waiting for another word. She marches quickly, with all of us following her.

We follow her into the forest where Vayna has just mass-murdered innocent Asterians.

CHAPTER 25

MELORA

¶ had felt when the Asterian land died, when the people in the forest had died. I felt it like a physical pain happening to me. I told Silas it had felt like my soul was being ripped from my body, but it was more than that.

I felt like my soul, the part that makes me whole, was being torn out of my chest. Like my head was about to implode from the pain that was radiating over my body.

I could do nothing but scream.

But now, as I walk through the forest and see the Asterian people, I feel an even worse pain. I feel their sorrow, their loss over the land and the people who lived here.

Our group walks through the Fallen Forest, past the people of Asteria who chose to live in the forest, who chose to stay in nature. Some are out of their homes, waiting for answers on what is happening.

They looked frightened.

I made eye contact with a man standing outside a lovely little cottage. He looked shocked and afraid. "Hello," I addressed the man as our group passed. "Are you alright?" I ask him.

The man nods but is slow to respond. "I am, my queen. T-thank you," he answered.

"Of course," I said to him as I continued on.

Silas and I led our group of Milo, Penn, Yara, Norik, and the twins. Everyone insisted on traveling with us to see the damage, to see what had happened.

We walked in silence, only talking to those we passed to make sure they were okay. Everyone said they were fine, but I could see the sorrow and fear in their eyes.

It fueled the already simmering rage I felt inside my chest, the rage I felt for Vanya and all she had done.

For all she has taken from me.

Push it down.

I told myself as we walked on. I needed to hold my emotions together.

"Oh my gods," Yara gasped as we approached a section of the land that had been affected by Vayna's dark magic.

It looked exactly like my vision; the land was barren, dark, and shadowy. It literally looked as though life had been sucked out of the land, like the energy and magic was taken straight from its source.

I stared at the once-green grass that was now grayish, the trees and shrubs the same. The once beautiful land was dead and rotted. Vayna killed everything in her path, only going halfway through the forest and affecting the closest to the mortal kingdom but doing enough damage to devastate.

She wanted to show us what she was capable of—I know it. She wanted us to be afraid of her.

Well, I will not.

The only thing I feel for her now is a wretched type of hate so deep in my soul that I feel as if it could rot me from the inside out.

I walked on, feeling the ground crunch beneath my feet as we moved on through the decimated land. Every crunch and snap of the affected land made my anger only increase.

No amount of calmness, of nothingness, could have prepared me for what I saw next. There were bodies, bodies of Asterian people who lived here in this part of the forest, crumbled and dead on the ground. Their skin was the same color as the forest; gray and dead.

I stopped, unable to move from the paralyzing sorrow I felt for my people, for the ones who have been murdered. I felt a tear slide down my cheek as I continued to stare at the fallen people.

"Mel," Silas said from somewhere near me. I could barely hear him; the ringing in my ears and the pounding of my heart drowned out all sounds around me. "Melora," he spoke again, but I ignored him and trucked on for the cottage I knew was in the destroyed part of the forest.

I picked up my pace and saw a tall male figure standing outside of Visha's cottage, staring at her cottage door.

Nicodem, the dryad who helped me return to the palace, stood outside the ruined cottage. "Nicodem!" I yelled to him, relieved to see he was alright.

He turned as I approached him, his eyes red and puffy. "She is gone." was all he had to say for me to know.

"I am so sorry," I said, taking the tall, tree-like man into a hug. "I am so, so sorry," I murmured, tears burning my eyes.

"Mel?" Milo questioned, and when I turned to look at him, he had a concerned look on his face.

I couldn't blame him, none of them knew this dryad, this friend who had helped me return home. "This is Nicodem," I introduced him; he only stared at the now-crumbling cottage. "He helped me return to the palace after I escaped the mortal kingdom. This is Visha's home." I explained to the now-formed group, standing and staring at Nicodem and me.

"I- I came to check on her. To see if she was safe after we felt the blast of magic." he stared straight ahead. "She is in there, in the kitchen. She is gone."

I felt like I could collapse, like I could just break down and let the wave of emotions take control of me.

But I couldn't.

Not when my people needed me right now. Not when they needed a leader, when they needed a queen.

I stepped forward to go into Visha's cottage and see what was left of her. I had to see; I was going to make myself see what Vayna had done.

Nicodem grabbed my arm to stop me, and I thought I saw Penn jolt forward. "I am sorry, my queen." Nicodem apologized for grabbing me, but I honestly did not mind; I knew he was only trying to protect me from seeing the horrors I knew were waiting. "You don't want to see," he said solemnly.

I looked at him and felt my face turn soft, understanding. "I have to see her. I need to see her." I told him and turned to the cottage.

"Mel," Silas said from behind me, following me into the cottage. "You don't need to."

"I do."

I stepped through the threshold to the house that sheltered me when I was at my lowest, when I had been hunted down by mortal men and was holding on to survive. Visha saved me, took me in, and helped me.

I owed her the respect to see her, to see what had happened to her.

There she was, just as Nicodem said, she lay in the kitchen. Her body lay crumbled and blackened, like ash coated her skin. Her face was hardly recognizable, her magic and life energy completely gone.

The impact that the floor had on my knees felt like nothing as I fell. I didn't even feel the hardwood under my knees as I collapsed over Visha's body.

I felt it then; through the wall I had been trying to build, I felt the pain and suffering that I was going through. I cried, sobbed, over her lifeless corpse.

"Melora-" Silas began.

"Get out! Please, just get out!" I yelled at him.

He listened, turned, and left me lying there on the cold ground.

I needed to be alone, needed to have a moment to myself as my emotions became unhinged and furious. I let it out; everything I was feeling I let come to the surface and break free in a scream and sob.

I am sure my sounds of sorrow could be heard outside the cottage, but I did not care. I mourned the loss of Visha and all those who were simply living in the forest and were now lost.

I mourned all that Vayna had taken from me; my life, my memories, my mother.

Loral.

The pain and sadness turned to anger as I thought of my friend, of her crumbled body that was much like Visha's now. How she looked at me in panic right before Vanya snapped her neck.

I was about to erupt; I knew I was almost there when I heard the wind blowing outside, the ruined trees scraping against the cottage.

Calm.

I thought as I tried to get a grip on my emotions. There was already so much damage and destruction here. I did not need to be the culprit of more.

I took one last look at Visha, trying to remember this moment, remembering it so it would fuel me to accomplish what I had set out to do: kill Vayna and destroy her plan to take Asteria.

I left the cottage, stepping out to the dim light coming through the forest line. It looked so grim, so morbid compared to what it once was.

My friends watched me as I stepped out of the doorway, watching me intently. I knew they were worried, and knew they most likely felt the stirring of my power when I was losing control in the cottage. I knew they feared for me, for what I must do, but I had to do this; I had to stop Vayna.

The familiar tug in my belly made me stop in my tracks. Usually, this is what I would feel before a vision, but no vision followed as the feeling traveled through my body, making me feel as if I needed to move—to go to the closest thing and touch it.

My body, my magic, was telling me to do this. Telling me that what I felt was right and I needed to listen to that tug, listen to my magic.

I turned my head to look at a nearby tree. Its bark and branches rotted and dead. But my magic told me, guided me, that it was, in fact, not. That maybe, just maybe, it was not gone.

I reached out for the tree, feeling my magic stir under my palm. Feeling my power push me toward the trunk as if it had a mind of its own.

I touched the trunk, feeling the rough bark under my hand. It felt like my magic was willing me instead of the other way around—not that it was controlling me but rather telling me what it wanted to do.

I obeyed.

I left my magic run free from my hand, tingling my fingers. I watched as the bark under my palm lit the slightest bit, shining ever so lightly.

I gave complete control over to my magic and let it run through my body, through my arms and hand. I closed my eyes as the sensation continued.

I finally opened them when I no longer felt the crusty and destroyed bark, but the bark of a normal tree, a healthy one. I opened my eyes to find the tree before me, the one I had just let my magic flow into, come back to life. It had returned to the beautiful piece of nature that it had been before Vayna laid waste to the land.

I restored it.

I restored *life*.

I turned around to find someone, anyone who could explain what had just happened. But when I turned, all those behind me were bent on one knee, their heads bowed.

"Silas," I said, slightly scared about what I was just able to do.

He looked up from where his head was bowed. "Melora, you just brought that tree back to life," he stated.

"I-I don't know how I did it. I-"

"She is the bringer of life; she has her mother's gifts," Norik said, astonished.

They began to stand after I did not say anything, too amazed by what I had just done to speak.

"They don't call her the 'Queen of Life' for nothing," Milo said, joy an undertone in his voice.

I looked at all their faces, they looked amazed by me, by my power. I felt...I felt scared. How was this possible?

I need to try again to see if I can do more. Heal more.

I kneeled to the ground, placing both hands on the forest floor. My magic came to life without me even thinking about it, without even willing it to work. The land beneath my hands starts to glow softly, my magic filling it.

I close my eyes and concentrate, pushing as much power into the land as I can. Pushing as hard as I can because I have to, because this must work.

I slowly open my eyes to green. Green grass, green leaves, and shrubs all around me where the destroyed forest once was only a second ago. I stare wide-eyed at what my magic has just done.

At what *I* have just done.

Thank you, mother.

I think to myself as everyone around me smiles and takes in the newly rejuvenated forest.

If I can restore life to the land, could I restore life to a person?

I take off back to Visha's cottage, Milo and Silas chasing behind me. I don't slow down as I cross the threshold into the home. I fall to the floor beside her and place my hands on her body. I try again, letting my magic take over and pulse into her.

I push and push, giving as much power as I can to her, to her life.

But nothing happens, no shining and no restoring.

She is gone, and I cannot bring her back.

"Mel, I am sorry." Silas says.

Tears fall again, but this time, they are tears of fury and rage instead of sorrow.

Vayna will pay.

She will pay in blood.

"Ready the army. We move out tonight."

CHAPTER 26

MELORA

Our large group traveled through the Fallen Forest all night. Silas and I have led our army, our friends, and others through the darkness to where we are now; the edge of the Fallen Forest that is closest to the mortal kingdom.

Ravenhall is in our sights. Only a short ride longer, and we will be in the small city. The ride here felt long, longer than it actually was. The anticipation of getting here and doing what needed to be done made me fidget with anxiety the whole ride, making my horse huff at me.

I gave her black coat a pet, trying to calm her.

Silas rode next to me on his horse for the entire trip, never letting me out of his sight. I know he is fiercely protective, and I love that about him, but I feel as though he is trying to keep me from doing what we all know needs to be done.

I love that he cares for me—so deeply, so truly, that he would rather let the world burn than endanger me to do what is right. But I need to do this. I need to be the one to end Vayna and take back her magic that my mother gave her under false pretenses. I need to do it for Asteria.

For my mother.
For Loral.
For Visha.
For *me*.

"Are you alright, my love?" Silas asks from beside me. "I can feel your magic stirring. What are you thinking about in that wondrous mind of yours?"

I smile and roll my eyes at him. Of course, he calls my reeling mind 'wondrous'. "I was thinking about you—you and Vayna," I told him.

"Hm. What an interesting combination. Both seem enough to make you mad." He teases me.

I laugh. "I was thinking about how protective you are. How you would do whatever it took to keep me safe."

"I would," he says seriously.

"As would I," I look at him, my brows furrowing. "I would do anything to keep you safe, to keep you alive."

I think back to when he was dying, when I struck the bargain with Vayna to save his life.

He must have thought of that, too, because he said, "I know you would, I would never forget it."

"Then you must know why I have to do this. Why I have to be the one who stops her and takes away her power. I need you to be safe, to live. I will do anything to make that happen, even risk my life like I know anyone here would do for me." I try to reason, try to make him see it my way.

"I know, and I understand." he paused, looking into the distance. "But it is hard for me to let you go, to let you put yourself in danger for me, for anyone. I cannot lose you again, Mel. I won't. And if that means that I am overbearing and overprotective? Then so be it because you are something I cannot afford to lose. I refuse to."

His tenderness warmed me, warmed the cool blood running through my veins at the thought of approaching Ravenhall. "Silas, I love you. And you love me. I will be safe, and I will live. I promise you," I pleaded to him. "But it was always going to be me who did this, who took Vayna head-on and tore her down. It was always me."

Silas began to speak, but the ringing of bells in the distance grabbed our attention. "They know we are coming," Kaius said from his horse behind us.

"Good," I told him.

We stopped our horde at the edge of the Fallen Forest line, right before we crossed into Ravenhall. We only stopped because there was an army of mortal guards waiting for us, standing between me and Vayna.

This is going to be fun.

The group stops, everyone behind me and Silas halts. We wait as an opening forms in the line of mortal guards on the front lines. Two bodies on horseback emerge from the wave of mortals.

I recognize who it is immediately; the mortal king and Arlan. I would recognize that blond hair anywhere, those snake-like eyes staring beadily at me.

We are some distance away, but I can see Arlan's reaction when he spots me. I wore my crown, even though I had not wanted to, but Yara said it would make a statement.

And I believe it has.

I hop down off my horse, Silas and Penn following close behind me. Milo has already shifted into his wolf form, ready for a fight. Yara and the twins follow behind us as well.

We will stand together.

We will fight together.

We walk to the middle of the green field that separates us from Ravenhall, stopping once we reach a close enough range to hear what they have to say.

"Hello, sister," Arlan says, a serpentine grin on his wretched face. "It has been a while. I see you have been busy since our last meeting." He says so smugly, referencing my crown.

"Yes, I have. I am the Queen of Asteria," I say loudly for all to hear, to let them know who stands before them. "And you will relinquish Ravenhall and give up your queen," I command them, my voice strong and regal.

"You will not find her here. She is in the capitol." the mortal king said, rather proud of himself.

"She must have run back to the capitol after what she did in the forest," Penn says from beside me, for only us to hear.

I take a moment and let the fury seep into my blood, let it have control over me, and give me confidence and strength for what is about to come because I do not care if Vayna is not here; Ravenhall will be ours.

"So be it," I call out to Arlan, staring him dead in the eye. "I will have your head instead," I say callously, the venom dripping from my tongue.

Arlan draws back, appalled. "You will have no such thing, you Asterian bitch!"

Milo growls beside me, as do the rest of his wolven brothers standing behind us. I smile as Arlan's face falls, hearing the wave of growls from behind me.

"Careful how you speak to our queen, *mortal*. I will rip out your tongue and feed it to you the next time you call her such." Silas steps forward and tells Arlan, anger written on his face.

Gods, he was sexy when he threatens life for me.

I smirk, tilting my head as I speak slowly to Arlan and the mortal king. "Relinquish. Ravenhall."

"Never." the king says, and that is all that needs to be said to let us know that this is about to turn into a battle.

I hold my head high as I take out the daggers that are strapped to either side of my thighs. My crown sits heavy on my head as I give a devilish smile to Arlan, to let him know I am coming for him.

Arlan and the king retreat back into the wave of mortal guards, not leading their fight as always.

"Attack them!" I hear Arlan shout from somewhere in the crowd of men.

The mortal guards start to run at us, moving quickly with their swords and battle axes. Our group of friends are the first on our side to take to battle, I will never be a queen who lets others do her bidding.

So, of course, I am the first one to engage in battle. My friends and I break into the front line of mortal guards, slicing and stabbing those who come near. A moment later, I feel the others at our backs. The rest of our horde comes into the mix, fighting their way through the large mass of mortal men.

I see flashes of fur every now and then, the wolves taking out mortals left and right. At some point, Yara shifted into her bright white fur, teeth snarling as she attacked a mortal with a sword pointed at her.

I knew he would be dead.

Battle ensues around me, people fighting everywhere I look. Mortal guards run at me, trying to take me out with either a slice of their swords or a chop of their ax; they miss every time. Fury and downright rage push me forward, push me to kill every man who raises a sword against me.

By the time I make it to an opening in the field, I am covered in blood and gore from head to toe. I feel trickles of blood running down my face as well as my arms. The black of my leathers is now stained red with the blood of my enemies. And soon, there will be more, because I have just spotted where Arlan and the king have taken up residency to watch the battle from a safe distance.

Anticipation floods through me, because I know today is the day I finally kill Arlan. I finally give him what he deserves.

I do a quick check of my surroundings; Silas is beside me, hacking down anyone even thinking of coming near me, his broadsword swinging through the air. Milo is on top of a man, tearing open his throat with his sharp canines. Penn is right behind me, never getting too far away from me, throwing punches at a mortal.

Guilt slips through my wall of madness as I watch Penn kill his mortal people. I know he knows the truth and has sided with us, but he probably knows these men, most likely trained some of them. I hope he does not mourn their loss as they try to kill him.

I shake out the thought, returning to the goal I have my eye set on: Arlan's head.

I run through the craziness of battle, never wavering as I make my way toward the man I hate the most. I duck under arms and swords as I race to where the two men sit.

I see it when he realizes I am coming for him, and satisfaction rings like a beautiful melody through my ears. I continue on, not stopping until I stand in front of Arlan and the king, who are still on their horses.

I wish I could see myself as I approach them because I know I must look terrifying, dripping in blood as my crown shines in the afternoon sun.

I viciously move towards my prey, walking slowly to take in the moment. I stop when I am close enough for them to hear me, and look up at them on their horses. "I will kill you and send your head to your mother," I tell Arlan.

He begins to speak, but his father cuts him off. "You will pay, you Asterian scum! I have not forgotten what you did to my son in the throne room in the capitol; you almost killed him!" he yells at me.

I am honestly not surprised that he is blaming me for protecting myself after Arlan was trying to hold me captive, trying to have me for himself. "I am not sorry for what I did," I told him. "If my people had not come to my aid when they did, your son would have raped me and kept me as his prisoner. Tell me, how is it my fault for his actions?"

Story of my fucking life.

The king starts to speak, but I have grown tired of him talking. I cut him off, throwing a dagger at his eye. The satisfying thud my weapon makes against his skull has me smiling, proud of my strike. He falls backward from his horse, dead before he hits the ground.

"You just killed him! You just killed the King of Morania!" Arlan shrieks.

As if I did not know.

"Yes, and you are next." I remind him as I feel a furry body next to my legs. I look down to see Milo standing next to me, his brown fur soft against my hand.

I return my focus back to Arlan, who is looking at Milo, scared shitless. I whip out a hand and pull Arlan from his horse with my magic. He hits the ground hard, grunting as he lands in the grass.

He knows his time has come to an end, and his panic is palpable. He scrambles to his knees quickly, his face pleading with fear. I hear him whimper, and it only fuels the fire within me. "Melora, please. I will do anything, anything!" he begs. "Please, do not do this. I—I am your brother. Please, Melora!" I listen calmly as he rambles on.

I stand tall, looking down at him, begging for me not to kill him. "I remember a time when I begged *you* for my life," I tell him slowly, maliciously. "You did not listen then, and I will not listen now."

I give Milo one last pet before he prowls forward towards a trembling Arlan. I make myself watch as Milo strikes, grabbing Arlan by his throat and tearing it wide open. I watch as life leaves his eyes, his body going limp.

I feel the presence of my friends behind me, and I know the battle is over and we have won. With my friends at my back and the body of my would-be rapist before me bleeding out, I have never felt stronger.

"Someone make sure his head makes it to the capitol."

CHAPTER 27

SILAS

I have never seen my wife so filled with anger, so filled with gut-wrenching rage as she had been as she stood above Arlan as he died. As he died slowly and most likely painfully. She watched as Milo relieved him of his head, watched and...and smiled.

He put her through hell, and I am not mourning his loss, but I worry for her. I worry that her anger and fury are going to push her too far, push her magic too far. I am scared she will push herself to a line she didn't even know she was going to cross. That she will become the thing she is trying to rid our kingdom of: a monster.

She did not notice, but as she conversed with Arlan, her anger grew. The longer they talked, the trees blew, the sky darkened, and a chill was in the air.

It was her, from her fiery emotions and her magic answering to her anger. She is so strong and ferociously brave, but I am scared for her as we continue in our plan to end Vayna and take her power.

I am scared for my wife.
For her safety.
For her well-being.
She has been through so much, so much that I could not even begin to question her feelings or her actions. But what I won't do, what I will never do, is stand by as she endangers herself for the good of the realm.

I refuse to.

I refuse to let my wife break herself to save others.

I am selfish, I know, but I promised to love her, to protect her forever. Even if it is from herself.

I stand in the dirt courtyard, watching as our army buries the mortals who died during our battle. Melora ordered it to be done after we rode into Ravenhall and took the palace, easily overthrowing the guards stationed here. She wanted the fallen to have an honorable death, to be buried and respected.

She is in the manor now, talking with staff and people who live in the castle. Mel ordered all of us not to harm any mortal who does not try to harm us. She does not want to play into the fear that Vayna has created against our kind.

She understands it is hard for us, for the Asterians who lived through the war with the mortals, not to want to get revenge for all they did. I was even tempted to rain fury on the mortals here, remembering what happened so long ago. But Mel reminded me that they knew no better, and it was not them who wielded the blade that drove the magic folk to the end of the realm. It was their ancestors...and Vayna. I calmed then realizing she was right, that this is what we must do if we want to change the realm and how people see Asterians.

I have been away from her for too long. I turn and walk into the castle to find her, needing to know she is safe. I know she is safe with Penn at her side, but I cannot help but feel the overwhelming urge to be near her at all times. To make sure nothing happens to her ever again.

I walk into the main hall to find Melora talking to a woman, a woman I recognize immediately. Lady Chapler stands in front of Mel, talking like they are the best of friends. She looks happier since the last time I saw her. I had only a glimpse of her in the carriage in Fallen Forest the night I took Lord Chapler, and she looked scared and miserable then. Now, she looks healthy and happy.

Probably now that her husband is dead.

I know this woman could not do much when Lord Chapler was still alive. I know that she could not stop a lord from having bruising hands and a devilish appetite for the things he put Melora through. I also know that she most likely endured his wrath as well as Melora did. But seeing her reminds me of that sad excuse for a man, making me think of all the things Melora never told me that happened behind the closed doors of Lord Chapler's study, and makes my blood boil thinking of what he did to her. Thinking of all the hell he put her through.

She helped Mel escape. She helped her come home. She got her out of this wretched place.

I remind myself as I approach the two women, trying to calm the heated temper that has arisen from just thinking of Lord Chapler. I wish I could watch Melora kill that fucker again.

Melora looks as beautiful as ever, her blonde hair tied back into a braided bun, little pieces falling out around her face and curling at the ends. Being queen suits her well. She carries herself as a leader, as a ruler. And it does things to me that could bring me to my knees and worship her in ways that I know she would love.

"Hello, my love." Melora greets me with a smile, wrapping her arm around my waist. "How are things?" she asks me, looking nervous about my answer. I see her fidgeting with her fingers again, showing her anxiety.

"Things are well. No one resisted as we entered the lower city to tell the people that we have taken Ravenhall. They did not resist at all, actually." I told her what Milo and Yara had told me. I am grateful that none of the mortals acted out against us because I feel as though Mel would be upset to kill them, to murder them because they know no better. They only know what they are told, and they are told to fear Asterians.

Just like she did not know better a time ago when she first came to me. When she first came to the kingdom she was born to rule.

Melora let out a relieved sigh, smiling in delight.

"That is because many here know the truth, that Melora is the Goddess of Life's daughter," Lady Chapler told us. "We know much more than Vayna and the rest of the crown think. We know she is evil, that she is the one who started all of this; the war against Asterians." Lady Chapler told me, and I was surprised at her statement. If that is true, why did so many men fight behind Arlan and the mortal king against us?

They probably had no choice and were forced to fight or die.

I feel bad for them, because they died anyway.

Melora seems nervous, anxious as she speaks to Lady Chapler and me. "I will address them today," she said, determination in her voice. "I want them to hear it from me that we are not here to harm them."

Later in the evening, I stand beside Melora as she prepares to address the people of Ravenhall, the people who were once hers. "This reminds me of when Ravenhall caught a flame, and Lord Chapler addressed the people and told them the Asterians were behind it." She smiled a bit, standing with her hands clasped together in front of her.

"That was also the first night we met." I remind her. Mel turns to look at me, and her face lights up as she remembers our night in the hot spring.

"That it was," she states mischievously, remembering our time together.

I tip her chin up so her gaze meets mine as I close the distance between us. "Are you sure you want to do this?" I ask her. "You owe nothing to them; you don't need to prove who you are to anyone."

She stares at me, intent on doing what she has planned. I know the look in her eye, and she has made up her mind. "I need to do this," she whispers to me.

I nod as she grabs my hand. She steps out of the castle's tall doors and onto a small dais that sits high enough that we can look over the people of Ravenhall standing in the courtyard. They go silent as she steps out, standing in the setting sun.

"Many of you may recognize me," she says loudly for all to hear. "May recognize me as the Moranian Princess. But I was never that." she paused, stepping closer to the small ledge, closer to the people. "I am the daughter of the Goddess of Life, and I am the true ruler of Asteria." She states strong and true.

The people murmur, growing agitated at her statement.

"How can we trust you!?" one yells.

"How do we know you are telling the truth!?" another yells.

I try to step in front of Melora, to shield her from the now heated people yelling and questioning her. She pushes past me, back to the front of the dais.

"I need to show them," she tells me harshly, throwing me a look that I know means I will be in trouble later.

She walks forward, off of the dais, and into the courtyard, where the people back away and make a space for her. She holds her head high as she looks around, looking at every person around her. They watch her with wonder and disbelief.

She kneels to the dirt, like she did when we were in the Fallen Forest and places her hands on the ground. I am unsure of what she is doing because the land here has not been touched by Vayna's magic; it is still alive and healthy.

I watch as she closes her eyes and concentrates. Penn and I are standing closely behind her, watching as her hands begin to glow. The shine is dim, only bright enough to light the small space under her hands. She continues to push her magic into the ground, and I am curious as to what she is doing.

I start to bend to hoist her up from the ground, to tell her she does not need to show these mortals that she is the true queen. But as I do, I feel her power surge around me and the ground quake beneath my feet. It is only a small tremble, but I feel it like I would feel her.

The mortals murmur and whisper as they watch, as *we* watch two massive trees come out of the ground side-by-side next to Melora. They are big and beautiful trees with greenery and leafy branches.

Well, that is new.

She just willed two trees to grow from the ground to their full height. Her power, her magic, it still shocks me at times. She is still learning, still understanding all she is capable of, but what she just did...that was life created before our very eyes.

Melora's head slowly looks up, and as she does, the crowd before her bows.

"It is true." someone in the crowd says.

"She is the Queen of Life." another says.

Mel stands as she looks over the mortals bowing to her. "I know I am not your queen, but I will protect you and keep you from harm as if you were my own people, because once upon a time, you were. I want to protect anyone who could be caught in Vayna's wrath, in which we plan to end." the people nodded at her claim, encouraging her to continue. "If you will have me, I will protect you more than Vayna has ever even thought to."

The people of Ravenhall cheer for her, cheer for the woman who just took their city and planned on killing their queen. They know the truth now: that Melora is the daughter of the Goddess of Life. They know that the goddess's blood runs through Melora, making her the closest thing to a god that they have ever seen.

And because of that, they will follow her until the end of time.

CHAPTER 28

MELORA

Milo and I sit in the war room as we look at a map of the Moranian capitol. He has been going back and forth on which way to approach in our battle plan, which way would work the best for us. I can't make a decision; I am too afraid to be wrong and lead my people to their deaths.

"If we go this way, we could have more of a surprise-"

Milo gets cut off by Kane rushing into the room, his face filled with worry. "Kane, what is it?" Milo asked.

"It's- it's Vayna and her army. They have moved to the border of the capitol. They are readying for a fight. They know we took Ravenhall." he says to us breathlessly.

I guess she got my present of Arlan's head.

They are ready for us. We need to move now, to meet them where they stand. We cannot let them make their way to Ravenhall and take back what we have accomplished.

"Ready the army," I say as Silas walks into the room quickly behind Kane. "We move out at sunrise," I tell Milo and Kane.

They nod their acknowledgment and leave in a hurry to get things moving.

I sit down and let out a ragged breath, covering my face with my hands. "They are coming", I tell Silas.

"Then we will meet them in the middle," he says simply. "They will not make it here if we leave at sunrise. They will not take back Ravenhall." Silas moves around the table, his large body coming to console me.

I need him right now, I need his warmth and love in my troubles. I just need him to be here with me as we wait to leave to head into battle.

He kneels in front of me and cups my face, his large hands covering my cheeks. I lean into his palms as he swipes his thumb over my lips. "I am scared," I admit to him, saying it out loud for the first time since we started this war.

He presses his forehead to mine, closing his eyes. "So am I."

We stay like that for a minute, letting our worries and fears spread, bearing the weight of each other's anxieties. It feels better when you can share the burden with someone who understands.

"I have a surprise for you," Silas says into the silence.

I laugh. "A surprise? Not another gift, I hope." He smiled at my comment about the engagement gifts he had given me, which seemed like forever ago. I love that he tries to take my mind from all that is happening around us. It works, his love already pushing back the rising fear.

He grabs my hands and gives me a tug to stand up. "This is different, and I know you'll love it."

Silas and I walked through the forest on the far side of the castle. I knew where we were going as soon as we headed toward the forest line that lined the back of Ravenhall; we were going to the hot spring.

I did not let on that I was aware of his surprise; I did not want to ruin it. It was a sweet surprise, something to take our minds off the inevitable battle we will see tomorrow.

I could barely contain my excitement as we reached the boulders that looked like skulls. The boulders made me think of Loral, who had told me about the hot spring in the first place.

There is so much I wish I could tell her.

"You know where we're going," Silas said, holding my hand and leading us through the forest.

I grinned at him as he looked over his shoulder. "I do."

We laughed together as we traveled on.

Only a second later, we were approaching the hot spring, *our* hot spring. I heard the bubbling of the water first, trickling in the short distance. We moved a branch, and there it was.

The spring looked as beautiful as I remember; the water was blue, bubbles formed on the surface, and green grass framed the bank. It was gorgeous and the setting for one of my favorite memories.

I have not felt true peace like I did since I last visited, true peace from relaxing in the hot spring. Floating on the surface, the sounds of the bubbling water lulled me into a peaceful state that cleared my mind, and I missed it.

"Do you remember it as clearly as I?" Silas asked as we walked up to the clear water. I could already feel the heat from the spring permeating the air.

I knew he was referencing the night we first met. "I do. I think about it all the time." I grinned, remembering how his lips tasted for the first time, how his lips were the first to touch mine.

"Come on," Silas said as he moved to take his clothing off.

"What? What are you doing?" I questioned as I watched him take off his shirt, his tanned skin making an appearance. "You know what, don't answer that. Just keep doing what you are doing." I teased him as I watched his muscles move as he pulled his shirt over his head.

"Curious little thing, aren't you?" Silas grinned that sexy grin and I knew I was done for. "Are you coming, or am I going to have to make you?" he toyed, and I enjoyed this teasing banter. It took my mind from the other things pressing to get in.

"You do not," I said as I started to unbutton my vest. I looked down for only a moment, my head shooting back up as I heard a loud splash coming from the pool. "Silas!" I laughed-yelled as I realized he had jumped in, just as he did our first time here.

I hurried to undo my pants and take off my blouse. I wanted to be in the water with him as soon as I could. However, my motions slowed as I watched Silas rise from the water. His body on full display as water trickled down his broad chest, making his tanned skin glisten in the night.

He looked like a painting of a sea witch I had once seen in the Asterian palace, magical and bewitching with his gloriousness. I never wanted to stop looking at him, never wanted to stop learning every inch of his body, of him. If I could, I would spend the rest of my life tracking the lines of his muscles, finding something new each time I look at him.

"Are you going to keep teasing me, standing there gloriously nude? Or are you going to join me, *wife*?" Silas asked from the water, his eyes taking in my stark-naked body. I shook my head and laughed at him, at the expression on his face. He was looking at me like he had never seen my body before, like it was the first time all over again.

His eyes bounce to mine, and I give a naughty little grin; I see his eyes widen as I run toward him, as I sprint for the hot spring and cannonball in. The water splashes about, creating a small wake in the water. I quickly come up above the water's surface, and Silas grabs me. I am glad he has a hold of me, because I cannot touch in this part of the spring, and I was starting to panic slightly when I was underwater and could not feel the bottom.

Silas has me, like always. He is here with protective arms and a possessive heart to keep me from drowning in our hot spring.

I latch onto him, feeling the warmth from his skin and the hot spring mixing beneath me. It is making me heady and hot, already flustered from the steam of the water. "I was not expecting you to jump in," Silas says into my shoulder, laughing. "Always surprising me, my queen."

Silas nuzzles closer, holding me tight and tucking his head into the crook of my neck. I gripped him tighter, too, matching the unyielding force at which he held me. We know what is at stake; we know what tomorrow will bring, but tonight is just us. It is just about us in our hot spring, enjoying a moment of peace together. And I will cherish every second I can get.

Silas pulled his head back, only enough so he could see my face. "Mel," he started, and his voice was worried, grim even. He knew what tonight was. It was the last night we had together before everything changed, for better or worse.

Tomorrow, we could win, killing Vayna and saving Asteria. Tomorrow, we could also lose, dying against Vayna's magic and letting Asteria be taken by her.

"Don't," I whisper to him, not wanting to talk about what could happen, about all the horrible things that have happened. "I just want to be here, Silas. I want to be here in this moment with you." I plead to him, emotion gathering in my throat and eyes.

He stared at me for a long second, understanding what I was saying. He understood because he felt it, too. He knew what could happen tomorrow, all the things that could go wrong, but he also knew that none of it mattered tonight. That tonight was our last time, our last sliver of happiness, before all hell broke loose.

Silas caressed my cheek, gently moving his hand to the nape of my neck. "Did I ever tell you what I was thinking the first night I met you?" he asks as I feel him fiddling with my braid. I nod that he has not, and so he continues. "When I saw you floating in the spring I almost did not want to disturb you, almost did not want to take the moment away from you. I had been tracking you, and I wanted to talk to you, to see what I was getting into." I rolled my eyes, making him smirk.

"And did you find out what you were getting yourself into?" I asked playfully as he combed my hair from the braid it had been in that he had taken out.

"I did," he looked deep into my eyes, his face soft. "I knew then that I would do anything for you. That I would fight for you, defend you, kill for you. I knew in that moment that I would love you, that I would love your strength, your grit, your viciousness. I knew that I was not only getting the Moranian Princess, but I was getting Melora, the woman I met before she knew who I was, before she knew that I knew who she was. I was getting a woman who knew her strength, who loved her friends, and would do anything for them. I knew you were like me; I could feel that you were meant for me."

I laced my hands through his wet hair as I looked at him, really looking at the man I love, not believing that he knew all of that on the first night we met...but I knew it was true, because deep down I knew the same thing. "I knew that I would love you, Mel. And I do, more than words or actions could ever describe."

I kissed his face as his tears began to fall, kissed away the wet droplets coming from his eyes as my own began to roll down my face. I love this man, love him more than I ever thought possible. Because here I am, ready to die for him if need be, and I would do it with a fucking smile on my face.

Silas kisses me, kisses me with a passion that is all-consuming, never-ending. He kisses me as one hand is laced through my curls and the other is holding onto me. I become instantly hot, immediately feverish from the mix of Silas's lips and the warm water around us. I kiss him harder, though, never not wanting to kiss him this way. Our mouths move against each other in perfect harmony, lips and tongues moving in sync.

I feel the head of Silas's cock against my entrance and instantly want him inside of me. I need him to be inside of me, letting me feel him in this moment, in our moment. I sink down lower on his body, letting his hard erection make entrance just enough for both of us to gasp against each other's lips.

He continues to kiss my skin, saying, "The feel of you, Melora." he purrs. "You are *fucking* perfect, all I could have ever imagined and more."

I hold onto his shoulders as he thrusts upward and fully inside of me, his head falling back in pleasure as he fully seats himself within me. "Look at me, Silas," I tell him, never wanting his eyes off of mine. He listens, his eyes snapping back to mine quickly. I place my forehead against him as we move together in the water.

This is perfect. This is how it should be: me and him, he and I, just like this.

Silas's thrust grows impatient, rapid in the movements. I feel myself clenching around him, getting closer and closer to ecstasy. I am about to implode, but I don't want to, not yet. I don't want this moment to end.

I run my hand through Silas's hair and grab his face, bringing his lips to mine. "I love you," he whispers on my lips. "I love you." again and again, as he continues to pull my pleasure from me.

My skin prickles, and the tension in my body feels as though it will unwind, leaving me spent and sated. "Come with me, my love. I need this. I need you, Mel-"

I hold onto him as shockwaves of pleasure explode through my body, causing me to shake and spasm around Silas's cock. He holds me through it, holds me as his own pleasure finds him, releasing himself inside of me.

We don't move apart after we catch our breath and stop quivering from the pure bliss we both just delivered. We stay like that, connected and clutching each other, never wanting to pull away.

Silas rests his head on my shoulder, my hair in his face, I know. I place my cheek on his shoulder, and soak in the feel of him, of my husband. We don't move to get out of the hot spring, and we do not move to untangle from each other. We simply stay here as long as we possibly can before the sun rises and it is time to go to war.

We stay here for as long as we can, cherishing each other, cherishing our time together because tomorrow is filled with what-ifs and so much uncertainty. Tomorrow could end us or bring us peace.

But knowing right now that we are together and safe, that in this moment we have love, passion, and never-ending devotion, is enough to give me peace in a time of war.

CHAPTER 29

SILAS

The light from the bright morning sun spills into the window of the bedroom Melora and I have taken over at Ravenhall. We came in after we returned from the hot spring last night, knowing we both needed rest for what was to come. Sleep had come easily, as it normally does when I have Melora at my side.

 I woke before Mel, who was still sleeping away, her hair tousled and her lashes fluttering as she snoozed. I watched her in this peacefulness, wishing we could stay here forever and never leave this bed. I know we will be moving out soon, making our move against Vayna, but even the shortest amount of time with her would be worth it, and I will savor whatever I can get.

 Her eyes open slowly, and a happy little smile appears as she sees me already looking at her. "Good morning, my love," she whispers, sleepiness still in her voice.

 Gods, she looks so cute like this.

"Good morning, my queen." I brush a piece of curly hair out of her face, just wanting to touch her really. "It will be time soon," I say regretfully because her sweet smile turns grim as she begins to move closer to me.

"Can't we just stay here a little while longer?" she asks, cuddling up closer to my chest and wrapping her arms around my body, pulling me towards her.

I smile, her cuteness taking over my heart. "As long as we can," I whisper into her hair, reveling in her touch, her smell, her love.

This is perfect. Even in the mitts of war, we still find peace in each other.

The door flies open only a moment later, revealing a worried Milo, who is dressed for battle. "They are coming," he says urgently.

"Good morning to you, too, brother," I say, annoyed that he barged in on Melora and I's last minutes of togetherness.

"Who is coming?" Melora asked frantically as she sat up, the sheets wrapped around her naked body.

"Vayna. They moved further in the night, approaching the territory between Ravenhall and the capitol. They will be here in a few hours." Milo walked to the bed, sitting at the edge. He was worried. I could see it in the way the lines around his mouth turned down as he looked between me and Melora.

"No." Melora began to get up and get out of bed, the sheet around her following. "We move out now and meet them in the middle. They will get nowhere near Ravenhall," she told him, holding the sheet around her tightly as she laid out the plan.

Even in a sleep coated voice, and in nothing but a sheet, she is a fucking queen.

"Agreed," I say from where I sit in the still warm bed, silently wishing Melora was still next to me. "We don't let them near Ravenhall or the Fallen Forest."

Milo stands to leave. "I will gather everyone. Give me five minutes."

After Milo left, Mel turned to me, her face solemn and scared. "It is time." she tells me, her brows furrowing at her own statement.

I stand and move to her, hating the distance that has already grown between us. "That it is, my love." I wrap her and her sheet up in my arms, wanting to hold her a moment longer than we had. "That it is."

Everything happened in a hurry, in a flash of rushing around to get things done and get people moving. A few hours after Milo left our room, we arrived in the territory that he spoke of, the land between the capitol and Ravenhall. We traveled on horseback, and did not let up our speed until we were well away from Ravenhall.

If things go awry, we cannot let Vayna take back Ravenhall.

The mortal army was here, here waiting for us. It was eerie seeing them all lined up and just standing or sitting on horseback. We stopped all on approach, waiting to see what they were doing and if they would move against us the moment we arrived. But it looked as though they were just waiting for us. Waiting for something.

Melora had led the army on the path that got us here, leading them in the front like I knew she always would. She was on her own horse, a white mare who loved Mel. I wish she would have rode with me, but I knew she needed to lead the army her way, do things her way, and I would always support her.

Of course, Penn and I rode beside her the whole way. Our friends were now lined up next to us on their horses, waiting for orders from their queen.

"You all know what we must do. Let us do it." Melora called out to our friends, and I could see their nervous faces and anxiety-ridden movements. She seemed to hesitate as she looked at them, at the friends she had come to love, at the family she had made.

"We are with you, Mel," Yara said from her horse.

"Always," Milo agreed.

My head snapped up as movement from the mortal army happened. The sounds of their armor were the only thing that we could hear as they moved forward the slightest bit. I saw Melora fidget, like she wanted to move closer to the army awaiting us.

"Mel," I got her attention quickly, trying to stop her from doing anything rash. "Stick to the plan." I remind her, not wanting her to get closer than we have to.

She nods her understanding and tries not to move as her anxiousness takes over. One of her hands travels to her hip, where one of her twin daggers is strapped in. She fiddles with the handle, trying to calm her nerves.

A blink was all that had passed before two figures appeared at the front of the mortal army, in the middle of the field where we waited. A lithe woman and a dark-haired man appeared. I knew who it was—we all did—and I saw Mel straighten at the sight of her once-mother.

Melora's face went red with anger at just the sight of Vayna.

This all seemed so familiar, like the battle that had occurred when Mel was taken. Fear ran through me at the memory, prompting me to say, "Remember your promise," I told Melora for only her to hear. "Please, whatever it takes. I will not lose you." I stare at her and wait for a response. I stare like it is the last time I will ever see my wife because, in the face of battle, there are so many things that could happen.

"I promised you, Silas. I will be with you," she assured me, but somehow, her words only made me more uneasy.

"Melora, my dear," Vayna called from where she and Simon stood. "Please come forward, I want to talk to you."

We all agreed that they would come to us, that we would not get close until necessary. We wanted to stay as far away from Vayna as we could for the time being, not knowing what she would do. So we sat there upon our horses and did not move. Vayna must have grown impatient because she, Simon, and some other guards walked forward.

"I do not appreciate you making me wait", Vayna said directly to Melora, who had slipped into the role of queen. I can see when she does it, when she knows she needs to be ruthless. I know her well enough to see the change from the loving and caring woman I married to the vicious and vengeful queen next to me. "I got your little gift", Vayna hissed, her dark brows raised.

She was talking about the head Mel had sent to her.

A nice touch, I may add.

"Ah, yes. My *brother.* I do hope you enjoyed it." Melora said to her, unbothered by the mortal queen's words.

Vayna drew back, anger filling her face. "Well, aren't you just a monstrous thing? Simon was right to gift you that enduring nickname."

He called her a *monster*?

I swear to the gods, to Melora's mother, I will end him.

"I am nothing but what you created, *Mother,*" Melora said back to her; I could already feel her magic stirring. She was getting angry.

Vayna breathed in a deep breath, as if she were calming herself. "Be that as it may, we are here today because of what you have done. First, you escape me after stabbing me in the chest, trying to kill me. We see how well that went as I am still standing here." she smiled arrogantly. "Then you go and marry that Asterian monstrosity next to you.

And if that was not enough, you took Ravenhall." She looked at me, disgust on her face. "You have done nothing but disappoint me, and that is why I had to do what I did to the Fallen Forest. To remind you who has the power here, who you want to kill exactly."

Melora seethes beside me, our friends growing agitated at her words of pure disrespect. "Yes, you did remind me who has the power to do such a thing like murder hundreds of innocent people. But it is not your first time murdering innocents, is it not?" Mel questions her. "I remember it well, as I remember the faces of all you have killed, everyone you have taken from me. That is why today will be the day I kill you, take your magic, and take the power you have over Asteria. For it will never be yours."

Vayna laughed; she actually laughed at Melora's words. "Oh dear, you think over highly of yourself if you think you can stop me from getting what I want. I got what I wanted when I killed the Asterians and made them flee. I got what I wanted when I captured your mother. I even got what I wanted when one of their own came to help me." I flinched at the mention of Simon, at his betrayal to our family.

I finally looked at him. His face was emotionless, nothing to tell what he was thinking.

He did not even react when Vayna mentioned killing people in the Fallen Forest, not even the slightest jolt. He is gone. I know the brother I once loved, who loved Asteria, is gone.

"Then today will be one of many first; you will not succeed, and you will die, and it will be by my hand." Melora sat straight, her head held high. "For all of those who have been taken from me. For everything you have done and all the blood you have spilled. I will kill you as I did your son and husband."

Gods, I loved this woman, her power, her fierceness.

"I will enjoy watching you try, and I may even enjoy watching you die." I froze at Vayna's statement. "But I will be saddened at your loss, for you were once my daughter." Vayna actually looked distraught, tormented for only a second at the thought of killing Melora.

"What once was will not save you now," Melora said to her, her words like ice.

With that, Vayna and Simon disappeared, most likely jumping to somewhere behind their army.

I watched as the mortal army took off for us, running and letting a battle cry ring. "They are coming," I stated the obvious as we all watched the wave of silver armor run towards us.

"That they are. Let us greet them." Melora said casually as she swung her leg over her horse. We all dismounted and readied for the horde of mortal guards to approach us.

Milo and Yara shifted into their wolf forms. Penn stationed himself next to Mel, sword at the ready. The twins made sure their weapons were strapped tight. We all stood together as the army closed in, only a short distance away.

I was ready, but I still needed one more thing before we faced battle head-on. I grabbed Melora and brought her to my chest, kissing her roughly, deeply. I kissed her and felt her melt into my hands as she kissed me back just as fiercely. We both knew what was at stake, what we could lose. So we kissed like it was our last time, our final moment together on this earth.

She pulled back, her eyes watery and her lips trembling. "I love you, Silas. Please, never forget that," she said as she caressed my face.

I brushed her cheek one last time as I said, "Never."

The mortals' footsteps shook the ground as they were now upon us, coming in fast. The time was now; the time to fight for our home was now before us.

"For Asteria!" Melora screamed, and her cry was answered by the battle cries of our army, ready to fight with a passion no mortal army could ever have.

This was more than a battle; it was more than a fight between two kingdoms for land or some other simple feud.

This was life or death.

And Melora has chosen life, life for our land, for our people.

And we will not let her down.

CHAPTER 30

SILAS

We all ran towards the oncoming mortals and clashed in the middle. The sounds of our people hitting the mortal army were enough to make one's stomach curl. Steel clashed off of armor, men grunted and cried out, arrows soared through the air. It was utter chaos right from the start, and he had only just begun.

I needed to keep my head on and focus on the goal at hand: keeping Melora alive and getting to Vayna. I would do whatever it took to make that happen. If it were up to me, I would be the one to take Vayna's magic and try to pull it from her. But Melora had made her decision, and I knew it was non-negotiable.

She is so headstrong, sometimes to a fault.

Men battled against each other on one side of me, hacking and chopping each other down. I focused on the mortal running at me, sword held high in the air, ready to take me down with a mighty blow. I brought him down in one quick slice, killing him instantly. I turned to my other side, where Melora was currently slicing a man's throat open.

Viscous.

My wife is *vicious*.

I loved it.

I fought on beside her, cutting down men who came near us with my broadsword, stabbing and fighting our way through the sea of men. Penn was next to Melora as well, hacking it out with a mortal guard and never leaving her for more than a few moments. His movements were strong and motivated. He knew what was at stake, and he would protect his queen with his life.

Milo ran past me on all fours, his paws moving him towards the enemy. I watched as he jumped and landed on a mortal who was going for Kaius from behind. Milo sank his claws into the mortal and gashed his chest open. Yara was doing the same, tearing open any guard that was brave enough to face her, her white fur now blood-stained.

Many had fallen already, but there was still much battle to be had. We were making headway, getting closer to the back of the mortal army, where we planned Vayna would be, where we knew she would be waiting. But that meant going through the middle of the battle, where all-out war was being waged.

It was a battlefield, filled with bodies, alive and dead, scattered everywhere I looked. The alive fight each other, leaving hardly any space in the grassy field. The dead were sprawled out through the field, some mortal and some Asterian. Too many had fallen already; too many had lost to the war waged by the mortal queen.

We needed to do this and we needed to do it now before Vayna has any ideas about using her magic to wipe everyone off of this land just as she did in the Fallen Forest. I know she would kill us all, even her own men if it meant getting what she wanted. She was ruthless, bloodthirsty, and would do anything for power.

Cries, grunts, and screams were all around us as we trucked on through the warfare. Melora kept both daggers in her hands, never leaving one in a man after killing them. The purple gems on the handles were now covered in blood, making her look like the warrior she was. The gift I gave her now came to good use, covered with blood from her enemies. I smiled at her when she caught my eye, flashing a quick grin at her. I wish I could tell her what I was thinking, that I was thinking of the night when I gave her those daggers. When I gifted her her engagement ring.

I wish we could be back in that moment, go back to that moment of pure happiness.

But we were here, and we had a mission to complete.

We have made our way through the majority of the battling, fighting side-by-side and back-to-back together. Penn makes it along with us, never getting too far from his queen. The battle is thinning before us, and we know we are getting close to where we planned for Vayna to be camping out during the battle. We need to get to her; we need to end this.

I turn to tell Melora such but am met face-to-face with my brother, my treasonous little brother, who stands before me, pointing a weapon at me. He has a sword, the same one that he put through my heart the last time we met on the battlefield. He watches me like a predator, waiting to strike.

I do not want to do this...but I knew it would happen eventually.

"Brother," I acknowledge him, waiting to see what he will do. Waiting to see if he will attack. "Come to apologize for your crimes?" I ask, knowing he would never. His pride is too important to him for that.

His jaw clenched, anger filling him. He narrows his eyes that look like our father's. "Tell me, how is our dear Melora? I missed the little monster after our wedding, does she remember our time together? Yearn for it maybe?" he started stalking around me, sword at the ready.

    He was trying to make me jealous, rile me up, and piss me off.

    It was working.

    "It is hard for her to forget the past when it is written all over her skin," I told him, talking about the scar he left her with, one I will return tenfold.

    His face went cold, like he knew I had decided that he would die, like he knew what awaited him. It pains me to do it, to kill my own blood, but after the things he has done to our kingdom, to our family, to Melora, he will not live.

    He jumped at me with his sword, ready to go. His sword clanged off of mine as they met in the air, clashing over our heads. His technique was horrible and his arms weak, but he was quick. We went at it, like the brothers we were, like the brothers we have always been. Hitting, swinging, and slicing. Hoping to end the other with our sword or our fist.

    Hoping to kill the other so they wouldn't kill us first.

    I punch him in the mouth with my free hand, causing blood to pour from his lip. He stammers back, shaking away the pain the hit must have caused him. He was slowing, his stamina weak and out of practice. I wish he had let me train him more, or even let Milo help him with his skills. Maybe then he would survive this fight.

    His sword strikes became sluggish and I knew I had him, knew I would end him. I felt the anticipation of killing him, knowing I must do it, but really not wanting to. Deep down he is my brother, but the man in front of me now was not the brother

I knew. He was not the brother I grew up loving and caring for.

If our mother were here, she would tell us to put down our weapons and fists and talk it out. She would remind us that we are brothers, that we are blood, and that we need to look out for each other. She would tell us that it is okay to be mad or upset with each other, but at the end of the day, we knew we loved the other.

I wish she were here. If she had been, Simon would not have become the stranger he is today.

"Is this how you thought it would end, brother?" I hit him with my free hand again in the gut; he keeled over and grunted. "Is this what you wanted?" I screamed in his face as he gasped for breath. He swung his sword, missing as I ducked. I popped up quickly, not hesitating, as I shoved my sword through his belly. "Was it worth it?" I asked him in his ear as he fell to his knees.

I went down with him, never leaving his stare as blood started to seep from his mouth. "It- it is- better this way. All I have done...it is better this way." he whispered, falling forward. I caught him, not wanting him to hit the ground. I held him as his eyes fluttered, as the pain from my sword traveled through his body.

I held my baby brother as he looked up at me, a gash in his stomach from my blade. "I am sorry I was not a better brother to you," I told him, and tears began to prickle my eyes. "I am sorry I was not there when you needed me most."

He coughs, blood comes up and sputters from his mouth. "I- I wish things would have been different," he whispered, staring up into my eyes. "This is what was meant to be."

His eyes close, and I lay him down on the grass field. I let my head fall as a tear falls from my eye for the brother that I once had. For the brother who was once loving, who was once trustworthy. I cry as I watch my baby brother die by my hands. The memory of what once was with it.

It hurts having to kill Simon. It hurts, and it will haunt me for the rest of my life. I will mourn him, mourn the person he used to be, the brother he used to be. I will not mourn the man he turned into.

I hear a sound that wakes me at night, that haunts my dreams, and even in waking, it torments me. Melora screams, and I immediately find her in the havoc of war. I will always find her wherever she is, even through a sea of men. She screams as she unleashes her power on the men standing before her, in between her and what she wants.

She incinerates them, leaving only dust in their wake. Gods...her power was menacing. More mortal men run at her, and she blasts her bright magic into them like she did the others, removing them from her path. They are gone in a second, leaving no one in between her and her goal.

There is nothing between her and Vayna now; it is just ground that Melora is quickly covering with fast feet and determined movements. I watch as Melora runs toward our enemy, and I watch as Vayna kneels to place her hands on the ground.

I stood quickly, leaving my brother's body lying on the battlefield ground. Fear, pure fear, made me move before my head could even tell me what was about to happen. But then I realized what Vayna was about to do; she was about to blast her magic through the land as she had in the Fallen Forest, killing everyone and everything in her path.

"No!" I scream at Melora, who does not hear me and just keeps running toward the threat.

"Melora! NO!" I scream for her again, my voice raw and scared.

I take off, trying to get to her before Vayna's dark magic can. I run and run and watch as Melora stops in front of Vayna, who is still on the ground. She looks up at Mel, her head tilted slightly and an evil smile on her lips.

Vayna thinks she has won, thinks she has outsmarted Melora, and thinks she is about to take out the most important people in Asteria with one quick blow. She thinks her plans are falling into place and that she will kill Melora and take Asteria herself.

Melora has other plans.

I can't get to her quick enough, still running as fast as I can for her as she plants her feet and raises her arms, hands splayed wide. I feel her power before I see it, before Vayna sees it. I feel it in the air and energy all around us, like a wave of power rolling through the land. It is her, though, all I feel is her.

Melora summons her magic and brings forth so much power, so much magic, that I knew the only thing fueling her is fury itself.

CHAPTER 31

MELORA

I know what Vayna is about to do.

We knew she would do this, or at least she would try.

I know what her next play is, know what she planned to do as soon as she saw me approaching her, ready to strike. She planned this from the beginning, just waiting on me to find her and make sure I was close enough for her magic to kill me as it kills everything it touches. She is willing to do whatever it takes to defeat us, even killing her own men. I knew she would kill everyone if it meant she won, won what she thought she owned.

I could not let that happen, I *would* not let that happen. Too many that I love are on this battlefield, too much is at stake, and we need to win right now more than ever. Now is the time to act, to take back what was not hers to begin with. To take back what my mother gave her to protect me, to take back the magic my mother granted her so long ago and the toxic power that came with it.

The fate of our kingdom lies before me, waiting for me to take it and make sure we live.

Fate...I truly never believed in such a thing until I met Silas, until his lips were on mine and he convinced me otherwise. Convinced me that fate is real, and it stands before me now, waiting to be changed.

I will not fail.

I cannot fail.

Now is my time, my fate and my purpose have led me to this moment, steered me in the direction all along. All I have done, all that has been done to me has led me here, ready to save the kingdom I once feared. I will save Asteria and all her people. The people I love and cherish more than anything in this life. And if it means I will relinquish my own, then so be it, because there are worse fates in this world than death.

I will gladly give my life in place of the thousands that live in Asteria.

I hear Silas yelling for me, his call in the distance over the sounds of battle still surging around us. He sounds afraid, scared, as he continues to yell for me to stop. I know he fears for me, and I know he will want me to stop and think before I act, but I cannot. We are out of time, and we are out of chances.

This is it.

I do not listen to Silas's screams as I focus and call forth my magic. I think of everything that has been taken, all that has been ruined in my life, and bring it forward. I bring the pain, the grief, the anguish; I bring it all forth to fuel me in what lies before me.

I think of everything Vayna has done and blamed me for her doing it. I remember how she glamoured me, made up an entire part of my life and family that I truly loved. I think about how she made me move to Ravenhall only to be abused by Lord Chapler for years and years. How she murdered and killed for the sake of it, just because she could.

I think of Loral.

I think of Visha.

She has taken so much, too much, and it ends now.

I am not her adopted daughter anymore, not her secret or her princess. I am a queen, and I am the queen she will fear.

My magic comes forth, ready to fight for what is ours and take what was given to her. I feel it vibrating through me as it travels to my outreached hands, moving to my fingers. I see Vayna's curious look as she watches me from where she kneels on the ground, her hands still placed on the field's floor. I envision what it will look like when the magic starts to be pulled from her body, when all her false power starts to be taken from her.

I watch her face turn from cold and calculating into fear and realization as she watches what I am doing. I can see the moment she starts to feel what I am doing to her. I can see when she starts to feel me take her magic. She tries to stand, but she is frozen where she kneels.

She will die on her knees, like the coward I know she truly is.

Just as I envisioned, her magic started to come from her, moving towards me in a dark cloud and out of her body. The darkness moves towards my outstretched hands, seeping into my palms as it comes to me. I feel her darkness entering me, her magic moving into my body through my hands as I continue to pull it from her. I keep willing it to come to me, keep pulling and pulling.

I keep using my power, keep pulling Vayna's magic from her body with my magic, even as pain starts in my temples and moves through my head. A scream climbs up my throat as pain begins to invade my every thought, but I will not stop, not when we are so close. Not when we are so close to the victory we have worked for and so many have died for.

I drop down to a knee to brace myself as a gut-wrenching screech comes from me. Fire fills my veins as I continue to take her magic into my body. I can still see Vayna, her body starting to cave in on itself, her once-perfect skin cracking and falling apart. I look into her eyes, seeing her confusion and surprise.

She did not think I would do it, she did not think I would kill her.

Oh, how she was wrong.

And it is working.

The pain is blinding, making my vision blur and go in and out, but I would never mistake the arms that embrace me from behind for anyone else. I would know his touch; even in blinding pain, I would know it was him.

Silas is here, wrapping his arms around me as I fall to the ground entirely onto my knees, still trying to use my magic on Vayna. "Mel! It's killing you! You have to stop!" he yells from behind me, his arms holding me tighter. I hear the fear in his voice, hear the emotion, but I cannot stop, not yet. "Please! Stop! Stop this!" he continues to beg.

Her magic is almost gone; I nearly have all of it. I can feel it as it enters me and leaves her, leaving her powerless and decrepit. Her body continues to wither away to nothing; she screams as I continue to pull her magic.

I almost have it, almost have it all, and she will never be able to hurt us again. I can't stop, even if it kills me, because we are so close, and it will be worth it. "I'm sorry," I whisper to Silas, unsure if he heard me as I continue to use my magic to take from Vayna.

I feel it when all of Vayna's magic has been taken from her and is now in me. I can feel her darkness running through me, mixing with my magic and creating something wretched, something evil. It hurts, her magic invading my every vein, like she is in me, her darkness is in me.

    I look to make sure Vayna is no longer alive. Her body has turned to ash, leaving nothing behind other than dust where she knelt. I stop my magic, stop pulling from her because there is nothing left to take.

    It is all in me.

    I collapsed fully into Silas's arms, he caught me as I fell to the ground knowing that I did it. I stopped Vanya and took her magic. I saved us. My friends will live. Silas will live. It is worth it, this pain I feel, to know that those I love will live.

    I feel myself fading, feel her dark magic rampaging through my veins and taking over my mind. We knew Vayna's magic was not right, knew it was dark, but feeling it inside me was different. I can feel all the horrible things she has done, feel all the hate and anger in her as her magic takes hold of me. The pain is overbearing as I continue to scream out.

    "Melora! Melora, look at me!" Silas screams from where he is looking down at me. He holds me in his lap, holding me up as all my strength is gone. "Melora! Look at me!"

    I feel my hands pulsing, pulsing like magic wants to escape from me. I hold up a hand over my face and look at it in the air. It's hard to focus as my vision goes in and out, but I can see this clearly...and it terrifies me.

    The veins in my hand have turned black, like the blood in my body has turned black and can now be seen underneath my skin. I panic at the sight, holding up my other hand limply to only find the same thing.

The pain is starting to become unbearable, making it feel like my very blood is aflame and dying to be let free. Like my insides are burning and turning to ash. "It hurts." I try to tell Silas, cries coming out with my words. "Silas, it hurts." I whimper to him, trying to hold on as long as I can. Trying to stay with him for as long as I can.

He rocks me while he holds on to me tight, his face wet with tears and laced with panic. "I know, I know, my love. It's her magic. You- you have to fight it. Fight it, Mel. Don't let it take you." he tells me, pleads to me.

I try to do as he says and fight it, but I feel her magic taking over my mind. I feel like I am slipping, slipping in and out of consciousness. Or maybe this is what dying feelings like. If so, I welcome death, for it means my friends and kingdom will survive. It means Silas will live and be safe.

I close my eyes, waiting for death to take me by the hand and lead me into the darkness, knowing that my people are safe.

"Melora! No! Open your eyes right now!" Silas yells, screams at me, and shakes me. "Open them! Baby, please! Open your eyes; let me see them. Let me see those beautiful eyes." He is stroking my face, moving my tousled hair out of the way; it is a soothing feeling as I wait for death.

I hear him, but I can't do as he asks. I feel like I am burning from the inside out, and the only way to stop it is to let death take me. My mission is complete, my goal is acquired. I can rest now that I know the things I love most will be safe. I can rest knowing we won.

I still hear Silas pleading for me to wake, can still feel him shaking me in his arms trying to get me to open my eyes. It hurts knowing he will have to live with this-have to live without me. I know he will blame himself, and I wish there was a way that I could tell him it is alright. It is alright because he is safe and I would do it all over again just to know him and our people will live.

He is strong, and our people will need someone to lead them after I am gone. He will do it; he will live on and will make sure our kingdom does, too. He will be the ruler he was born to be, and he will be a great one.

It is a comforting image as I drift off into the nothingness of death.

It is a funny thought that all my life, I have been welcoming the feeling of nothingness to get me through the unthinkable, the most horrible things that have happened to me, and here I am once more, welcoming the feeling of nothingness again like an old friend.

CHAPTER 32

SILAS

She is not dead.

I know she is not dead.

She can't be. She cannot be gone. There is no possible way that she is gone, and I will not entertain that thought for a moment longer.

I hold on to my Melora, my strong and fierce girl. I hold onto her as she lies limp in my arms, in my lap. I cradle her head in the crook of my arm as I continue to look down at her, waiting for her to open her beautiful blue eyes.

She is not dead.

She is not gone.

She made me a promise, and I know she will not leave me.

"Silas," Milo comes next to me and kneels beside me. I don't even look at him, not wanting to take my eyes off of Mel for even a moment. "Silas, she is gone. Look at her." He says quietly, his voice wavering. I can hear him crying, hear the emotion in his voice as he talks to me.

I feel the others at my back, Yara and the twins gathering around us, watching the scene play out before them. I see Penn drop to his knee next to us, looking at Melora. He lets out a sob as he reaches for her head, his hands covered in blood and shaky as he reaches for her. He places a hand on her wild hair and cries. "She is gone," he says.

They are starting to piss me off.

"She is not gone. She is alive, I know it." I try to tell them. "Just- just give her a minute. She promised. She promised she would not leave me again. She is going to be okay." I feel more tears start to shed as I rock her back and forth, her limp body laying weightless in my arms.

I pull her closer, pull her to my chest, and her arms don't wrap around my neck like how they normally would. I hold her tighter, not letting the thoughts of her being gone come into my mind and make me crazy.

"Silas," Milo says, reaching out for Melora, trying to take her away.

Rage flows through me at the thought of anyone touching her, even my best friend, who I know loves Mel. I growl and pull her away from his reach. "No." is all I say, rage in my tone.

Milo understands with this one word and pulls back, giving me space. "You can take her. We just need to get her back to Ravenhall. We need to go, Silas." he reasons with me.

I guess we won the battle after Melora had taken out Vayna. I noticed the sounds of war has ceased, and there was no longer men battling around me. I had hardly noticed anything going on around us after Mel had gone down, nothing else mattered besides her.

I heard Milo giving men orders as we walked through the battlefield, orders I did not pay attention to because it was all on Melora. Men, Asterian and mortal, lay scattered about everywhere, blood and gore on the grass.

Milo was trying to order our men around, trying to get things in order and have some structure in the aftermath of war. But I could hear his voice, have known him long enough to know that he was fighting back emotion.

Yara ushered me quickly back to our horses, where we mounted and took off back to Ravenhall.

The hour and some ride back to Ravenhall was tortuous. Mel still had not moved as I held her to my chest while riding on my horse, watching her closely. She still has not moved as I brought her into the castle and took her to our room. I carried her through the halls and into the room we had taken over.

She still has not moved as I laid her down in the bed we shared only a night ago.

She lays so still in the large bed, so still she could be dead.

No.

She is not gone, I remind myself.

She is *not*.

I examine her as I hold her hand, kneeling next to her as she lay motionless on the bed. I hold her hand and rub her arm, not wanting to stop touching her. I look at her arms and hands, the veins are still black and stand out under her soft white skin. I think about when she was screaming in pain, lying in my arms on the battlefield after Vayna was finally dead, her eyes...they had turned black. The river blue I knew and loved had turned dark as night. I had never quite felt fear like that before, not before I saw my Melora, my wife's eyes turn as black as her veins.

I can only see her like that now, eyes and veins black, screaming that it hurts while laying in my arms. Grief threatens to invade my mind, take over my every thought. I will not let it happen, because I know she is alive. I know she will wake up.

Penn is on the other side of the bed with Milo, both having returned back to Ravenhall shortly after us. They are both looking down at her. Their faces are morbid, eyes red and puffy from crying. I know they love Melora, know they would die for her, but I know they are wrong. She is alive.

Penn bends to Melora and kisses her forehead, whispering something to her before he stands and leaves the room quickly. Milo is still with me, watching her lay there in bed. "Silas-"

I cut him off before he can say another word about her being gone, because he does not know that for sure and I will not hear another word about it. "I need to clean her up. She cannot have all this blood on her when she wakes. She will panic." I told him.

I don't see his face, but know the look he is giving me. He is worried, worried and sad.

"Can I help?" Yara asks from behind me; I hadn't even known she was there. But as always, she is right there beside me, ready to help me care for the woman I love.

I nodded that she could because I knew Mel would want her to. Yara comes over and looks at Melora. She really looks at her, and she sees what I see. Her body is bloodied and covered with dirt, her veins black with Vayna's magic, and her face resting beautifully. "We need to wash her."

Yara and I wash Melora off, cleaning her of blood and dirt from the battle. We change her out of her torn and tattered clothing into a silky soft nightgown, one I know she likes. I want her to be comfortable when she wakes, not scared.

Yara leaves sometime after we change her, quietly slipping out of the room. But I do not. I stayed with her through the night, holding her hand and talking to her. I remind her of our story, of how we met, how we fell in love, how we were meant to be with each other. I tell her how much I love her, how she is a part of my soul, and there is no part of me that does not belong to her.

I reminded her of her promise, her promise that she would not leave me again. "You promised," I told her. "You promised not to leave me, please, Melora. Wake up. Please." I begged her.

But she still has not woken, still has made no move to wake. She lays there in our bed, lifeless. I climb in next to her, wanting to hold her one last time because I finally see it. I finally see what my friends tried to tell me; that she is dead.

Denying the truth doesn't make it hurt less.

I hold her as I sob, as I sob so loudly, so painfully, I know the castle can hear me. It hurts, knowing she is gone, knowing I will never hear her laugh again, or feel her never-ending love. It hurts knowing she died for me, for our kingdom. It all hurts, and there is nothing I can do. There is nothing I can do to bring her back to me.

I lay with her, trying to soak up as much of her as I could. I try to leave, knowing and understanding that she is gone, but I can't bring myself to do it. She is gone, and it feels like she took my heart with her, like she took my soul into death with her. It belongs to her, after all, my heart and soul, so taking it into death with her makes sense.

A part of me is missing as I finally leave her lying in bed; a part of me is gone as I leave my wife. I walk aimlessly until I find the room I know my friends will be in, know they will be together in. I open the door, my eyes planted on the floor before me as I walk into the room. I don't want to see their faces or see their expressions when I walk in because I already feel too much of my own pain; I do not need to feel theirs, too.

"She is gone," I whisper, the room going silent. "She is gone," I say again, this time letting the strength leave my knees and falling to the floor. I have no more strength to give, no more life to live if Melora is not doing it with me. I do not know how I will go on after feeling her love, after knowing what her love was like. I simply cannot.

Yara and Milo are at my side in a flash, consoling me as I scream in agony. As I cry into the hands that once held Melora. Yara holds on to me, and I shake with the pain of losing the only thing in this life that has given me peace. The only person who has given me love when I thought love was an unreachable thing for me.

Someone hands me a drink, Kane, I think. I take it, not caring that I haven't drank in over a month. Whoever it is, I appreciate them because the taste of whiskey is easier to bear than knowing I will never see my Melora again.

Just as I bring the glass to my lips, I see the sunlight coming in from outside disappear. "What is that?" Yara asks as we all stare out the window, at the sudden change in light. The wind is blowing and the sun has completely been covered by dark clouds. Thunder rumbles, and the wind whips, shattering glass somewhere in the distance. "What is happening?" someone else asks in a panic.

I know what is happening.

I know what is *happening*.

"Melora," I whisper just before I take off back to our room.

I run fast, as fast as I can, as the group of friends are right behind me, keeping up. We turn a corner and come into the throne room to get to where Melora lies in bed. But as we enter the throne room, I see her.

I see *her*.

I see Melora stand.

I see Melora *alive*.

Melora is standing facing the thrones, staring at them blankly. She stands so still, the skirt of her nightgown flapping in the wind she is creating. "Melora," I called to her, to try and get her attention away from the thrones.

She turns to us, and an audible gasp leaves the group. "Oh my gods," Yara says in a hushed tone at what we all see.

We all watch as Melora looks at us, her eyes pitch black as they were on the battlefield. Her veins stand out more under her skin, the black matching that of her eyes. "Melora, it is me. It is Silas." I try to remind her, try to get her to see through the darkness that is in her.

She tilts her head to the side and gives a menacing look. It hits me then, that she does not recognize me, that she does not recognize any of us. She does not recognize her friends standing behind me.

She narrows her black eyes and walks towards us, her pace a viciously slow walk. The glass that shattered earlier must have been in the throne room because as she walks towards us, she walks barefoot over the broken window pieces. She leaves a trail of blood from her feet as she walks unbothered by the crunching pieces beneath her soles.

She looks absolutely terrifying, like death incarnate is coming for us, walking right toward us. But I know she is in there; I know she is still there.

"Vayna's magic has taken her over. It's in her mind, corrupting her. We need to bring her back." I tell the group, hoping they can help me.

"Mel, it is us." I try to reason with her, but before I can get out another word, she cuts me off.

"Bow before your queen!" Melora screams at us. "Bow before the one they call 'Queen of Life'!" she screams at us again as more wind whooshed through the room. Thunder crashes, and lightning strikes outside as we all drop to our knees.

I need to get her back; I need to get my wife back. "Melora, it is Silas. It is your husband. Remember. Remember our wedding on the beach, when we danced and laughed with all of our friends." I tell her, and she straightens like she recognizes what I am telling her. It is working. "Remember that I love you. Your friends love you. Penn. Milo. Yara. Kane. Kaius. We are all here for you. We are all here, Mel." her face has gone stark, she is listening to me.

"We are here, Mel!" Yara shouts.

"We will always be with you, Melora," Penn calls her.

She shakes her head and stumbles backward. The chaos around us stops abruptly, the wind stopping and the thunder going quiet. I see it when she changes back to the Melora I know, I watch as her eyes change back to the beautiful blue that reminds me of the ocean. She holds herself as she looks around, her face scared and her body trembling. She stops when she finds us kneeling before her, staring at her. "Silas?" she cries, I know she has to be scared.

    I rush to her and take her in my arms, relieved that she is alive.

CHAPTER 33

MELORA

"The last thing I remember is seeing Vayna die, seeing her body wither away. I remember watching her, making sure she was completely gone before I let myself go. Before I let myself fall into the darkness." I explain to everyone as they stand around the living area in Silas and I's room.

Their faces are grim, they keep looking at me like I will snap at any moment. I honestly feel like I could, like the darkness within me from Vayna's magic is begging to be let free. To wreak havoc. To make me into the monster that I was trying not to become.

I scared them; I know I did. I scared myself when I came to and saw what I had done. I walked across broken glass, made my friends bow to me, commanded them to bow to their queen. I know it was not me doing it, not actually me, but the darkness of Vayna's magic within me making me act.

I can only remember bits and pieces of what happened, snippets of the horrible event that happened when I woke. But I remember enough to know that I was terrifying, that I was evil alive. I know it is not me; it is Vayna's magic. But it is me acting on what it wants. It wants power; it wants blood.

"I feel what her magic wants." I continue to tell my friends. "It wants power. It is so hungry for it that the magic has turned so dark, so wretched, that it will do anything to have that power." I continued, still feeling it under my skin, just itching to be led free.

"Just like Vayna," Milo added from where he stood near the liquor cabinet. This room in Ravenhall was nowhere near as equipped with alcohol as our room in Asteria is, but it will do.

"Exactly," I say, looking down at my black veined arms, at the magic beneath my skin. "When I took Vayna's magic, I took her darkness, her...want for power and pain."

The realization of what I have in my veins, mixing in with my own magic, hits me. I- I am turning into Vayna. I am turning into the monster I tried, tried so hard to not turn into. I battled and fought with myself to not become the monster I felt I could be, yet here I am. I feel her magic in me, wanting me to be the ruthless queen I was in the throne room. It craves it. It craves power and fear, and when it takes me over, that is what it takes.

"Well what do we do now?" Yara asks, but I don't hear her. I don't hear any of them as they converse about what is inside me, about what we should do next.

All I can hear, all I can see, is the faces of my friends, of Silas, in the throne room. They looked scared, scared of me and the monster I became. I can't become what Vayna was; I can't let her magic take over my own and turn me into something I am not.

I would rather die than turn into her.

"Mel," Silas's voice is muffled in my ears. I can barely hear him over the pounding in my head, the pounding of my heart as anxiety and fear take over my body. "Mel," I hear him again, but I can't talk; I can't move as the fear of what I am becoming sets in.

I stand abruptly, not able to sit here any longer. I walk quickly to our bedroom, it is attached to the living area, but I just need some distance from everything. I need to be able to take a breath for a moment; I need to think.

I walk into our room and place my hands on my knees, bending over at the waist and bracing myself. I feel like I can't breathe, like I am panicking, and the pressure is pushing my chest down. Like the weight of the world is crushing my chest to nothing.

I know what is happening; it is as Penn once said, it is a fit of fear. I need to breathe like he taught me, but I can't come down from the panic I am feeling. I continue to suck in air rapidly, unable to catch my breath or my rising anxiety.

My body shakes, and tears begin to burn my eyes, at least until I feel a warm chest press up against my back. Silas's hand laced around the front of me, a hand on my chest, and a hand on my belly. He holds me tightly against him, grounding me in this moment of panic.

"Breath with me." he sucked in a deep breath, prompting me to do the same and follow his movements. "Breath for me, my love." he continues to breathe deeply, the rise and fall of his chest helping me control my own breathing.

Finally, I calmed down. I regain control of my emotions and breath normally. Then, the tears came in full force. I cry, I cry and let my head fall back onto my husband's chest. He holds me up as my knees threaten to give out. He holds me to his chest and lets me cry, whispering soothing words into my ear.

"It is alright, my love. Let it out."

"I am here for you. I will always be here."

"I love you. I love all of you, every part, the light and the dark, the good and the evil."

I listen to his words and let them soothe me. I calm down and let my body melt into his. "Silas," I whimper, turning to face him and placing my hands on his chest. "I'm scared, Silas. I don't want to become her." I admit to him; I admit out loud.

He hugs me, pulls me into his arms, and squeezes me in a comforting hug. "You will never be like her, Mel." He whispers into my hair, holding onto me. "Never."

"I feel it in me. It- it runs so deep, I don't know what to do. I- I don't know what to do." I cry to him again.

He moves pieces of hair out of my face, pushing the strands behind my ear. "We will get it out of you; we will get her magic out," he promises. "You are alive; that is all that matters, Mel. You are here," he tells me and the look in eye, the look of never-ending promise, tells me that he will make it happen or die trying.

I nod, understanding I am lucky to be alive. I am lucky to be still standing, even if it costs me. I was lucky in the battle, but others weren't. One in particular comes to mind. "Simon," I say his name in question, wondering what happened to him. "What- what happened to Simon?" I ask Silas.

"He's dead," Silas said mournfully, his face falling. "I killed him," he told me, his forehead falling to mine.

"Silas, I am so sorry." I tell him, holding his cheek, running my thumb over the scruff of his chin. "I am so sorry."

I hated that he had to kill his brother, to end the life of the one he was supposed to protect. But I knew why he did it, and I would not question him. I just know it will haunt him, hurt him for a very long time.

"We are all safe now," Silas reminds me. "She is gone, he is gone. We are all safe," he says, sounding like he is also reassuring himself.

We stood there, in each other's arms, feeling all the emotion and hardship we have been through. It helps, having someone to help bear the weight of it all, all the loss, all the death. In Silas's arms, the darkness flowing within me doesn't feel so bad.

"What now?" I ask, thinking of all the things we now need to do. "Where do we go from here?"

He looked at me, his face smoothing out and relaxing as he took in my features. "We will take it one step at a time", he said, his voice calm. "The realm needs a ruler now that Vayna is gone." He gave me that look, and I knew he meant me.

"We got lucky in Ravenhall," I reminded him. "The rest of the realm will not be so easily taken." I tried to tell him.

He shrugs. "You never know until you find out." He raises an eyebrow. "We take the capitol first, tell people the truth of what happened, just like we did in Ravenhall. We tell them all of it." He lays out the plan.

I smiled. "I like that plan." I feel my magic do a little flip in my gut, and it is *my* magic, not Vayna's. "My mother," I said. "We must free her from the capitol. She is priority number one." I tell him, demand, really.

He nodded, understanding how important she was to me. "She may also know how to free Vayna's magic from you, how to take her darkness out," he says, hopeful.

"She may, but getting her out is the most important thing to me," I tell him, making sure he knows I need to free my mother before all else. I need her, I need her guidance and...I want a mother. I want a true motherly presence to be there for me, to hold me and love me only like a mother ever could.

Silas's brow scrunched, worry lining his face. "Are you feeling okay?" he asked timidly, like he didn't want to scare me. "You...you're sweating." he held my face and examined me closer.

I touched my forehead and felt the dampness on my brow. I was starting to feel hot, like my skin was too warm for my body. My hands turned clammy as I opened and shut them, trying to shake the feeling of magic coming to life.

I knew what was happening as Silas's face turned pale. He knew, as I knew, that Vayna's magic was taking over again.

I started to feel pain in my arms, like my magic wanted to be used but was being overrun by Vayna's darkness. My blood felt like it was on fire, like it was vibrating in my veins and trying to get out. I looked down and the black veins were still there, sticking out more prominently against my light skin.

The urge to give in to the darkness, to the evilness whirling inside me, came over me. Vayna's magic wanted me to act on its will, to do all the horrible deeds it wished to act out.

It craves power, craves blood, just as Vayna did.

And now it was in me. Her magic was in me, and it wanted to use me to get what it wanted.

"Mel, look at me," Silas said, getting my attention. I must have spaced out because I hadn't fully heard him, only the brief muffling of a voice. "Melora, listen to me. Do not let it take you. Fight it."

He kept talking, kept repeating what he was saying. But I can't hear him. The pain was now in my head, pulsing and pounding against my skull. I felt like I could implode; it might feel better than this.

I fell to my knees, trying to brace myself against screams trying to come from my throat.

Silas was in front of me, trying to hold me and get me to focus on him. I wanted to; I wanted him to be the only thing I could ever see, ever feel. But my vision was blurring, and I couldn't hear any of the sounds coming from his mouth.

"Silas," I wheezed out, trying to gather enough strength to tell him to run. "Go. Please. You need to leave." I groaned as I talked, the words painful in my mouth.

His hands were on my shoulders, holding me up as my body continued to give out. "I will not leave you. I will never leave you."

I was holding on with the last bit of strength I had to not give in, to not let the darkness of Vayna's magic take hold of me. I was doing everything I could to push it down, to not let it invade every sense, every part of me.

But it was doing just that; my hold was slipping, and time was running out. "RUN," I begged as I let out a shriek that echoed off the walls.

And just as it did before, the darkness of Vanya's magic took over my mind. Took over every thought I had and threatened to break me into a million pieces.

I slipped into darkness, into the nothingness, as I heard Silas beg me not to give in.

CHAPTER 34

SILAS

"Fight it, Mel! Do not give in!" I yell at Melora as she is screaming, hanging on for life as the darkness threatens to take her over once again. Her scream rings through the walls, and as I knew he would, Milo runs into the room. He is panting, and fear is apparent on his face. I knew he probably made the others stay back...stay out of harm's way. Stay out of Melora's way.

"Oh, gods," Milo said, stopping when he saw Melora on the floor of our room screaming bloody murder.

She is shaking, trying her damnedest not to let Vayna's magic take over her again. Shaking and trembling in my arms as I try to keep her up and not let her fall completely to the floor. She only grips her head and continues to shriek.

"Throw me in a cell!" she screams to us. "Keep me away!" She continues to try and plead for me to lock her up, to put her in a cell.

No way that is happening.

"Milo," I tried to get his attention. He is staring at Mel as if the evil queen from the throne room has returned already, ready to take her place on the throne. Not yet; she is still my Melora. "Milo!" I yell for him, and he snaps back into the moment. "It is going to take hold; be ready when it has her. We need to-"

I stopped talking when there was only silence in the room. I was cut off by the sound of nothing, by the silence that was only a moment ago, agony-filled sounds coming from Melora. She stopped screaming, stopped pleading for me to lock her away. Stopped everything as she kneeled in front of me, her head bent forward.

The silence was deafening as I looked at her; her head hung low and her hair fell around her face. I tried to bend lower to see her, to see her eyes. I couldn't see her, but I felt it when the magic that was not hers took her over. I felt it when the darkness that is Vayna's filled Melora.

"Mel?" Milo asked quietly, testing to see if our girl was still in there.

Her head was still down, keeping us from seeing her face. Her breathing steadied, and a low laugh started to rumble from her. A laugh that was not hers, not the beautiful sounds I had heard before when Milo and I teased her. It was dark and full of promise, promise of destruction.

"Melora," I say to her, trying to bring her back as quickly as possible. Trying to bring back the woman I love. "Melora, listen-"

"Fools," she laughs as she slowly stands. I rise with her, taking a step back as she rises to her full height. She stands on sturdy legs that were threatening to give out on her only a second ago.

Melora looks up, bringing her eyes to mine slowly, carefully. They are black, black as a starless night, just as her veins are. She tilts her head methodically, looking at me like I am a challenge. Like I am a challenge she must conquer.

She looks at Milo and does the same, looking at him as if she were a hungry lioness, ready to strike. Ready to take down anyone in her path that is keeping her from power, and right now that is us.

"Listen to us, Mel-" Milo gets cut off as he is thrown against a wall by Melora, by the magic that is mixing with her own. He lands with a loud grunt as things around him crash and shatter. Milo groans, trying to get up and holding his now bleeding head.

Melora turned her sights to me next, and I am truly afraid. I am truly terrified by my own wife in this form, when she is not herself but a version of herself that has been taken over.

Her hand whips through the air, and I am thrown backward into a shelf. I hit hard, feeling the wooden furniture against my spine. I roll to my side and onto broken glass. I try to get up, try to stand, but I am frozen where I have landed. I feel Melora's magic keeping me in place, keeping me pinned to the floor.

Melora just laughs as Milo and I lie on the floor, watching us struggle to get up. She lifts her head high, her black eyes gleaming as she looks down at us, as she looks over us like her subjects. "You will die," she says wickedly. "You will all die. I will take what is mine, what has always been mine. I will kill you all." she vows, promise in her voice.

It can't happen like this; it is not supposed to happen like this. I just got her back and she is gone again, taken by the darkness, taken by something we cannot fight. I cannot let her go; I will not let her go again. "Melora!" I scream at her from where I still lay on the floor, still pinned by her magic.

Her head whips to me, her curls flinging as she turns. She looks at me, looking at the fear I have for her on my face. I know she is in there. I know my Melora is still in there, and she sees me scared. She has to see me in there. I know she is *somewhere* in there.

She stares, sucking in a sharp breath as she hunches over. Melora screams again; this time, it is with power instead of pain.

"Silas!" Melora screams, trying to keep herself standing. It is her; it is my Melora and not that evil thing trying to take her. "I can't hold it back! Go! Get out of here!" she yells again.

I stand, finally free of the magic that was keeping me locked down. I step to go to her, ready to grab her and hold on. "I am not leaving you!"

Melora is shaking, trying to hold onto the power she has over the darkness in her. She holds out her hand and keeps me in place with *her* magic, not the darkness inside her this time. "Stay away! I will hurt you!" she pleads, still holding me with her power. I see her look behind her, look into the full-body mirror in the corner. She stares at herself, her now blue eyes filled with tears.

Before I know what she is doing, the glass from the mirror breaks, Melora turning and punching straight through it. The mirror shatters to the floor, pieces flying everywhere and scattering across the room.

I watch as Melora, as my wife, picks up a shard of broken glass from the mirror, a large piece, and holds it to her throat. She looks at me, crying as she presses the glass against her perfect skin on her neck.

I know what she is about to do.

"NO!" I scream, trying to take a step to her. "Melora, no!" I struggle against her magic.

She still holds out her free hand, still stopping me in my tracks with her magic. I try to overpower her, but it is no use. "It is better this way," she whispers, crying as she looks at me with the piece still at her throat. "You were always my fate, Silas. But so was this." she moves to slice her throat, blood starting to trickle from the pressure of the sharp end.

Another sound of glass breaking startles me, and I fear I may have just lost Melora forever. But then I see Yara standing behind Melora who falls to the floor, her magic hold on me gone as I fall to the floor. Yara hit her over the head with a vase, shattering the thing to pieces over Melora's skull.

Everything moves in slow motion as I crawl to Melora, as I crawl to her motionless body on the floor. I get to her and place my hands over the small cut on her neck from the glass she had been holding.

I feel tears stream down my face as I hold her neck, hold her close to me. I feel the anguish rolling inside of me because I know what I need to do.

I will do anything to keep her safe, even if it means keeping her safe from herself.

Yara falls to the ground next to me as I still hold on to Melora for dear life. "I am so sorry." she pleads to an unconscious Mel. "I didn't know what else to do."

I applied pressure to the cut Melora had made with the shard of glass, saying, "It is alright, she is alright. We have to keep her safe. We have to..." I trailed off, not wanting to finish the sentence but knowing what needed to be done.

"Silas," Milo says, still lying on the floor holding his head. Yara goes to him and examines the still-bleeding cut. "We need to put her away. We- we need to do what they did in the capitol. You know we must do it if it will keep her safe." he says, and I know he is right.

I know he is right, but I do not want to put my Melora away in a cell with wards written in her blood around it so she will not be able to use her magic or Vayna's magic. I do not want to do the same thing my brother did to her, the same thing that has plagued her with nightmares since returning home.

But it is the only way that will keep her safe, keep her safe from herself and the darkness that is running inside her. It will keep her safe until we find a way to get the darkness out of her, until we find a way to get Vayna's magic out of her. It is going to hurt like hell to do that to her, but I must do it if it keeps her alive.

Because a life without Mel is not a life I will live. I will not do it, not without her. I need her; I need her love and her light. And she needs me; she needs me more than ever right now to protect her and keep her safe. I made a vow to do so, and I do not plan on ever breaking that promise, even if I throw her into a cell.

"We...need to get her to a cell," I tell Milo and Yara, wanting to get started and do it before I change my mind. "It can't be like the one she was kept in when she was held in Morania. We—we will put things in it, things that she loves." I begin making a mental list of all the items I will put in her cell, in the prison I was about to place her in.

Yara nods, understanding that I do not want to put her back into a cell that would remind her of her time being held captive. She is still tending to Milo's cut head as she says, "We can put her bed in there," she tells me, her eyes hopeful but worried. "We can put books in, too; she loves books."

I need to move; I need to get Melora to safety before she wakes. I need to get up and get moving, but I cannot move as I hold my wife, who is unconscious with a partially slit throat. I hold her and look down at her, at the amazing woman who has every part of me to herself. I look down and wish that things were different, that the

circumstances were different. But they are not, and what is meant to be will always find a way to be.
    Fate is before us, and it has found a way.
    Fate has found a way to take away everything I love.

CHAPTER 35

MELORA

The glass slit my throat. I slid the shard of glass against my neck, killing myself. Saving everyone around me, saving everyone I love from the darkness inside of me. The glass killed me, killed the darkness using me to rain havoc and chaos, killed the magic that is not mine.

I know it did not happen like that, that I did not actually succeed in real life. But my dreams often show me what could have been, what could have happened. Of what I could have done.

Guilt flows through me at the thought of what I have done, and the thought that I was willing to leave Silas. I want to keep him safe, I want to keep everyone safe, but leaving him like that is selfish. I regret even thinking about it and even trying to act on it. I thought I was doing what would keep him from harm, but my being gone was the furthest thing from safe for him. He needs me, just like I need him.

There has to be another way, a way where I do not die and I do not leave Silas in this world. There has to be a way to take Vayna's magic from me like I did from her, but without killing me, of course. I wish Visha were here; maybe she would have some insight into what to do. Maybe she would know something, anything that could help me. I wish my mother were here. I wish she was here to comfort me and tell me it will be okay. I know she will help me; she will know what to do.

She has to know what to do.

The pounding in the back of my head pulls me from my thoughts, making me groan in pain. It is a thumping, hammering pain that radiates through my skull and down my back. I touch my head lightly to make sure it is still intact. Sure enough, it is still there in one piece, even though it feels like a chunk has been taken out of my brain.

I feel something scratchy as I let my hand travel down to my neck; it's a bandage. A bandage had been placed over my neck where I had cut it, where I had started to slit my own throat. It hurts, but not as bad as my head. And not as bad as knowing I was ready to leave this life, ready to take myself away from Silas.

I look down into my palm and see another bandage, the white gauze spotted with blood. It is not the hand I held the shard of glass in, so I know it is not from a cut. It definitely feels fresh, but I have no idea what it is from.

Not until the realization of where I am hits me.

I sit up and take in my surroundings. I am in a cell...of sorts. There are bars lining the wall, but it is much more comfortable than the cells I am used to. Much different from the cell I was kept in in Morania.

I sit on a bed, a small bed like my old one I used to have here at Ravenhall. It could very well be the same one for all I know. The blankets are different, they are soft and comforting as I run my hands over them. A rug has been laid on the floor, covering the hard ground of the cell. A copper bathing tub sits in the corner, as does a small wardrobe. In the other corner, a short bookcase with dozens of books stands.

This is a very homey cell.

A cell I can almost guarantee from the fresh slice on my hand that is warded on the outside with my blood. It is warded to keep me from using my magic or Vayna's magic. I am glad they did this, glad they warded me in the cell to keep the darkness at bay until we can find a way to rid it from me.

But I know it was Silas who sliced me, drawing my blood to make the symbol I had told them about. I know he would never let anyone else use a blade on me, even if it was for my own protection. It pains me that he had to do that, because I know it was hard for him, it would be hard for anyone.

"It is the best I could come up with while you were out," Silas says from the other side of the bars, startling me. I find him in the dimly lit space, his eyes puffy and tired. His hands are in his pockets, and his face is grim.

"Silas," I stand and quickly run to the bars, flinging myself against them to try and get as close to him as I possibly can. "I am so sorry. I am so sorry for what I did. For what I was going to do." I hold onto the bars as he stares at me, his face sad and lips trembling. He looks at me, stares at me like I could drift away at any moment.

The sight of him almost rips my heart out. I know this is killing him, putting me in here, imprisoning me. I know it is hurting him seeing me like this.

He finally reaches for me, reaching between the bars to cup my face. I close my eyes and lean into his touch, feeling the immediate comfort his skin brings. "I could never live a life in this world if you were not in it. If you would have succeeded, I would have been meeting death right alongside you, holding your hand," he says, his voice low and shaky. "I am sorry it had to be this way. I want to keep you safe, even from yourself," he tells me, sorrow on his face.

I try to inch closer to him, but the bars are a thick separation between us. "*You* will be safer this way; our people will be safer," I assure him. I do not want him to feel bad for doing this, for doing what had to be done.

This was my idea, after all, an idea I thought of when I was writhing in agony, but still my idea. I did not want him to feel bad for this; he did not have to bear that burden on his already heavy soul.

"Is Milo okay?" I ask, partially remembering throwing him into a wall. I cringe as I remember what Vayna's magic had done.

Silas nods, "He is fine. A little bump on the head, but he will be okay."

I try to think back, try to remember anything else from the last time I was conscious, but nothing comes to me. "How long have I been out?" I question, wondering how much time has passed. "Have you taken the capitol?" I ask urgently, thinking back to the last conversation I fully remember.

He shakes his head no. "I was waiting on your orders, my queen," Silas says, a small smile gracing his lips.

I want to roll my eyes, but now is probably not the best time. "Do the same as we did here in Ravenhall. Tell the truth; do not hurt anyone." I make it sound so easy.

"I will not act without you." he tenses. "You are our queen."

"And you are the king." I stopped him. "Our people need a ruler, and you will rule until we figure this out. They need you, Silas. They need a ruler."

He doesn't answer for a long time, frustration and anger prevalent. Finally, he meets my eyes again. I can see the green, the color like the Fallen Forest. They are watery as he speaks. "I have already sent men to free your mother from the capitol. She will know what to do," he tells me. "She has to," he whispers to himself.

"She will," I promise him, holding his hands tighter.

I wish I could promise him more, that this will all be okay and everything will work out. The truth is, I have no idea if she will know how to take this magic from me, take this darkness from me. If it would even be possible to take Vayna's magic from me after I took it from her. My mother is the Goddess of Life, but this darkness is rooted so deep in me that I fear it will never be taken out.

Silas holds me through the bars, brings me as close as possible with the bars in between us. "I vow to you, I will free you from this cell." his voice wavers and I know he is fighting back tears. "I will take away the pain her magic is causing you. I promise, Mel. I will do whatever it takes."

A sob breaks free and tears roll down my cheeks. "I know, I know you will, my love." I cry more at the thought of being away from him rather than being in this cell. "Please, just stay with me for a while. Don't leave me, not yet." I plead and try to cling to him. "I love you, Silas. I love you."

Silas brushes the falling tears as he says, "I love you, Melora. I will love you if you are the Queen of Asteria or the queen I saw in the throne room." he tells me as a sob breaks free from his lips, as tears stream down his cheeks. "I will love you no matter what the circumstance, because our love is meant to be, and nothing, *nothing* will keep me from you." I cry harder at his words, at his never-ending love for me. "Even with the darkness in you, you light a place inside me that will never be extinguished. Our love is fated, written in the stars, and I will not let Vayna come between us again. It is you and me, Mel. You and me forever."

  I hold on to him, hold tight in fear that he will slip away from me. Fear that some way, somehow, he will be taken from me. I fear that fate has plans for us, plans that have been written long before we ever even existed in this realm.

  I fear for fate.
  I fear for the future.
  I fear for my destiny.
  "You and me. Forever, Silas."

About the Author

Sarah Teasdale

Sarah is a romantic fantasy author publishing her second book, Kingdom of Fury of Fate. Sarah brings deep emotional connections, bad-ass female protagonist, and the perfect amount of toe-curling spice to her writing. Born in Eastern Ohio, Sarah is a small-town girl at heart. When she is not typing her little heart out, you can find her working her 9-to-5, binge-reading romance novels while having a glass of wine, or being disgustingly in love with her fiance. You can follow Sarah Teasdale's work on her social media account: @sarahteasdaleauthor

Also read her monthly newsletter on her website through the QR code below.

Made in the USA
Middletown, DE
23 April 2024